Me

Megan's Game

TONY DRURY

Megan's Game

Published in 2012 by City Fiction

Edited by Laura Keeling

City Fiction
c/o
Sue Richardson Associates
Minerva Mill Innovation Centre
Station Road
Alcester
Warwickshire B49 5ET
T: 01789 761345
www.city-fiction.com

A CIP record for this book is available from the British Library.

ISBN 978-0-9572017-0-5

Printed and bound in Great Britain by TJ International, Padstow, Cornwall

Megan's Game is set in London and Aberdovey, West Wales, in 2011.

It is based on the legend of 'The Bells of Aberdovey'.

The Bells of Aberdovey

If to me as true thou art
As I am true to thee, sweetheart
We'll hear, one, two, three, four, five
From the bells of Aberdovey.
Hear one, two, three, four. . . five, six
Hear one, two, three, four, five and six
From the bells of Aberdovey.
Glad's a lad his lass to wed
When she sighed, "I love you!"
When but today on air I tread
For Gwen of Aberdovey.
While the heart beats in my breast
Cariad, I will love thee, by
One, two, three and all the rest
Of the bells of Aberdovey.
When I cross the sea once more
Love comes knocking at my door
Like one, two, three, four, five and six
Of the bells of Aberdovey
One, two, three, four, five, six
Like one, two, three, four, five and six
Of the bells of Aberdovey.
Little loves and hopes shall fly
Round us in a covey
When we are married, you and I
At home in Aberdovey.
If to me as true thou art
As I am true to thee, sweetheart
We'll hear one, two, three, four, five, six
From the bells of Aberdovey.

The composer is unknown. The words were written in the nineteenth century by John Ceiriog Hughes. The song is based on the legend of the submerged former kingdom of Cantre'r Gwaelod (Lowland Hundred) situated within Cardigan Bay. In the sixth century, Gwynddo King of Ceredigion built twenty fortified towns and ports. A great dyke with watch-towers was constructed to prevent the tides flowing onto the land. Prince Seithenmin, a mighty warrior, was in charge of the guards – but he was a drunkard and he allowed the fortifications to weaken.

One night a great storm swept through the dyke and the area has been covered by water ever since. Prince Seithenmin died as he waded out into the incoming tides.

It is said that if you walk the shores of Aberdovey at midnight you may hear the church bells ringing a tune, known locally as 'The Bells of Aberdovey'.

Publisher's Note

On 27 June 2011, Prince Charles, the Prince of Wales, visited Aberdovey. One of his main objectives was to launch the new Time and Tide Bell, the fourth of twelve to be installed in the United Kingdom. Crafted by the sculptor Marcus Vergette, it will respond to the incoming tide and resonate with the legend of 'The Bells of Aberdovey'.

Megan's Game

Prologue

The early morning sky was unusually cloudy as Lance Corporal Rhys Williams of the 1st Battalion, The Welsh Guards, tried to cushion his body from the bumps inflicted by the uneven and dusty road leading back towards southern Basra. They had been out since before midnight, patrolling an area they did not know, protecting a population they could rarely see, against an invisible enemy they could not identify. Within 500 yards they would be in the secure zone – although this particular division seemed arbitrary and uncertain.

Rhys was tired, thirsty and tense. He had allowed his concentration to wander back to a discussion he had had two nights earlier with his friend from the Royal Irish Regiment. Even at this early stage in the conflict neither of the soldiers could fully understand what they were trying to achieve.

"They all just want to bloody kill somebody as far as I can see," said his friend. "Killing for killing's sake. It reminds me of Kosovo during my first posting."

"It's early days," acknowledged Rhys. "I still believe there may be a real reason for us to be here."

The Irish soldier took a piece of crumpled newspaper out of his pocket. It was a report of a speech given by his boss, Colonel Tim Collins who, on 19 March 2003, in an address to his troops at their Kuwaiti desert camp, Fort Blair Mayne, had said:

"If you are ferocious in battle remember to be magnanimous in victory. Let's bring everyone home and leave Iraq a better place for us having been there."

Rhys quietly repeated the phrase: "Let's bring everyone home. . ."

The men were less than fifty yards from the secure zone when the roadside bomb was detonated. The four soldiers were thrown into the air and tossed down beside the burning vehicle. Two died instantly and one was caught in crossfire. The fourth soldier remained alive, but barely.

As Rhys lay on the ground he did not feel any sensation,

although he was aware of a gradual numbness creeping through his body. He could hear the wail of sirens. What was he thinking about? Home. He could see a cottage and a fair-haired girl, an elderly woman, a river and a beach. Some words formed on his lips.

But he was struggling. "Meg. . ." "Mam. . ." He tried again. "Meg. . ." "Meg. . ." There was a sudden spasm of agonising pain. "Megan!" he cried.

The sirens grew louder and then stopped. The British soldiers opened fire on three fleeing figures who were disappearing into the sun-drenched sands and isolated grey buildings.

The sergeant watched his squad for a few seconds and then examined the four bodies lying on the road. He moved slowly from one to the other. When he reached the last soldier he checked for a pulse and then wiped his own forehead in dismay.

"Bastards," he mouthed.

He stood up and returned to the armoured vehicle.

"All dead, sir," he reported to his colonel.

PART ONE

Storm Clouds

Chapter One

Despite the sun pouring through the open window, Megan Williams was struggling to get out of bed. She slammed her head back down on the pillow and shut her eyes.

"Megan. *Mae rhaid i ti siapio'I,*" she cried. She really needed to pull herself together.

In recent weeks she had struggled to maintain the discipline which, as a graduate sports teacher and former international hockey player, was her personal benchmark. She was trying to ignore the fact that it was now a struggle to reach the existing hole in the belt of her jeans, and that over the last few evenings she had twice opened a second bottle of wine as she lounged away the hours, listening to music from her favourite shows. And, of course, last night had been another disappointment.

She was being honest with herself. It had not been solely Gavin's fault. Megan knew about Julia and realised there was a shared responsibility. When their night together had ended in embarrassment she had lashed out in pure frustration. She now regretted the words she had chosen.

She needed to get dressed quickly; she didn't want to be late. She looked around her untidy bedroom, clothes strewn everywhere. She couldn't now remember why there was a photograph album half opened at the end of the bed. She stared dully at the empty bottle of wine on the dressing table and what appeared to be the remains of a bread roll.

"Ugh," she moaned.

She followed her daily routine of taking off her night shirt and going straight into the bathroom. She stood on the scales and tried to lower the digital output by putting all her downward pressure on the left side. It reduced the reading by one pound. The figure was still depressing.

She dressed quickly, pulling on a light coloured top and, after breathing in, her jeans. After washing out a mug from the pile of unwashed crockery in the sink, she made herself a black coffee. She looked at the invitation pinned to the notice board.

"*Duw*. It's after nine," she said. Nerys had asked if she could be there no later than 9:30.

She stepped out into the fresh air and got into her red Ford Mondeo, preparing to leave her stone and slate cottage. She lived in the village of Abergynolwyn, in the County of Gwynedd, on the west Welsh coast.

Despite the time, Megan wanted to enjoy the spring scenery. The early, lush green growth contrasted with the harsh slate hills. She turned south out of Tywyn onto the coast road. There were five miles to travel to Aberdovey. She looked to her right and watched the blue and green waters of Cardigan Bay in awe. She had lived here for much of her life, and yet she had never lost the almost childish excitement the coastal seas summoned in her.

When she was only halfway to her destination she pulled off the road into a parking area. On the beach side were some of the eighteen holes played by members of Aberdovey Golf Club. The early starters were now on the sixth fairway.

It was, however, the graveyard on the other side which was the focus of her attention. Her mood changed as she stared up the hill at the rows of tombstones cut into its side. She wiped a tear from her eye. She knew she did not have enough time to reach the burial place she wanted to visit. He would still be there later in the day, but it was now that she wanted to be with him.

David Rensburg was lost in his thoughts as he joined the M1 motorway travelling north out of London. He was listening to the third of Rachmaninov's four piano concertos. He eased his BMW 7 Series into the outside lane and put on cruise control, which he registered at seventy-five miles per hour. He had six points on his driving licence and was being more careful. When he crossed the border into Montgomeryshire he would reduce his maximum speed to seventy. The Welsh traffic police seemed rather more vigilant than their English counterparts.

Although his two sons were with their mother in France for the Easter break, David laughed to himself thinking about them. He knew what Matthew and Josh would say about his immaculate, new white shirt, his black slacks and matching shoes. When he arrived in Aberdovey he would change straight away into shorts and a top – but, as he often told his sons, you could never be sure who you might meet on the way. Though his hair was now flecked with grey, David had decided that using hair dye was the same as cheating. His dark eyebrows hooded piercing blue eyes and his clear skin reflected his athletic regime. The daily session in the gym in the basement of his London office and the weekly appointment with his personal trainer on Primrose Hill meant that he was in good shape.

The car phone rang and he answered using his hands-free set. He listened to a foreign voice before speaking.

"But I thought you promised to move at least two million shares at 12p each," he said.

He assessed the reply while swerving to avoid a lorry which was drifting out of the inner lane.

"This isn't what we agreed. The mid-price in London is 14p. I must have moved two million shares, and preferably at 12p, by the time we open on Tuesday. You have three days, Stephan."

He absorbed the response from Zurich.

"Yes. I agree. Markets are difficult. But Stephan, I expect you to use your own funds if needs be. We're not talking about a lot of money. I don't need to remind you of the March deal. You made a lot of money, Stephan."

When their conversation ended, he rang Jemma.

"Hi. Sorry. Still asleep are you? When you manage to reach the office, can you email Jackson and tell him that Stephan is struggling but I'll get him there. Can you then phone Martin Van Dijl and ask him to fax me an investor list for Trafford Discount Stores on my Wales number."

There was a cry of protest from a bed in West London.

"Yes, Jemma. I know. Martin's a shit and has wandering hands. But it's all in a day's work, madam, and you're being paid double time for the bank holiday."

They both laughed and the call was terminated.

He stopped on the Shrewsbury bypass to refuel and have a coffee before settling back to enjoy the country roads beyond Welshpool and on to Machynlleth. He now turned west to Mallwyd and then travelled along the Dovey river valley into

Aberdovey. His knowledge of the Welsh language was limited to a few words, but he knew '*aber*' meant 'river mouth' or 'estuary'. As he turned the final corner and saw the harbour in front of him, he gave a small gasp. He still did this nearly every time he arrived. It was the Aberdovey effect that has thrilled people over the centuries, including the Romans whose road is still accessible along parts of the river bank.

He passed the entry to the Outward Bound Trust where the students were preparing for the day's activities on the water. He drove under the railway bridge and through the village to the west side, where he turned left and parked his car. After collecting his cases, he opened the front door of his three-storey holiday cottage. It was called Swn-y-Don, 'the sound of the waves'. He noticed that the winter storms had left deposits of sand piled up in the corners of the slate-based front garden.

Albert Payne ordered a large scotch and added a small amount of water. He was watching the TV screen which filled much of the wall of the North London pub. Despite the lighting there was a depressing atmosphere, the result of decades of cigarette smoke, spilt beer and the occasional fight. Albert would add that Arsenal's failure to win further trophies in recent years probably added to the gloom.

His own mood wavered as he felt the familiar surge of pain across his lower abdomen. The Sky Sports newsreader was prettily announcing that Chelsea were to play their home match against West Ham United. Albert wanted to hear whether John Terry was playing, but the call of nature sounded its alarm.

For a few moments he experienced the most acute spasm of pain yet in the six weeks since his difficulties began. He almost fell off his bar stool, but managed to stagger towards the men's toilet. He opened the wooden entrance, the matchstick man on its outside contrasting with the matchstick lady on the adjacent door.

To his relief the urinals were clear, but he decided to use a cubicle anyway. He shut the door behind him and took off his jacket. Holding his penis over the basin, he strained to empty his bladder. He heaved and pushed and groaned and eventually there was a trickle of water. And then suddenly a hot stream of urine ejected into the bowl. He pulled up his trousers and tied his belt – he was beginning to feel better. But, as he looked down, a wet patch began to spread over his groin area.

He decided he could not return to the public bar and so took the back exit and wandered into the high street. It was a half mile walk to his flat. He would pass the doctor's surgery and he wondered briefly whether he should try to see somebody. But he was feeling better, so he decided to go home, change his clothes and return to the pub. There was a game of bar billiards awaiting him and he didn't want his ex-army pals to find a replacement player.

Megan had now reached Aberdovey. She indicated left and turned into the parking area of 'Wrth y Mor' – rather an unadventurous name for an eight-bedroomed mansion with its own swimming pool and tennis court – and yet it was 'by the sea', in that Cardigan Bay lay behind the sand dunes. It was low tide and the hard sands lay exposed to the seagulls who were feeding on the small sticklebacks at the water's edge.

She shut the car door and saw that Nerys Griffiths was already striding towards her. Megan knew that she was meant to call her 'Nerys'. She found it so difficult. Rhys' mother had been in the Griffiths' service for over forty years, following the premature death of her husband. In that time she had missed only five days, and only then when she could not reach Tywyn and the railway to Aberdovey on her bike because of the snows. Megan could recall several occasions when she had walked from Aberdovey to Wrth y Mor to wait for Rhys' mother before catching the train home. Back then she had been taught to stand up and acknowledge M'dam Griffiths. This had become Mrs Griffiths as Megan had reached her teenage years. When Rhys' mother finally retired, Nerys had continued to take an interest in Megan and invited her to their regular social events. It was when she and Rhys began to visit the house together that she had been told to address her host as 'Nerys'.

"Megan, my dear," Nerys exclaimed.

They kissed and strolled into the house. It was the weekend of the Griffiths' annual tennis tournament. There would be eight couples and some other guests attending. The mixed doubles would start on Saturday lunchtime and go through to Sunday afternoon. The organiser, referee and loudspeaker commentator were all Gareth Griffiths wrapped into one.

Megan was helping with the preparation of the salads. She began work at ten o'clock, tasked with peeling potatoes and washing lettuces, and finished at four in the afternoon. She told Nerys and Gareth how much she was looking forward to the next day.

"You'll win, you and Dennis," laughed Gareth, as he closed Megan's car door.

She turned left and arrived at the Cemetery Beach car park in under ten minutes. She left her vehicle, crossed the road and entered through the iron gates. She climbed past rows of graves in various states of upkeep. When she reached the top, Megan knelt down in front of a green tombstone. She tidied the soil with her fingers and re-arranged the flowers she had placed there two days earlier. She brushed some sand away from the writing etched into the marble and, with her fingers, she slowly traced the wording.

"Lance Corporal Rhys Williams, 1st Battalion. The Welsh Guards. Born 22 April 1980. Died by enemy action in Iraq 16 September 2003. Beloved husband of Megan and son of Cerys Williams."

Outwardly Megan no longer cried. But she often recalled every single inch of his six foot two frame. He laughed a lot – though when it came to Wales playing international rugby at the Arms Park or any other national event he became more serious.

Theirs was a love story and they adored being together. They would walk the beach from Aberdovey to Tywyn, climb the Snowdonia Hills, play tennis, go sailing in the estuary waters and occasionally drink a little too much. She remembered the time in a pub in Dolgellau when a local farmer had put his hand on Megan's bottom while Rhys was fetching some drinks. It had taken Megan fifteen minutes to treat Rhys' bruised knuckles.

She and Rhys had been born in the same village and attended the same schools. They became closer during their teenage years and stayed in contact while she attended university and Rhys joined the army. They had both tried different relationships, but when Rhys told her he was being posted to Iraq they quickly married. It was a small and private ceremony in their local church. They were to have fewer than sixteen weeks in each other's company before Rhys was killed. She missed him desperately.

Megan stayed lost in her thoughts until she sensed that the sun was sinking in the west and the temperature was falling. She stood up slowly, keeping her eyes on the grave.

"Happy Birthday," she mouthed. "*Bendith Duw arnat,* Rhys."

As she arrived back at her cottage twenty minutes later, she noticed a small, hunched woman dressed in black struggling down the lane. Megan parked her car and ran towards her. They embraced.

"Have you been?" asked the woman.

"Yes, Mam. I have had time with him."

"He would have been thirty-one today." The woman stumbled and Megan held her upright.

"Mam, we need to get you inside."

"Why Rhys, Megan? Why my son?"

David spent the whole of Good Friday in Aberdovey. He spoke to Matthew and Josh, who seemed to be enjoying their holiday in France with their mother. David thought that his elder son sounded a little subdued, but Matthew had inherited some of his mother's personality and David was never completely sure what he was thinking.

He spread the contents of his briefcase over the dining room table. He knew high tide was well gone and so, after a breakfast of yoghurt and fresh fruit, he left the house and ran across the hard sands to the water's edge, where he slowed to a walk. He turned to cover the stretch along the estuary before cutting across the rocks and pools and heading towards Tywyn. He reached the pipes within an hour and turned back again. He returned at noon, refreshed and clear-headed, took a shower and settled back down to work on his business files during the afternoon.

At around four o'clock he received a phone call from Gareth Griffiths and confirmed that he was looking forward to the next day's events. They discussed a recent share sale which David had organised for his host.

An hour later he dialled a telephone number in Zurich. He wanted to speak to his Swiss banker colleague, who was part of the fundraising team of investors put together by the stockbroker, Martin Van Dijl. This was the way the City operated. The funds required for the deal he was currently working on were £3.5 million. The stockbroker put together a group of investors who each agreed either to invest directly or raise some of the amount required from other investors.

"Stephan Andrew, please. . . David Rensburg. . . of Park Avenue Capital. . . yes, how are you?. . . Florence. . . excellent. . . is he in?. . . ah, Stephan."

They discussed the agreed share placing. Stephan explained that he had found a buyer for one million shares at 10p per share and would be working on the balance over the weekend.

David then spoke to Martin Van Dijl. He thanked the broker for the faxed list of investors and explained that Stephan was on his way to selling the two million shares allocated to him. He tried to discuss the price of the shares and his worries that 10p was too low, but Martin terminated the call. David could hear he was out with a raucous crowd.

He cooked himself a dinner of steak and roasted vegetables, listened to a CD of Miles Davis playing jazz in New York, read a hundred pages of his latest thriller, and went to bed.

When David arrived at Wrth y Mor at around twelve o'clock on Easter Saturday, he left his tennis kit in the changing rooms by the pool and found Gareth struggling with sheaves of paper. His host explained to David that organising a tennis tournament for eight pairs should be straightforward, but bloody Dennis Jones had just been called by the police to clear his cattle out of Happy Valley.

"I warned him David. 'Get your bloody fences repaired, Dennis.' That's what I said. Did he listen?" Gareth returned to his list of players.

David found his partner and they sat together at a poolside table and caught up on their news. They had lost the final twelve months earlier, which still annoyed David. She told David about her husband's promotion and their two girls' progress at school. She then announced she was going to change into her tennis outfit as they were due to play their first match at one o'clock. She went into the changing room, took off her clothes, did some rather vigorous stretching exercises, and pulled her calf muscle. She spent the rest of the afternoon with her leg up in an ice pack, drinking champagne.

"Well," announced their host. "You've lost your partner and Megan's is chasing bloody cattle around the valley." So Megan and David were introduced to each other. Megan had been away for last year's tournament, but they recalled briefly meeting two years earlier, although not on the tennis court because Megan and Dennis had lost in the first round.

Within twenty minutes they were on the court together and winning with ease. The semi-finals followed at four o'clock and provided a much sterner test of their abilities. They won in three sets. They would play together in the final at twelve noon the next day. Their opponents would be Gavin Davis and his long time girlfriend, Julia Etherington.

Megan was in the changing room when she realised that David and Gareth were on the other side of the wooden divide talking in hushed tones. But she could hear well enough.

"Well, Gareth," said David. "That *was* a pleasant surprise. Thank you!"

"Megan's gorgeous, isn't she?"

"She can play tennis, Gareth. I'll say that. She really moves well and has some lovely shots. I've seen her before in previous years but never really noticed her, if you know what I mean."

"She lost her husband in Iraq in 2003. She's been finding it tough. Understandably."

"She certainly appeared a bit casual. That dress of hers needed ironing and she's carrying some extra weight."

David continued to mull this over in silence.

Megan returned home, entered her cottage, slammed the door, stormed into the kitchen, opened a bottle of chilled white wine from the fridge, and slumped down on her sofa. She drank a glass rather too quickly and went back for a refill. When she had finished that, she put down the empty glass and covered her face with her hands.

She went upstairs and changed into shorts and a top. She rushed down the steps, ducked under the beam, filled a bucket with water, went outside and cleaned her car. She returned inside with her tennis equipment. She used whitener on her shoes and changed the laces. She checked her racquet and straightened some of the strings. After this, she cleaned her kitchen and filled two black sacks with bottles and waste.

Happily tired from her exertions, she climbed the stairs. After stripping off her clothes, she cleaned her teeth and turned on the shower. She allowed the hot water to pour over her. After drying herself off, she viewed her reflection in the mirror. She sucked in her stomach and tensed her buttocks. She opened a drawer and took out a tennis outfit. She tried another and then a third, but returned to the first dark blue choice. She nodded approvingly at her reflection. After placing her carefully selected clothes on a chair, Megan went to bed naked and fell deeply asleep.

Martin Van Dijl stretched out on his settee. Justine was standing on the balcony of his eighth floor flat looking out over the London Docklands. The Thames was flowing quickly and several barges were chugging upstream. She could see the Essex coastal area in the east.

"Try Stephan again, Justine," he barked.

Martin was a self-made stockbroker, born and bred in the slums of London's East End. He made money by buying shares at one price and selling them at a higher one. This was the motivation that drove him to work hard and to play hard. He made money. He spent money. And he fucked Justine.

"He's on his answerphone, Martin," Justine replied. "He's probably enjoying the Zurich nightlife."

"He'll be playing chess. He has two things in his life. His banking business and the games of chess. When he came over here last week I had to take him to *Simpson's-in-the-Strand* for breakfast so he could study the pictures of Fischer and Spassky." Martin knew there was a third activity occupying another part of Stephan's life, but declined to mention it here.

Martin's East End upbringing had taught him two lessons:

how to survive and how to read human nature. It was the latter which had propelled him up the ladder. He had discovered share trading during the 1980s when Margaret Thatcher privatised much of British activity in her zest to create a community of private investors. Martin joined in and began to understand the elixir of greed.

His colleagues in the stockbroking office where he learnt his trade became used to his customer rhetoric.

"Of course, Gerald. I may call you Gerald? I understand that you have limited cash available and this is a very brave decision. Don't worry about me. I've already sold these shares once – but I do really like you, Gerald. That's why I retained five thousand pounds' worth for you, but no worry, I'll complete with my other. . . are you sure, Gerald? I'll be worrying all night if I think you aren't happy. . . you are? OK. Deal done."

Martin had known that Gerald's greed would eventually overcome Gerald's fear.

"Will Stephan place the shares?" asked Justine. She struggled to understand all the terms used in the office. Why were shares sometimes called 'equity'? And why did some of the older brokers use the words 'call' and 'put' instead of 'buy' and 'sell'?

"He will place them, Justine. Stephan's a good friend to me."

Martin stood up. He was around six foot tall, with a shaved head and a cruel, sinewy figure. He wore a ring in his left ear. He went over to the cocktail bar and poured two drinks. The hi-fi was playing a Queen song. He handed Justine a glass. She could see the look in his eyes.

"I'm fucking good, ain't I, Justine? I never fail."

"No, Martin. You never fail."

He put his hand up her skirt and held her inside her panties.

"And what's my reward for being so fucking good, eh?"

Albert cried out in pain as his bladder desperately tried to empty itself of urine.

He wanted to phone his son to ask for help but he knew that difficulties at his business, Payne Printers, were occupying his time. He wondered about going down the high street to the surgery. He must make an appointment to see a doctor.

David drew in his breath sharply. Walking towards him, among the guests at Gareth and Nerys' Easter Sunday party and the final of the tennis tournament, was Megan. Her blue tennis dress and white shoes caught the warm lunchtime sunshine. She had removed yesterday's headband and her hair fell loose around her shoulders. She was smiling and waving at various people. As she reached David he attempted to give her a kiss, but she moved her head away.

"I watched our opponents yesterday," he said to Megan. "They're good."

"Gavin's weak on the backhand when it's hit deep. Julia is fast and clever. She'll lose concentration at some stage."

"Right. Spoken like a professional," said David.

They sat down at a table and Megan poured two glasses of fresh orange from the jug in the centre. The ice cubes had melted but it was refreshingly cool.

"Well, I *am* a professional," said Megan.

David looked at her quizzically.

"I'm a PE teacher at Dolgellau High School. I teach hockey, tennis and a little golf."

Megan then stood up and strode over to a table where three women were sitting. David checked his mobile phone.

Their match began at twelve noon. The tennis court was built at the base of the hills behind the house. It had been refurbished last year and had a green playing area and a sand-coloured surround.

Megan realised immediately that Julia knew about her Thursday evening with Gavin. Within forty minutes David and Megan had lost the first set 6-2.

"I'm glad they've got that out of their system," said Megan, as the players toweled down.

"We're struggling," said David.

"Play on Julia, David. She'll crack."

In the second set Julia did not weaken. The games became closer and Gavin somewhat frustrated as he found himself isolated in a number of the rallies. On three occasions, when at the net, he came across to intercept the drives aimed at Julia. With two of his volleys the ball ended in the net on their side. Julia initially hugged her partner. On the third occasion she uttered an expletive. Megan turned and winked at David. But the game still went to a tie-break.

Megan ran up to David. She put her arm around his neck and whispered in his ear, "Every shot now goes to Gavin."

Megan and David won the tie break 9-7.

At the start of the second game of the deciding set, Megan sprinted forward to relieve a Gavin drop-shot which she lobbed back over his head and just inside the base line. She toppled over the net and found herself splayed at the feet of her opponent.

"Fucking whore," Julia spat.

Megan knew they were going to win. Their opponents' shots were a little shorter and David, at long last, could free his arms. He propelled a range of drives, the last one drawing applause both from Megan and the roughly forty people watching the match.

Megan was now tiring. They reached match point. Gavin lobbed her. She raced back, turned, and unleashed a backhand past a despairing Julia who slammed her racket unsportingly into the ground.

David grabbed Megan and hugged her. He felt her breasts sink into his chest. Megan wrapped her arms around him.

"Megan. *Ti'n ferch lwcus,*" she said to herself. In the next few weeks she was to discover that she was indeed a lucky girl.

Chapter Two

Three hours later David was standing in the drive of Wrth y Mor waiting for Megan, who had driven back to Abergynolwyn to change. When she finally arrived, David watched as she alighted from her car. She was wearing an emerald-green cocktail dress and a hint of make-up. A silver pendant hung around her neck and David noticed a small tattoo – a red dragon – above her left ankle. He knew it was the Welsh legend. As Megan stood before him, the lowering sun in Cardigan Bay caught her in its light. She shook her hair to allow it to settle around her neck. David was enraptured.

They strolled together around the house and toward the group of guests. It was four o'clock and everybody knew it was time for Gareth's annual speech. Nerys dreaded it. Most of the invitees simply drank more champagne and pretended to be engrossed. But this year was to be different. Gareth spoke at length about his joy at the result of the March referendum, which had granted the Welsh Government more powers. The fact he was wrong, in that the only real effect of the referendum was to transfer the authority for sealing new regulations from Westminster to Cardiff, simply did not matter. His dream of an independent country, free of the bastards from across the River Severn, produced some stirring rhetoric. The applause rang out; Nerys breathed a sigh of relief; Megan nodded in approval; David groaned; and Gareth introduced Brigadier Harmsworth Davies-Butler.

Same introduction, same joke.

"My friends, please welcome our great friend, the Brigadier. As you know, Brigadier Davies-Butler is president of the Golf Club. Each year they hold a 'Bells of Aberdovey' tournament. I have stolen the idea and our trophy is called the very same. The Brigadier has just handed me a writ for copyright infringement." Everybody laughed politely. Gareth beamed. "Ladies and Gentlemen – the Brigadier."

"Gareth, Nerys, ladies and gentlemen. Can I start by reminding Gareth that Westminster still holds the purse strings. But watch Scotland. They are on their way and Alex Salmond knows what he is doing. Gareth, I promise, one day your dream will come true."

This time the applause was loud and enthusiastic.

The Brigadier continued by thanking Nerys for her hospitality and all those who, each year, made the occasion so enjoyable. He then picked up a silver vessel.

"'The Bells of Aberdovey' trophy," he announced. "May I ask today's runners-up, Gavin and Julia, to come and collect their award."

They strode up to the Brigadier. Julia was dressed in a figure-hugging yellow trouser suit, which pushed the Brigadier's blood pressure up to dangerous levels. She accepted the cup for second place with a grace she did not feel.

"And now, ladies and gentlemen," boomed the Brigadier, "The winners of the 2011 'Bells of Aberdovey' trophy are. . . Megan and David!"

David pushed Megan forward and the formalities were almost completed. But first David had something to say.

"Brigadier, Gareth and Nerys. It is impossible to find words adequate to express our appreciation for this wonderful event. It was a great final. Gavin, you are a terrific player and I think Julia now has the right partner."

There was a mixture of applause and laughter and Julia's mother wondered if she would soon be buying a wedding hat. David continued.

"We won this marvellous trophy because I was lucky enough to have a terrific partner. Thanks Megan. Thanks everybody."

The afternoon came to a close and the guests began to leave. Thirty minutes later David caught up with his co-winner.

"Lovely speech," said Megan.

"Megan" said David, in a quiet voice. "Will you sit with me on the harbour steps?"

They strolled slowly out of the house and retraced David's route back to the village. They passed Swn-y-don and crossed the bridge onto the wooden quay. Together, they sat on its edge and watched the boats riding the incoming tide.

"Cardigan Bay at its best," said Megan.

Her blonde hair caught the onshore winds. Her skin reflected the cloudless early evening skies.

She noticed that David was massaging the inside of his left forearm. He stopped and flexed his fingers.

"Problem?" asked Megan.

"I think I've strained a muscle. During the second set."

Megan continued staring out over the estuary waters. Several seagulls were hovering over the water, searching for their supper.

"When we were kids we were taught a song" she said.

"Which song?"

"It was called 'The Bells of Aberdovey': the same as the trophy we've just won. I can only remember a few of the lines. I'll sing them to you, if you'd like?"

"Of course."

"*While the heart beats in my breast, Cariad,*
I will love thee," sang Megan.

"Cariad?"

"Sweetheart."

"Sweetheart," repeated David.

"Or lover."

David looked out across the bay.

"I think I prefer 'lover'."

Megan looked at him. Their eyes met. For a few moments neither moved a muscle.

"Is it your song?" asked David.

"No," laughed Megan. She continued by speaking the words:

"Glad's a lad his lass to wed
When she sighed, 'I love you!'
When but today on air I tread
For Gwen of Aberdovey."

"So," said David. "Megan's out and Gwen's in."

"Not a chance," said Megan.

They stood up and walked back into the gardens. At the Harbour Master's office David read the tidal charts. The next morning's low tide was due at 6:42am. He was already looking forward to his pre-breakfast walk over the sands.

They continued to talk. They reflected on the tennis, on

Gavin and Julia, about Megan's job at Dolgellau High School and David's work as a corporate financier in London. He talked in particular about the stress of his work. He told Megan that one of the joys of Aberdovey was his walk at low tide from the harbour, round the estuary, along the coast to Tywyn and back again. "It takes just over two-and-a-half hours and it's where I find peace of mind. . ."

He said he would be walking it the following morning. "Low tide is at 6:42am – I'll be leaving at 5:30."

They walked back to David's home on the sea front.

"You can use the spare room, if you like," said David.

Megan looked surprised.

"Nice offer, David, but I think I'll go home." She was planning to clean the rest of her cottage during the Bank Holiday Monday – and they'd only just met.

"Let me call you a taxi then," offered David. "You've been drinking."

Megan had an abrupt change of heart. "What the hell," she thought, and decided to accept his hospitality.

Once inside, David showed Megan two spare bedrooms on the top floor. She selected the back one which looked out on the rock face behind the house.

Twenty minutes later they settled in the lounge on the first floor. David poured two brandies and put on 'Porgy and Bess' by Miles Davis.

Megan listened to the classical jazz interpretations of the Gershwin opera: 'Bess, You is My Woman Now', 'It Ain't Necessarily So', 'I Love You Porgy' and 'Gone'.

"This recording was made in 1958," said David. "And it's still the best thing he ever did."

Megan sank back and closed her eyes as 'Fisherman, Strawberry and Devil Crab' filled the room.

Half an hour later Megan rose and yawned. "Time for bed," she said. David tried to put his arms around her neck, but Megan gently pushed him away.

"Good night, David, and thanks for a lovely day."

Earlier that evening Albert Payne had waited for over an hour to see the emergency doctor. He had twice rushed to the surgery toilet and felt embarrassed by the messes he had caused. Initially he had used his handkerchief to mop up the spilt urine but on the second occasion he had nothing left once the toilet roll was exhausted.

His name was called and he was instructed to see Dr Shepherd in Room 8. He walked down the corridor, knocked on the door and when he heard a voice respond he went into the room.

Immediately panic rose up in his chest and he thought about walking out, but he thought better of it and sat in the chair being offered to him.

"You've not been to see us for some time, Mr Payne," said the doctor. "Two years ago, to be exact, when you had a dose of shingles. You've also not taken up the offer of a 'flu jab for the last three winters. They are particularly effective for somebody your age, Mr Payne." She paused, "Anyway, how have you been keeping? What can I help you with today?"

At the question, Albert became embroiled in a sea of confusion. He coughed and brushed the thinning strands of his hair across the crown of his head. Finally, he looked Dr Shepherd squarely in the face.

"I'm having some trouble peeing," he said.

"Right," she said. "First things first. How is your general health? Are you eating regular meals?"

"Yes."

"And sleeping well?"

"No."

"Are you taking anything? Your notes don't indicate that we've given you any prescriptions recently?"

"Nothing," replied Albert.

"Do you smoke, Mr Payne?"

"No."

"Do you drink alcohol?"

"Yes."

"How many units a week, do you think?"

"What?"

"Right, Mr Payne. On an average day what do you consume?"

"Consume?" Albert was becoming increasingly confused.

"Drink, Mr Payne. Do you go to the pub?"

"Two or three times," he said.

"A week?"

"A day. Except on Mondays, when I do my washing."

"So what do you drink at the pub?" asked Dr Shepherd.

"In a morning, three pints of lager. In the afternoon, some scotch. In the evening I drink wine and I like a brandy."

Dr Shepherd wrote in the file: 'Heavy drinker: eighty units a week.'

The calculation was short by around twenty units.

"Right, Mr Payne, I would like to take your blood pressure. Please roll up the sleeve on your left arm." The rubber coil was wrapped around the limb and Dr Shepherd pumped air into the cushion. As the readings were registered, she wrote down the figures of 195 and 110.

"Now, please tell me specifically about your problem," she continued.

"That's what I came in for. . ." blustered Albert.

"Yes," said the doctor. "When are you experiencing trouble with the waterworks exactly?"

"All the time," he said. "That's why I'm not sleeping any good. I have to keep getting up and I've. . . er. . . started to wet the bed." Albert went bright red in the face.

"Right, Mr Payne, let's have a look."

"At what?" he asked.

"At the waterworks. I need to examine your penis."

"No. Absolutely not. I just want some pills!"

"Mr Payne," said Dr Shepherd, "I am trying to help you. Please slip your trousers down."

"But you're a woman!" cried Albert.

"I'm a doctor, Mr Payne."

She watched as he stood up and dropped his trousers. She carefully examined his genitals and asked him to sit down.

"Mr Payne, I can test with a blood sample, but I think you may have a problem with your prostate. I need to examine it, and I will do this by inserting my finger up your rectum."

"You will do what to my what?!" Albert was horrified.

"Mr Payne. Please relax. I'm going to help you. All men have a prostate. It is a small, doughnut-shaped gland inside you, down here," Dr Shepherd placed her hand on the base of the abdomen. "It produces seminal fluid which is used in the sexual process."

"I haven't had sex in twenty years. My missus died in 1990. No doctor, I don't want sex." Albert started to get up.

"Please sit down, Mr Payne. The problem is that in older men the prostate enlarges and pushes upwards on the urethra. This means you have a problem passing urine. I cannot be sure without doing some tests but I am fairly sure that is your situation. Now, please let me examine you." She stood up and put a rubber glove on her right hand.

Albert looked at Dr Shepherd. "Can I just go home now, please?"

Matthew Rensburg sniffed at the wine and took a small amount into his mouth. He swirled it around and then swallowed. He gazed at the log fire and frowned.

"*Je pense que le vin est un Chardonnay*," he said.

His mother laughed. She picked up the bottle and handed it to him.

"Oh," he said "Chablis."

Michelle le Grande moved over and sat beside him.

"So, how's your father?" she asked.

Matthew put both the bottle and his glass down on the stone floor.

"You know I don't like these questions," he replied, moodily.

"But I care about my family."

"Mum, your family is here with Maurice. You divorced Dad, remember?"

She rubbed her left eye, which Matthew noticed was slightly swollen, irritably. She then put her hand on her son's knee.

"Please, Matthew, is your father happy?"

"He's lonely, Mum. All he does is work. Josh is at boarding school and I know technically I live at home, but with all my uni stuff I often don't get back for three or four nights in a row. I've suggested to Dad that he moves into a flat but he loves Primrose Hill. He walks for hours around Regent's Park. Mind you, he spends most of that time on his BlackBerry, I bet."

"So there's nobody else?"

"If there was, I wouldn't tell you." Matthew paused. "What's wrong with your eye?"

"Nothing. I must have a bit of grit in it or something."

"Well, it looks kind of bad."

"Matthew, it's fine. Don't be silly. Now, I must go and check on Josh."

Early on Easter Monday, David finished his fresh fruit and left a note in the kitchen. *'Megan. I'll be back by 7.30 and will cook you breakfast. My scrambled eggs are delicious. . . David.'*

He opened the front door. Despite a clear sky it was slightly chilly. He crossed the road towards the beach and stopped. There, sitting on the wall, was Megan, dressed in a rugby shirt and rather large white shorts. She was bare-footed.

"Mind if I join you?" she asked.

"What the hell are you wearing?" he laughed.

"I found these in one of the drawers. Is that ok?"

"Ha," he said. "It's my elder son's kit. Ok fine, let's go."

And so David and Megan commenced their walk. Quite soon they were striding along the estuary and out towards the sea. The curve took them round the headland and north towards Tywyn.

At first they were quiet. The sand was firm by the water's edge. Megan told David to avoid the pools of water left by the outgoing tide. "Because of the weever fish," she said.

"Weever fish?" he asked. "What's a weever fish?"

"It's a horrible little critter with a single poisonous spine. It buries itself in the soft sand. My friend once stepped on one, just around here. She ended up in Tywyn Hospital. Her foot was paralysed."

"Wow," said David. "I've been coming here for years, and I didn't know that."

After an hour or so they reached the two massive drainage pipes which carry the inland rainfall into the sea at Tywyn. They turned back and began talking gently. Megan told him about her beginnings in Abergynolwyn. "Dad died quite early," she said. "I still miss him." Her mother was now in Canada. "I see her every two years, she has a new partner." David learned that Megan was educated in Cardiff and at Loughborough University. "I played hockey for Wales," she told him. "Once I graduated, I taught in Birmingham and then nine years ago moved to the High School at Dolgellau. It's great. Most of the girls are boarders and of course there is a real sporting tradition. We won the Welsh Schools' Tennis Championships last year."

They slowed a little as the conversation continued. Megan was enjoying splashing through the incoming waves as the tide was turning.

"Gareth told me about your husband," David said. "I'm sorry."

"Rhys was my life," said Megan. "We grew up in the village and moved into a cottage as soon as I inherited some money from my father's will when I was twenty-one. We were married when he was posted abroad. He was part of the invasion of Iraq and was killed a few weeks later."

"So you've been alone for quite a time?"

"I have a full life at school. I still miss Rhys but with him being in the army we didn't really see that much of each other. . . but it was good when we did. He was a proud soldier. He once told me he was indestructible. I see his mother regularly in the village. She still can't really cope with his death."

They had now reached the point where the River Dovey emptied into the ocean and they followed the curve of the estuary back towards Aberdovey harbour.

"So you have two sons?" asked Megan.

"Josh and Matthew. Josh is thirteen and at boarding school in Wiltshire. Matthew is nineteen and at the London School of Economics."

"Do you see them often?"

"They're both at home at weekends but they have been away quite a lot. . . Michelle, my ex-wife, went off with another man. A Frenchman. She met him at an exhibition opening in London." He paused and reflected on the frequent rows when he had not wanted to spend another Friday evening at some charitable arts event. "The boys are fair and try to support her. She lives in France now and they go over there when they can."

"Do you know Michelle's new partner?"

"Husband. They're married."

"What's he like?"

"He's ok. I quite like him. He's treating Michelle and the boys well. And he's fine with me. I offered them financial support and he was quite polite. 'Non, Monsieur, non.'"

Megan splashed through the water's edge and wondered if she was asking too many questions.

"So why did Michelle go off with him?" she asked, eventually.

"There were. . . issues. . ." said David.

They were now reaching the slopes of the beach at the edge of the harbour. It was becoming busy. Several early morning fishing boats were on their way up the estuary. Megan noticed that her close friend and shoulder to cry on, Charlie Bartlett, had arrived. His wife, also called Megan, ran a five-roomed nursing home in Tywyn and they had agreed to take Rhys' mother when she became too frail to look after herself. He had taken his leisure boat, *Mikatcha,* off its mooring and tied it up at the jetty. He would be taking a party of fishermen out later. She knew Charlie would moan about the price of diesel. The recession was hitting the Aberdovey community badly.

"Issues?"

David hesitated. He was confiding in a woman he had met less than two days earlier. She turned and smiled at him.

"I got involved with somebody else."

"Was it serious?" asked Megan and immediately regretted her question.

"At the time, yes."

"Well, no wonder your wife left you," said Megan. "You told her, I suppose. Most men confess in the end."

"It wasn't that simple," said David. "I allowed myself to get carried away and I think I promised that I would leave Michelle and marry her."

"And then you didn't?"

"No. The problem was she then kept phoning Michelle and writing her letters. She went on and on about how she gave me the sex life Michelle never had."

David seemed to become lost in his thoughts, but then continued.

"We were married in our early twenties."

"And Matthew is nineteen?" mused Megan.

"We had to get married. Her father was awful. He was a Church of England minister and her mother was a doctor. I liked her and she accepted things. But, as far as Michelle was concerned, somehow my career, my frustrations, my ambitions simply passed her by. She said she could forgive the affair but not that I had discussed our sex life with *'that other woman'.*"

"What was her name?" Megan stopped. "I'm sorry - I'm being nosey. Let's talk about something else."

"Carolyn," continued David. "She was a client, which made it even more difficult."

He paused and looked across the seaward part of the Dovey Estuary towards Ynyslas. The waves of the incoming tide were breaking over the sandbanks.

He turned and faced Megan. "She took me out to dinner at the Dorchester Hotel. We had drinks and we talked a lot about our lives. She was interested in what I did. We just ended the evening by going to bed. She'd booked a room. It felt natural."

"And afterwards?"

"Depressed and guilty. I had cheated. I couldn't look Matthew in the face."

Some early morning residents were starting out on their beach walks. They covered the final stretch of the beach in silence.

"What happened? Can I ask?"

"Michelle left me. Carolyn wouldn't speak to me and changed company advisers. My bosses were furious that I had lost a client."

They arrived back at the road and quickly entered Swn-y-Don. David went into the kitchen and handed Megan the note he had written her earlier.

"Scrambled eggs!" she exclaimed.

They were indeed delicious.

After breakfast, David slipped into the front room to make a phone call.

"Is Jemma there please?. . .Tell her it's David. . . She will know. . . Jemma, sorry, yes, at home, sorry, it is early. . . But I'll never get Jackson at a weekend. . . Did the second list arrive from Martin Van Dijl?. . . It did?. . . And what was the total? What, seriously?! Christ. No. Thanks. I'll see you tomorrow. Bye."

David started to move upstairs, but his mobile phone rang. Megan answered and handed it to him as he reached the top of the steps.

"John Pearman?"

David held the BlackBerry to his ear. "John, nice to hear from you. Yes, looking forward to seeing you. . . Well perhaps it would be best if we covered the ground at the meeting. . . Yes, I am sure he is. . . Please don't worry, we'll have a full explanation tomorrow. Yes. Cheerio, John."

"Will you?" asked Megan.

"Will I what?"

"Have a full explanation?"

"It's a matter of managing expectations," said David.

"In other words, 'no'."

David wiped his forehead.

"I thought Martin was well on his way," he muttered to himself.

At around ten o'clock they left the house and walked down the road towards the local shop, where David bought *The Times* and the *Financial Times* and Megan *The Daily Post*.

As they strolled along the pavement they agreed to spend the rest of the morning on the beach. They passed *Nandoras*, a boutique catering for the wealthy West Midlanders who owned properties in the village. David put his hand under Megan's arm and guided her into the shop. A few minutes later she had selected a pretty La Senza bikini.

They settled in a sand dune on the Aberdovey beach. They talked. They read the newspapers. They dozed in the bright sunshine, although David twice took calls on his phone. As the sun grew hotter, he smothered Megan in suntan lotion. He watched as she stretched up and walked slowly to the water's edge. The dark green colouring showed Megan's figure at its alluring best. David watched intently as she splashed sea water over herself.

They decided to spend the afternoon on the beach, and so Megan returned to the house and collected a picnic basket. She packed some plates, several glasses and a bottle opener. She then ventured into the village for supplies.

They lingered for a long time over lunch. "The wine is Chateau Dyfi," announced Megan. "The best Londis had to offer!" She handed David a slice of ham pie and some tomatoes.

"Excellent choice," he said. "But I can't eat too much of the pie. I have my medical next Wednesday." He patted his flat stomach. "I must weigh in at twelve stone two."

"Aren't you well?" asked Megan.

"I'm fine," said David. "But I have an annual medical."

"And the doctor is happy to do it?"

"Well, I pay him enough."

"Ah, you go privately."

"Of course," said David. "Dr Elson has been looking after me for three years now. He's good. A South African."

"So what happens in this medical?"

"It will take two hours. I start by talking to Dr Elson for about thirty minutes about my general state of health, my training regime, a few personal issues, male things, you understand, and any other matter I want him to consider. He then gives me a full examination, takes a series of tests, blood, urine and so on. He will weigh me and he is expecting me to arrive at the weight I told you. I also had raised blood pressure last time so he will be particularly concerned about that. When he has finished I have an ECG exercise which tests my cardio-respiratory fitness. I go on the treadmill. That's a revolving platform on which I do a series of runs. The incline is increased after each four minute period. I have electrodes attached to me and the computer monitors my blood pressure with the heart under pressure. Dr Elson will write to me about a week later with a full report, a copy of the blood test and the results of the treadmill exercise. The blood test is important because it measures the blood fats. People talk about their cholesterol. There are six different readings because there is good cholesterol and bad cholesterol. The blood test measures blood counts, haemoglobin, that sort of thing, and checks for diabetes, liver and enzymes."

"Enzymes?"

"I don't really know what they are," replied David. "But Dr Elson says they're important."

"How much does this cost?"

"Dr Elson will charge around £500, the various tests are billed separately by the laboratory but will be around £180, and the ECG test is £150."

"Over £800. *Duw*!"

"You can't pay too much for your health."

"No, not if you can afford it."

Megan straightened her towel and lay face down in the sand dune. As she reflected on what David had just told her she felt a hand slip onto her bikini bottoms. She decided to let it stay there.

"That's one test Dr Elson need not worry about," she thought.

They arrived back at Swn-y-don in the late afternoon. David intended to leave for London by six o'clock and Megan would return to her cottage.

They stood together outside the front door. Megan reached up and kissed David on the cheek.

"*Diolch am dydd hyfryd, David,*" she said. It had been a lovely day; a lovely three days. She watched him carry his case to his car and leave for London.

Matthew paused and turned towards his younger brother.

"Tell me, Josh. I want to know."

Josh looked around at the evening lights which were illuminating the market square of St. Marguerite. He watched the families finishing their evening meals. A squabble broke out between two young girls, each of whom wanted to take the King Charles Spaniel for a walk. A tug-of-war developed over the lead.

"She kept asking me to sit on her lap. Bit weird – I haven't done that for five years. And she kept trying to hug me."

"And you saw her through the bedroom door?" said Matthew.

"Briefly. I can't be sure. It happened quickly and then the door was slammed shut."

"But you saw her fall over?"

"Think so, Matt."

The offices of Park Avenue Capital were shuddering with the force of the explosion from the company chairman.

"Fucking FSA rules! Fucking compliance! David, do something!" yelled Jackson Holmes.

"Nothing I can do, Jackson. We've had to put the meeting back a week. Our Compliance Department say they've not finished their checks on all the directors. We can't sign the documents until they do."

"Fucking Cameron wants us to stimulate enterprise in this country and I'm bogged down with fucking rules!"

"Jackson," said David. "You might want to review our internal processes. I wonder if this situation might have been avoided."

"You're a bloody partner. You do it!"

David decided to refrain from telling his colleague that in Park Avenue Capital nobody did anything without the permission of the chairman. He thought instead about how much he was looking forward to collecting Matthew and Josh from Heathrow airport that evening. He sent a quick text message.

"Coming to Dovey on Thursday evening. Will you join me? David."

He was surprised to receive an immediate reply.

"No. Thanks for asking. Megan."

He went out for lunch with a lawyer who acted for a number of their clients. They discussed their concerns over the continuing depressed state of the London markets. She had just returned from Hong Kong and told David about the contrasting vitality and growth in the Far East.

He returned to his office and sent another text message.

"Any point in pleading my case?"

The reply came an hour later.

"None whatsoever, but you are a lucky boy. My shift at Outward Bound has just been changed. I'll be with you at 8:00am Friday. Megan."

David was shocked by the surge of excitement which shot through him. The next two days went happily quickly. Matthew and Josh settled back home, although David thought his elder son was a bit subdued.

He reached Aberdovey in the early hours of Friday morning and, after three hours sleep, rose and went for an hour's run on the beach. He was changed and ready when Megan arrived at 8:30am. After a breakfast of fruit and coffee, and David excusing himself to take a phone call, Megan moved upstairs to the lounge and switched on the television.

Over an hour later David realised Megan had not returned. He climbed the stairs and stepped into the front room. The curtains were closed and tears were pouring down her cheeks. He glanced at the screen.

The bride was walking up the aisle to the coronation anthem 'I Was Glad' by Sir Charles Parry, from Psalm 122. The 1,900 guests in Westminster Abbey watched the service progress, enraptured. David knelt beside Megan and put his arm around her shoulders. As Prince William and Kate Middleton kissed, she dissolved into fresh emotion.

David let her watch the procession to the palace and then put a glass of chilled white wine in her hand.

"The Duke and Duchess of Cambridge," he said.

"She's very pretty," Megan replied.

"Not a patch on you."

"That's because she's about thirty pounds lighter than me, David!"

The next day, in the afternoon, they took a picnic onto the beach. They drank more than a bottle of wine and talked endlessly. At the end of the day they said goodnight and went to their separate beds.

The next morning, when David returned from his walk, he found a note in the kitchen.

"Taking Mam to chapel. Back late morning. Megan."

After making a number of calls, he left the house and walked around the harbour. He then settled on one of the benches circling the lawns in the centre of the village and enjoyed a leisurely read of the weekend papers.

The time passed and there beside him appeared Megan, carrying a blue and white holdall.

"Are you going somewhere?" he asked.

"Outward Bound have just swapped me again. It's because I'm single. The married staff are always changing shifts. . . So I'm now free. They want me on Monday afternoon."

She sat down beside him and they watched the growing numbers of holiday makers.

"Better this year," said David. "It was dire for nearly the whole season last year, what with petrol prices and the recession."

She interrupted. "It wasn't all bad news, mind you. The jetskis are doing alright. Do you know it costs £80 to rent one for the day? I hate them. Their waves destroy the estuary banks."

"Really? I think they're great," said David. "Both boys have got one. I take them down to the Solent. They love it."

"David, they're a menace. They damage the ecology, they scare the birdlife. . ."

"If they're used responsibly they're fine," said David. "And, if I may say so, the jet skiers bring the money to Aberdovey."

"They're too noisy," said Megan, and she walked off towards the jetty where she waved to the Outward Bound crew as they launched one of their boats.

Thirty minutes later they were walking at the water's edge, watching the waves come in as the estuary began to gather the tidal waters.

"So you work in London?" asked Megan.

"Yes, the office is in Curzon Street in Mayfair. Right by the Saudi Arabian embassy."

"What's the firm called?"

"Park Avenue Capital. It's owned by a chap called Jackson Holmes. I joined him four years ago."

"What do you do?"

"We're AIM Nomads".

"Um, sorry – you're what?"

"Sorry," acknowledged David. "I'm a corporate financier. I specialise in helping companies to join AIM. That stands for the Alternative Investment Market and it's owned by the London Stock Exchange. It's the most successful junior stock market in the world".

"So what's an AIM Nomad?"

"Nomad stands for 'Nominated Adviser', hence the term 'Nomad'."

There was a loud siren as the Aberdovey Sailing Club began their 1:00pm race.

"Sorry David, I'm lost."

"OK, try it another way. I help companies raise money. They do so by putting their companies on a stock market, in my case the AIM. They sell shares to institutions and private individuals."

"It's another world."

"Not really, Megan. You're familiar with the big names: Marks and Spencer, Tesco, BT and so on, but the economy depends on encouraging smaller companies to grow. On AIM there are young retail businesses which, if they have access to capital, can grow into the Marks and Spencer of tomorrow."

"Is it like that programme I've seen on television – what's it called? 'Dragon's Den'?"

David groaned. "No, nothing like it."

They sat down at the water's edge.

"Megan, I'd love to show you Primrose Hill."

"Is that where you live, in London?"

"Yes."

"Do you have photos?" she asked.

"Why would I have photos? said David, looking puzzled.

"You said you wanted to show me where you live."

"Yes, I want to take you there," said David. "If we leave now we'll be in London by eight o'clock."

Megan looked at him in complete amazement.

"London! Now? You're crazy! How will I get home? Where will I sleep? I've only just met you. . ."

"But you haven't said you don't want to, have you?"

Chapter Three

The journey to London took nearly seven hours and it was a little before 11:00pm when David and Megan reached the inner suburbs of London, just to the east of Lord's Cricket Ground and to the north of Regent's Park. They parked the car and entered the four-storey Edwardian house on the eastern edge of Primrose Hill. David showed Megan to the top floor and opened a door leading into a bedroom.

"There are bathrooms on this floor and two downstairs," he said.

They returned to the ground floor kitchen where David made them each a cup of coffee, which they took into the lounge. He put a CD on the deck and pressed the start button. The voice of Elaine Paige filled the room. When David went into his study to take a phone call, Megan took the opportunity to stroll around the house. The opulence, the furnishings, the decorations were things she had never experienced before, with the exception of the occasional visits to Gareth and Nerys' home.

Megan stood up and stretched out her arms. She decided that this was something she could get used to.

"Well, David. It's never dull with you," she said.

She kissed him on the cheek and went to bed.

The following morning Megan was in an exhilarated mood and they walked together along Regent's Park Road. There was an atmosphere of holiday gaiety as they purchased fresh bread and fruit from the pavement vendors and bought papers from the newsagent.

After breakfast David disappeared for an hour, but he returned mid-morning and suggested a walk. They left the house, crossed the road and entered Primrose Hill through the iron turnstile. They strolled together up to the top, where Megan was transfixed by the views across London. She walked over to the stainless steel display board, scanned the etched outlines and read the names: Canary Wharf Tower, St. Paul's Cathedral,

London Telecom Tower, Mill Bank Tower, Battersea Power Station. . .

David sat back and watched her. She was wearing a pale green cotton shirt and pure white slacks which were cut away at her calves. From there elegant muscles led down to her feet where, from one, the Welsh Dragon streamed out over her ankle. At this point David did not know there was another tattoo hidden elsewhere. His eyes lifted and he studied her buttocks. In a purist sense they were possibly slightly large but the effect was a rear of supreme attraction. He carried on past her waist and made out the outline of her underwear. He reached her blonde hair which was gently catching the mild winds.

Megan turned towards David. He watched her thighs rippling with health and energy. He could see her white panties and, higher up, the curve of her full breasts. Her fair hair was full of vitality and her face radiated happiness. She was wearing no make-up, no jewellery. But it was the smile that seduced David. Her mouth was compact with slightly red lips. Her skin was tanned; her eyes blazed.

"The wheel is missing," she said.

"What wheel?"

"You know, the one that goes round with people in it."

"The London Eye."

"Yes, it's not there.'

"Hmm, go back and read the bottom right hand corner."

She returned. "Greater London Council 1986."

"So when was the Eye erected?" asked David.

"Oh. The Millennium. 2000," said Megan. "They should have added it."

David stood up and put his arms underneath her shoulders. He lifted her up and swung her around. Her hands locked behind his neck. Megan knew that she should resist but his vitality was infectious.

They walked down the hill, across Prince Albert Road, over the Grand Union Canal and into Regent's Park. Megan absorbed the smell of cut grass and the people doing what people do in parks. Some were just walking and thinking. Some were running, keeping fit. Some couples were simply together.

That evening they had dinner in Primrose Hill. David had booked a table for two at a local French restaurant.

They strolled back to the house at around eleven o'clock. Megan refused a drink and simply kissed David goodnight.

The following morning was May Bank Holiday. Before dawn, Megan caught a pre-booked cab to Euston Station where she began the six-hour journey back to Aberdovey. She wanted to be at the Outward Bound school by mid-afternoon.

When David reached the kitchen he found a note.

"Adore Primrose Hill. Thanks. Megan x."

The next morning a meeting took place at Park Avenue Capital in Curzon Street, Mayfair. It was chaired by Jackson Holmes, chairman and chief executive of the corporate finance advisory company, and included David Rensburg and Jemma Shah, together with Martin Van Dijl, the chief executive of Mulins Rowland and Julian Bearing of solicitors Bearing and Russell, together with the directors of Trafford Discount Stores plc.

"These are the best fucking market conditions I've ever known," announced Cyril Trafford. "The fucking crisis is perfect for our business. Interest rates are down to half a percent, the fucking bank is now asking me for business and I've got five new stores ready to launch. And you fucking clowns now tell me that the £3,500,000 I was told would be available this week . . ." He turned to David, "THIS FUCKING WEEK, David. . . and now you are telling me you haven't got it?!"

"There is a delay, Mr Trafford," said Jackson.

"How much have you got and what is the delay we are talking?" asked Margaret Drummond.

She was Cyril Trafford's daughter and she protected her father with a frightening intensity.

"Margaret," replied David, "it's not that easy. I explained to you recently that we may have lost our lead investor and that means we cannot be sure whether others will drop out too."

"I know what you bastards are doing," interjected Cyril, in the direction of Margaret and John Pearman, the chief executive of Trafford Discount Stores. "Didn't I tell you? They are going to tell us the price is too high." Cyril then turned to David. "12p a share is what we agreed and 12p is what stands. Got it?" Cyril's face was turning redder by the minute. He was extremely angry.

"So what happens now?" asked John.

"We're simply asking you to allow us to extend the placing period by another four weeks," replied David. He was referring to the placing of shares. This was the language of the City. In practical terms he was talking about persuading investment funds and private individuals to buy shares in Trafford Discount Stores. If they decided to do so, and as the action lay outside normal stock market activity (where shares are bought and sold through stockbrokers), the terminology used was a 'placing' of shares.

"But we have to make a market announcement," David added.

"Two things need to happen," said Julian Bearing. "We need to hold a Board Meeting now, which we can do because I have proxies from the two non-executive directors, and then Park Avenue Capital needs to make an announcement to the AIM. Can I suggest we extend the closing date to Friday 13th May?"

"No," said David. "Friday 20th May is better."

"For whom?" asked Cyril.

"Cyril, trust me, please. I need the extra time."

"Have we any fucking choice?"

"David," asked Margaret, "can you reassure us that you will raise the money?"

David sighed, but before he could answer the question Jackson Holmes spoke in a quiet voice.

"David never fails," he said.

"Mr Trafford," interrupted Jemma Shah, "we need to leave. We are introducing you to Mainstream VCT at 12 noon and I think the cab is here. It will be at least thirty minutes to London Wall."

"Just remind me what a VCT is, Jemma, please," said Margaret.

Martin Van Dijl raised his eyes to the ceiling.

"A Venture Capital Trust," replied Jemma. "They invest their shareholders' funds in British businesses."

"Well, I'm fucking British!" shouted Cyril. "They can write out their sodding cheque today!"

"Cyril, you know the ropes," said Jackson. "You need to sell yourself."

The three executives exited the meeting without further words. Margaret smiled at David as she left the room.

Jackson produced a bottle of gin and four glasses. "Right," he said. "Martin, let us go through the list."

Martin read out twelve names and said that he had placing agreements for £1,220,000. "We then have Atlas, who seem weak. They were in for £1,000,000."

"I spoke to them this morning," said David.

"And?" asked Martin.

"Martin, you're the broker. This is getting stupid. You will earn big sums of commission on the amount raised and I'm doing all the work."

"Jackson," said Martin. "I promise you my team have been working all weekend. It's all very well Cyril Trafford saying the recession is over but we're still finding conditions tough."

"So what about Atlas?" asked Jackson.

"You need to go and see them," said David to Martin. "It requires your eloquence. I sometimes seem to get on the wrong side of female executives. That Kate Livermore. . . she scares the life out of me."

"We need some more documents," said Martin.

"OK, I will call at the printers this afternoon. I don't think Jemma will be back."

As David walked towards Green Park tube station he received an email on his BlackBerry. "Kate Livermore, Thursday 10:30. I can't make it. Thanks. Martin."

Megan tapped firmly on the door and walked into the room.

"Megan," said Gillian Edwards, "come in and sit down."

Megan poured two cups of tea, one of which she handed to the principal of Dolgellau High School.

The school was the place Megan had found stability and the chance to rebuild her life following the death of her husband. In the six years since she had joined the teaching staff she knew she had made a positive contribution to both school life and the team ethos. She enjoyed coaching the individual sports and there were now three girls heading for golfing honours. Her tennis teams rampaged around Wales and she had, in the last two years, ventured into England. There was a group of players at Cheltenham Ladies' College who were still recovering from last autumn's whitewash.

But for Megan it was team sport that gave her the greatest fulfilment. Her hockey sides were the fittest, best trained and most skilled in the black arts of the sport. She took this belief into her work at Outward Bound. She relished the opportunity to take kids from deprived backgrounds and mould them into successful groups. Megan did not waste time thinking about social issues. She accepted that they fornicated, took drugs and stole. But they were human beings and she knew that there would be some who would watch, listen and begin to enjoy her approach to life. She watched them overcome their prejudices. They slowly edged towards her. They started to confide in her, and received the Megan treatment. "Hard cheddar. So your Dad's in prison. Let's row round the estuary once more." It worked. She could reach inside these kids. If there was something there, Megan would find it.

And the person who most appreciated her special qualities was the woman sitting opposite her.

"Megan," continued Gillian, "firstly, I appreciate you coming in. I gather you were at Outward Bound yesterday. You look better today. That's a nice tracksuit you're wearing. I always like the way your teams are turned out."

"Thanks, Gillian. 'Look smart, play smart.' That's the rule we play by."

"What about, 'look happy, be happy'?"

"Sorry?" Megan asked.

"You know what I'm saying, Megan. In the last few months your attitude has changed. You are, at times, a bit morose. Others have commented about it to me."

"But my results are still good. . ." Megan felt defensive.

"Megan, nobody doubts your ability. You have that special quality of relating to the girls." She took a polite sip of tea. "But it has been observed by several of your colleagues that in the last few months you have seemed. . . shall we say, dispirited. If you are to be given added responsibilities I must be sure that you are ready for the promotion."

"But, Gillian, you've promised me sole control over all sporting activities next year. You know how much it means to me," pleaded Megan.

"And so you will have, Megan. But I want to see you in this frame of mind all the time. When you are positive you are the leader we want."

Megan smiled. "Thank you," she said quietly.

"Emily Bowden?" continued the principal. "I've had a letter from her mother. The marriage has broken up and neither parent can take her in July. Mrs Bowden is moving into a new house and says that from August onwards Emily can live with her."

"I like Emily," said Megan. "I'll sort it out. She's a good hockey player. I'll ask at Outward Bound to see if she can stay there."

"In Aberdovey?"

"Yes. I have several friends there. They are full throughout the summer and I guess Emily might be a help to them."

Their conversation continued during a second pot of tea. Was Gillian imagining things? Was she detecting something different about her colleague?

Megan left the principal's office and went over to the playing fields.

David Rensburg could not hear the answer to his question because of the noise being made by four printing presses. He therefore followed the direction of the pointed arm and entered a dingy office.

"Thomas," he said, when he realised the owner of Payne Printers, his company's print suppliers in North London, was sitting there, "I need a reprint of the documents covering Trafford Discount Stores' share offer. About five hundred copies. OK?"

"When?" the printer asked.

"Friday."

"I'll deliver them by 9:00am in the morning."

"Are you feeling all right, Tom?" asked David "You look a bit pale."

Thomas closed the door of his office and switched on an electric kettle. The water heated and he handed David a steaming cup of coffee. "Sugar?" he asked. David declined and Thomas started talking.

He explained the problems Payne Printers were having. "It's always the same, David. As soon as there's a credit crunch people stop paying their printer. I've been fighting for nearly four years. Ever since that Northern Rock collapsed. Bloody banks. My Dad and then me, we have been with the same bank for over fifty years. What did they do last year? They called my overdraft in because they said we were high risk. I had to find £200,000."

"Did you?" asked David.

"Yes. I cashed in my pension. My financial adviser went mad. We trade in credit now."

His mobile phone rang and he listened for several minutes.

"My Dad," he said. "He's off colour."

"Is he ok?" asked David.

"He'll be back tomorrow," said Thomas. "Tell me, David," he continued, "this document about Trafford Discount Stores. . . is it a good business?"

"I think so," said David. "They've now got over fifty stores around the country, although most are in the North East and North West. Cyril Trafford has travelled the world buying in DIY stock, and with the housing crisis more people have undertaken home repairs, and of course vast numbers are improving their homes. But his real success has been his range of home insulation goods. With the rise in energy costs he's cashed in at just the right time."

"Sounds like a good investment."

"High risk, Tom." David finished his pint. "All small companies are high risk."

"So where is the risk with Trafford Discount Stores?"

"I'll tell you something, Tom. I'm not sure I understand risk anymore after the banking crisis. I had never heard of sub-prime and I can't work out how the banks did what they did."

"It was more than just the banks," said Thomas. "You want to live round here. I can see society breaking down. That bloke Cameron keeps talking about mending our broken society. Etonian twat. Born with a silver spoon. I see street fights, drug dealing, drunkenness, shop thefts every week. You want to talk to my guys out there. I pay as well as I can but they're struggling. All of them."

Thomas paused. "And, David, I'll tell you where it might end up. Civil disorder."

"Meaning what?"

"The recession is so deep that our basic structures have broken down. The police are overwhelmed. There are no-go areas everywhere. It's every man for himself. I tell you, there'll be mayhem on the streets."

David reflected that Primrose Hill seemed somewhat safer.

"Anyway, I'm prepared," Thomas went on. He opened the middle drawer of his desk, took out a gun and put it in front of him. "That is my answer," he said.

David looked at the weapon and then at Thomas. "Put it away, Tom," he said quietly.

"It's the only answer, David," he said. As he went to pick up the gun he knocked it onto the floor by accident. David reached down and picked it up. "Put it away, Tom," he repeated, as he returned it to the frightened printer.

Albert Payne put the receiver back on the phone.

He limped back up the stairs and went into the bathroom. He looked into the toilet bowl and at the globules of blood on the surface.

He knew he had to return to the surgery to get the results of his tests.

He went downstairs and into his kitchen. He looked at the mess and selected a glass. He poured himself a large scotch. He decided he would not go to the pub tonight.

On Thursday morning at 10:15am David left Liverpool Street station and walked into Broadgate, the area of the City where many of the institutions had their offices.

He never understood why he was invariably nervous when he visited 'the City'. The term itself was still accepted by most commentators to mean the country's financial centre and that meant the Bank of England in Threadneedle Street, opposite the Royal Exchange where David often met clients for coffee. But, for many, it was now the Docklands, where the Financial

Services Authority was located, that was the new pulse point. Many an executive had travelled the Docklands Light Railway down to Canary Wharf for a meeting with the regulators.

There was an arrogance about the City which David found difficult to accept. It was based simply on finance. Forget ethics. The driving force had always been the making of money. In the City there were two main routes. The first – inherited wealth. The community is dominated by public school landed gentry who are raised to believe that they are different. The prime minister himself owes his social position to his late stockbroker father.

Secondly, there are those who have made money from the markets. The traders, brokers, dealers. Their riches are baffling.

In recent years there had been a drift towards Mayfair and the West End. David much preferred Curzon Street and the Park Lane vicinity for his daily work.

He entered a thirty-storey building and asked for Atlas VCT at the reception desk. His photograph was taken as the receptionist phoned through to announce his arrival.

He caught the lift up to the seventeenth floor and then entered the foyer of Atlas VCT. His feet sank into the carpet as he was asked to sit down. He browsed through the *Financial Times*, looked at his watch several times and checked his BlackBerry. He answered an email with a single word.

At 10:50am he was shown into a spartan meeting room which had a table and six chairs, six glasses and a jug of water.

He looked through the all-glass wall and out over the panoramic view of Finsbury Square and City Road. He thought about the person he was due to meet. Kate Livermore was an investment manager. She was responsible for three funds. These effectively take other people's money – usually from pension companies and private investors – and try to earn a better profit than might be available by putting the money in a bank. This was often achieved by identifying smaller growing businesses and backing them. Kate's record was good.

The financial sector is, to some extent, dishonest. They operate peer group measurement. Kate's job and bonuses depended not on the absolute, or true, returns on her funds, but how she measured against other funds. During the recessional years which had started in 2007, Kate had lost less money than most other similar funds. For this she received industry awards because the denizens of the City love giving each other prizes. The newspapers that write about the funds receive annual awards from those same funds, allowing Mr Murdoch and his colleagues to tuck away the advertising revenues.

But David knew better than to buck the system and he needed Kate Livermore's money.

At 11:05am the door opened and Kate entered. "David," she said, "this is Natasha Naylor-Simmonds."

They all sat down. Kate and David faced each other across the table. Natasha Naylor-Simmonds reposed at the end of the table. She crossed her legs and eased her skirt above her knees. She then adjusted her hair band, which was holding together a group of jewel encrusted braids. She stared out of the window.

"May I say how much I appreciate. . ."

"David," interrupted Kate, "just over three-and-a-half years ago," she stopped to examine the file, "15th November 2007, to be exact, we invested £2,000,000 into Trafford Discount Stores plc. at 22p per share. They have missed all their sales projections and the price is now 15p. And now you come here expecting me to agree to another £1,000,000 at 12p per share. I'm more inclined to ask for our money back."

Natasha continued to look out of the window.

"And I strongly suggest that you refrain from trying to sell me the advantages of averaging down because if you do I'll sell you the disadvantages of throwing good money after bad."

David took a sip of water.

"And now I'm going to get cross. You agreed with me that it was unacceptable for the finance director to be the daughter of the chairman. But what do I read? 'Finance Director: Margaret Drummond FCA'."

She took a drink of water before continuing her tirade.

"I've been in this industry for twenty years and, David, I tell you from bitter experience that there must be a wall between the chairman and the finance function."

"Kate," said David, "as always you are making some interesting points. . ."

"And you will no doubt be able to explain to me why Cyril Trafford, three months ago, sold 5,000,000 shares at 16p per share, just before the company put out a trading statement and said it would be raising more money."

"Kate, please. You told Martin Van Dijl that you would invest £1,000,000."

"Martin Van Dijl!" exploded Kate Livermore, as Natasha uncrossed and crossed her legs. "Why, David, does your firm use Mulins Rowland? They're discount brokers. You don't need them. We prefer to deal with you."

David sighed.

"Kate, this is a deal I want you to consider because I believe that the target price of 30p can be reached within two years. That requires pre-tax profits of £32,000,000. The fundraising will be used to improve liquidity and fund the opening of five more stores. I've prepared ten key points that I want you to think about."

He waited while Kate considered the contents of the single sheet of paper in front of her. Natasha left her copy unread.

"We saw so many businesses struggle in 2009 and 2010, Kate. None of us saw the credit crunch coming. Cyril Trafford was working twenty hours a day, week after week. He got it right with the new range of home insulation materials. People were never going to respond to climate change issues. Escalating energy bills were the impetus to Trafford's expansion."

Natasha stood up and walked out of the room.

"I'll think about it," said Kate, as she closed the file in front of her.

"May I phone you?" asked David

"No."

She accompanied David to the lift and turned on her heels.

As David left the building he used his BlackBerry to send an email. "Thanks for your time, Kate. Sincerely, David."

As she read the message, Kate nodded to herself. She looked at the page on her desk. "Commitments June 2011." Against Trafford Discount Stores plc. she wrote, "Trust David Rensburg. Will consider."

Albert Payne reached across the bar and grabbed at his glass of scotch. He consumed nearly the whole amount. As he did so another spasm of pain seared across his abdomen.

"Oh God," he cried.

The barman came out from behind the pumps and helped Albert onto a stool.

"Shall we get you home, Albert?" he asked.

"I've got a doctor's appointment," he whispered.

Without saying another word Albert fell off the stool and lay prostrate on the floor. The barman bent down and held Albert's hand as the staff awaited the arrival of the ambulance.

Megan and David were in daily contact via mobile. On Thursday evening Megan received a text. *"Swn-y-Don 11:30 tomorrow night?"*

When they met at the house late the following evening both were tired and they agreed to miss supper and go to bed. David said that low tide the next day was around midday.

They spent Saturday morning on the beach and began the walk around 12 noon. The May sun was hotter than the previous weekend and the sands around the water's edge were firm. Megan wore a tee shirt and bikini bottoms. David smothered himself in suntan cream and settled for shorts. Both went barefoot.

Megan had to wait for David, who seemed preoccupied with his left foot.

"I may have a neuroma," he said.

"What's a neuroma?" asked Megan.

"Rather serious. It may require surgery."

"David, tell me what a neuroma is."

"It's a foot injury. I looked it up on Google. My foot has been hurting all week."

Megan sighed. "A neuroma is a thickening of nerve tissue, David. In the foot it is called a Morton's neuroma. It usually occurs between the third and fourth toe and sometimes requires surgery. I've been teaching PE for ten years and have never come across it."

They continued their walk.

"How did you know about a neuroma?" asked David.

"I studied hard," replied Megan. "There are more problems with feet than any other part of an athlete's body. There are twenty-four separate joints in the foot alone."

David was impressed.

"And my mother had one three years ago. I never saw it because she lives in Canada but she kept emailing me photographs!"

They had been talking non-stop since breakfast, with Megan telling David about her new responsibilities at Dolgellau High School and David expressing his worries over Trafford Discount Stores.

As they reached the headland and began the long stretch towards Tywyn, David turned to Megan.

"Megan, your accent. . . It's not – well – deep Welsh, is it?"

"David!" exclaimed Megan. "I am as Welsh as you can be. I speak Welsh most of the time unless I'm with English invaders such as you. But you're right, I suppose I've spent quite a bit of time away at Loughborough University and teaching in Birmingham and my accent's not as strong as it was."

They walked on. "I'm so Welsh I even played hockey for Wales," she said.

"When was that?"

"Well, actually, I played for Great Britain. I was selected for the Olympic qualifying tournament in New Zealand in 2004. We all thought we were on the way to Athens. . . We lost. It was my one and only match: Auckland 2004 – the peak of my career."

Megan paused and then continued: "Just think, I might have been in Beijing in 2008 if things had turned out differently."

"So what happened?"

"The school had been supportive with time off but I felt I wanted to return to concentrate on my career."

"No regrets?"

Megan did not reply. They were well on the way to Tywyn and for the next twenty minutes they walked in silence. They turned around and began the return walk to Aberdovey harbour.

Megan began to sing quietly.

"Mae hen wlad nhadau yn annwyl I mi,
Gwlad beirdd a chantorion, enwogion o fri;
Ei gwrol ryfelwyr, dwladgarwyr tra mad,
Tros ryddid collasant eu gwa'd. . ."

"Is that the Welsh national. . .?"

"Gwlad, gwlad, pleidiol wyf I'm qwlad;
Tram or yn fur I'r bur hoff bau,
O bydded I'r hen iaith barhau."

"What's that word, Megan, *Gwad* or something like it?" asked David. "I thought the chorus starts *Wales, Wales. . .* isn't that *Cymru*?"

"Oh *Duw*," laughed Megan. "This is the translation – and just enjoy the poetry, David."

"The land of my fathers is dear unto me,
Old land where the minstrels are honoured and free;
Its warring defenders so gallant and brave,
For freedom their lifeblood they gave."

"And the chorus starts Gwlad which means home –"

"Home, home, true am I to home,
While seas secure the land so pure,
Oh may the old language endure."

"Dylan Thomas," said David.

"Um, what's he got to do with it?"

"He wrote it – the national anthem."

"Try Evan James from Pontypridd," said Megan. "He was the owner of a woollen mill. The story is that his brother emigrated to America and wanted Evan to join him. The words he wrote tell why he wanted to stay in Wales. I think his son James wrote the music."

"Well, it was lovely," said David.

"There are another two verses. . ."

"Hmm, it was not that lovely," smiled David.

"Seriously, David, Welsh is a beautiful tongue. There are over half a million of us who use it as our native language."

"It is the sound, Megan, that makes it so difficult. '*Llan*', for example, I just can't say it."

"'*Llan*' means a church or a village. What you do is position your tongue to say 'l' and then you breathe out. Try it."

"Flaann. . .er," stuttered David.

"*Llan,*" said Megan. "Mouth the letter 'l' and put your tongue in place and breathe out. *Llan*. It's easy."

"*Llan,*" said David, triumphantly.

"There you are. You probably know more words than you realise. What about '*ar werth*'?"

"Never heard of it."

"You see it all the time, David," laughed Megan. "Try 'for sale' – and what about '*Aber*'?"

"*Aber*?" David thought. "Estuary?"

"Estuary or river mouth," said Megan. "Hence 'Aberdovey'. The estuary of the river Dovey."

"And what does Dovey mean?"

"'*Dyfi*' means 'dark one'. *Aberdyfi*. . . 'the mouth of the dark one'."

She splashed happily through the gentle surf and chuckled as David ran back to avoid a stronger incoming wave.

"Tide's coming in," he announced.

"No it isn't," said Megan. "It's going out."

"What was that bloody wall of water that just soaked me, then?"

"It was the seventh wave."

"The what?"

"Every seventh wave is much stronger than the others. It's a well known fact."

David stood at the water's edge and watched as the Cardigan Bay waves came in. He was counting, and when the seventh wave hit he was splashed up to the bottom of his shorts.

"So how do you know the tide is going out?" he asked Megan.

"Look at the boats in the harbour. You can see several from here. Look at where the anchor is. If the tide is going out the boats will be being pulled away from their base."

"Right."

"And also I checked the times of the tides in the Harbour Master's office!"

They continued on until Megan broke the silence. "I have a surprise for you," she said.

"What is it?" asked David.

"What's what?"

"What are you up to?" he said.

"Hmm, does *Mikatcha* mean anything to you?" she laughed.

"*Mikatcha*?"

"It's a boat. The name is made up of the first letters of Charlie Bartlett's three daughters' names – Michelle, Katherine and Charmain."

"Who's Charlie Bartlett?"

"He owns the boat. He runs fishing trips. I've booked him for Bank Holiday Monday. That's in two weeks' time."

"Who says I'll be here?" asked David.

Megan pulled David towards her. "Be honest, Mr Big Noise from the City of London. You can't resist coming to see me, can you?"

David pulled away from her and wondered about asking the question on his mind. He decided to bide his time.

On Tuesday evening of the following week there was a knock on the door of Megan's cottage. She opened it to be confronted by a man holding a board.

"Can you sign here, please Miss?" he asked.

"Sign for what?"

"Your car," he said and stepped aside. Behind him was a jet black sports coupé with the Alpha Romeo badge showing proudly on the bonnet.

"It only came off the production line last week. You must be able to pull strings. Some of the cars I deliver have been ordered three months ago." He pushed his board under Megan's chin. "Please sign here. You are Megan Williams, I assume? It says 'by order of David Rensburg'."

"But I already have a car," said Megan.

"I'm taking that away, Miss. Come on, I'll show you the controls. There's a full tank of petrol."

Thirty minutes later Megan was driving the eleven miles to Aberdovey. The top of the car was down and her hair streamed behind her as she accelerated out of Tywyn and along the coast road, past the cemetery and the golf club and into the village. She posted a note through the letterbox of Swn-y-Don.

On Friday morning David phoned Megan to say he would not be arriving in Aberdovey until early on the Saturday morning. Megan was organising a tennis training weekend at Dolgellau High School and so they agreed to meet for lunch on the Sunday. "I'll prepare something light for us," Megan told David, "after I've given you a spin in my new car, of course!"

What David did not tell her was that he was having a few problems with Matthew and Josh. They had caught on to Megan and wanted to know everything. David had found it very awkward when Matthew had asked whether they were sleeping together.

At 12 noon in the offices of Park Avenue Capital, Jackson Holmes chaired a team progress meeting. There was one topic to cover. The fundraising for Trafford Discount Stores was floundering. The review centred on the role of Martin Van Dijl. Jackson was confident.

"I've worked with Martin for many years. He's all you say. His communications are awful. But he raises money. We must stick with him."

As David walked towards the Ritz Hotel at the top of St. James's in Mayfair he received a text message. *"You have six fucking days left. CT."*

It rained all day on the Sunday and so after lunch they settled down in the lounge of Swn-y-Don. David sensed a slight atmosphere between them and tried to establish what the issue might be. Megan was not responding to David's questions. He decided to change the subject.

"In three weeks' time," he said, "Matthew and Josh are staying in London with me. Will you come down and meet them?"

"I'm not sure I can."

"Oh, school duties?"

"No, we're in the middle of term and I'm really just finishing off preparing for the next year's groups."

"So come to London and meet the boys," repeated David.

Megan frowned. "Aren't you worried that this is all a bit sudden?" she asked. "We've known each other for just over five weeks. You've bought me a car costing a fortune and now you want me to come to London again to meet your sons. Why?"

David rose from his chair and went over to Megan, who was lying on the sofa. He put his arms under hers and lifted her to her feet. He then put his hands on her shoulders and looked into her eyes.

"Megan," he said, "if you want time that's fine by me. I'm sure of my ground, but I can wait for you." He gently kissed her. She wrapped herself around him briefly and then pulled away.

"David," she said. "It's not that easy. Please don't take this the wrong way, but I have never met anybody like you." She paused. "I promise you I'm not looking for another Rhys – because I know he doesn't exist." She took a step back. "You are. . . you are. . . well, that's my problem, David. I don't know who you are."

Chapter Four

Thomas Payne pushed the tube to one side and lent over the bed so that he could wipe the damp flannel over his father's face. He reached for the glass of water and held the rim to his father's lips. Some dribbled down his chin and Thomas carefully dried this up with his handkerchief. He looked around the ward but could not see any medical staff. In the next bed was a moaning, slumbering figure. He had been sick on the floor.

"Dad," said Thomas. "I expect they're short staffed. I'll go and see what I can do."

Albert grabbed his son's arm. "Please, Thomas, get me out of here."

"Dad, it's not that easy. They've started your treatment. We're going to get you better."

Albert grimaced with pain as another spasm sent red hot arrows around his groin.

"Please, Thomas," he pleaded. "It's not going to work. I'm too far gone. They said I should have gone to the doctor earlier. I just thought I was having trouble peeing."

A nurse arrived at the bedside and began straightening the covers. "And how are you this morning, Mr Payne?" she asked.

Thomas stood up and indicated he would like to talk to her. They moved away from the cubicle.

"As you know, Mr Payne, your father was brought in yesterday in agony. His kidneys were not working properly. He was seen by the surgeon late on. Although there are still some more tests to be done I'm afraid we are pretty sure it's a prostate problem."

"Cancer, you mean?"

"Well," said the nurse. "As I say, there are still some more results we are waiting for, but the surgeon spent well over twenty minutes with your father and, to be frank, the disease is so far advanced that there did not seem to be much doubt."

"So what happens now?" asked Thomas.

"We're hoping he'll see the surgeon again later this afternoon. We can control the pain. When the surgeon has been we will know what the course of treatment will be."

"Can't it be removed?" asked Thomas, increasingly desperate.

"Perhaps, Mr.Payne. I can't say."

"Can I see the surgeon?"

"You have to phone his secretary to make an appointment. Sorry, Mr Payne, I must go."

As the nurse rushed to the far end of the ward Thomas returned to the bed. His father seemed to be uncomfortable.

"What is it, Dad?"

Albert opened his eyes. "Please, Thomas, get me out of here."

Bank Holiday Monday started like so many summer days in Aberdovey. To the south west there was a mass of black cloud hovering over the southern part of Cardigan Bay. The sky above the coast remained bright and clear. To the north there were layers of grey and white cumulus and an onshore westerly wind was blowing.

This would be one of the busiest days of the season. By mid-morning the car park was full and late arrivals were forced to drive under the railway bridge and out towards the grass verges on the outskirts of the town. From before breakfast time the pier had been crowded with kids crabbing, which they did by lowering their lines into the sea beneath the wooden jetty and pulling out three, four or even five crabs at a time on one line, having been tempted by the meats on the hooks supplied by the butcher in Church Square. The crabs were put into buckets and would eventually cascade back into the water when the youngsters tired of their sport.

A number of the fishing vessels had left their estuary moorings early in the morning and by mid-afternoon most had returned, coming back in on the tidal waters as the hour of the high tide approached around four o'clock. On the Ynyslas side of the estuary the incoming waters were crashing over the sand banks.

Megan thought David had seemed preoccupied during the morning. He had spent more than an hour in the front room sending emails and had taken several calls. He later told Megan that one was from Matthew. He had not sounded his usual self.

As the sun disappeared behind a bank of cloud, David became more aware of the weather conditions. When he wandered over to the beach he registered a fall in temperature and noticed that some holiday makers were beginning to pack up their wind-shields and chairs and were returning to their cars.

"Are you sure about this sailing trip?" he asked Megan.

"We need to pack a waterproof each," she replied and a few minutes later she was standing at the front door of Swn-y-Don, dressed in white jeans and a blue sailor's top. As David put his key in the lock she reached into the pocket of his trousers and took out his phone. She went back into the dining room and left it by his laptop. Their eyes met and David hesitated. But he left it where it was.

The skies had cleared and they made their way to the harbour. They reached the mooring stairs leading under the pier at the agreed time. *Mikatcha* was riding the water and its white and dark blue hull was gleaming in the sparkling sunlight.

Charlie Bartlett waved to Megan.

"Come on board whenever you want," he cried.

They eased themselves over the side of the jetty, down the metal ladder and stood on the rear deck. Megan introduced David to Charlie and the two men shook hands.

Megan briefly explained Charlie's background. He took over and seemed keen to tell David about how he had relocated his family from the Midlands many years ago and how he had built up his business.

"You're happy about the weather conditions?" asked David. "Are there life jackets on board?"

"David," Megan said, "Charlie is the best sailor in Aberdovey. He's a former RNLI Helmsman and this boat. . ."

"This boat, my friend," interrupted Charlie, "is fitted with a Volvo D12 engine and meets the MCA Code of Practice category 2." Charlie paused and looked at David. "Don't worry, I don't take risks."

He released the boat from its mooring ropes and eased his way through the various craft which were occupying the outer harbour spaces. When he saw it was clear he eased the throttle and picked up speed. The exit out of the estuary is marked by a series of buoys which at night provide flashing lights. All boats need to hold their line until they are well out into Cardigan Bay. As that point was reached Charlie turned to starboard and began the journey towards the Barmouth Bar.

David was beginning to relax and he looked around the boat. Charlie was sitting in the front cabin faced by the control panel. Every so often the radio would come alive but David noticed Charlie appeared to ignore the conversations. Opposite the skipper's chair was a seating area for six people and in the bow there was a small kitchen area.

Megan was standing at the back of the boat and had been thinking of climbing the metal steps to the two seats positioned on top of the cabin where there was a second control panel, allowing Charlie to navigate outside if he wished.

She saw that David was talking to Charlie and decided to join them.

"We're going up to the Barmouth Bar," said Charlie. "It's one of three causeways in this area. They're the stuff of legends – there are all sorts of daft stories about sunken villages. In fact they are simply moraines."

"Which is what?" asked David.

"It's a line of rock left by a glacier."

"Is that where you take the fishing trips?"

"We go where the fish are," replied Charlie.

"And how do you know that?" asked David.

"The seagulls mainly. Where they are so you will find the mackerel and the sea bass. The eels will be deeper down." Charlie smiled. "I also have my depth searcher."

David looked at the instrument panel which illuminated the sea to its bottom.

"Makes it rather easy," commented David.

"There are more than enough fish," said Charlie.

Megan returned to the stern and allowed her hair to stream in the wind. It was a warm evening and she thought about taking her top off.

However, the seas were growing more agitated and she looked at the cloud bank to the south. She shuddered and after a few minutes returned to the cabin and put on her rain jacket.

David was now standing in the stern of the boat surveying

all around him. He counted the fishing rods in their holders and attached to the rear of the cabin. There were twelve. To his right he could see the coastline and behind that the hills and mountains of the hinterland. But much of this was obscured by the mist. He moved over to the ocean view and thought he saw a flash of lightning on the far west horizon. He could see no other boats in the water.

As he studied the weather patterns he noticed that Charlie had leapt out of his seat and pulled out two life jackets. He handed one to Megan and came over to David. "Put this on," he instructed. "And please come into the cabin. The weather is turning against us and we're going back."

"What's going on?" asked David.

"As I said, we're going back," replied Charlie. "There's a weather warning, that's all. We'll be in the harbour before anything happens."

"Should you not have foreseen this?" asked David as he struggled to fit into the jacket.

"That's exactly what I am doing. We'll be back in Aberdovey within twenty minutes, well before the storm arrives. In Cardigan Bay these squalls can happen quite quickly. Just relax and enjoy the rest of the trip."

David sat down beside Megan and watched intently as Charlie listened to another radio message and then began to turn his vessel to port and start the journey back to the Dyfi estuary.

Five minutes later Charlie became involved in an urgent radio interchange. He pulled out a chart of the coastline and seemed to be trying to identify a particular area. "Just west of the bar," they heard him saying, "please repeat. You are sure we are the nearest?"

He came out of his seat and turned towards Megan and David.

"They've picked up a distress call and the Coastguard has asked me to go to their help."

"Whose help?" asked David.

The seas were now beginning to swell and Charlie grabbed onto the wooden rail surrounding his cockpit as his feet slid away from under him.

"It's a yacht called *Aunty Betty*. It's lost its mast and there are some injured people. We need to go straight away, so sit tight."

"No," said David. "We're going back to the harbour. We are your passengers and we have the right to ask you to ensure our safety. Why can't the lifeboat go to the rescue?"

A crash of lightning exploded over the horizon and the whole area darkened. *Mikatcha* was now being thrown around as the waves smashed against the side of the hull.

"The lifeboat is coming but we are thirty minutes ahead of them. So shut up and let me do my job. Not another word from you. Understand?"

David stood up but was forced to grab for a rail as *Mikatcha* was caught by a surge of tidal seas. Megan dragged him down and back onto the cabin seat.

Charlie settled back to his controls and changed the direction of the boat. David felt him power the engines and they seemed to surge forward away from the coastline and out towards the north west extremity of the Barmouth Bar.

Megan whispered in David's ear. "He has to go, David. It's the rule. Charlie knows what he's doing."

The waves were now crashing over the bow of the boat and Charlie reduced his speed to eighteen knots. He was continually on the radio. He called Megan over to him. As she rose from the seat a larger wall of water hit the port side and Megan crashed forward, hitting her head on the cabin wall. She struggled to her feet and shrugged off David's attempt to help her.

"Megan," instructed Charlie, "try to get the first-aid equipment from the front. Go carefully down the steps. There are three boxes. . . ok Megan, well done, lass. Bring them up. David, help her."

The first container Megan lifted into the cabin crashed across the floor and hit the retaining plank. David grabbed it and put it on the seat they were occupying. They soon had the other two in place.

"David, come here," ordered Charlie. "Look," he said, and as they peered into the storms ahead they were able to see a mastless boat about thirty yards ahead of them.

Charlie throttled back and within minutes they were able to assess the conditions aboard the vessel. The mast of the 32-foot sailing craft was lying down the deck and over the stern. The sails were draped around it. There were two women, both wearing life-jackets. One seemed roped to the port side railing and the other was clinging to the wheel. Both were screaming and pointing to the water. There was a young man in the rear of the boat.

Charlie was maintaining a distance between him and the other boat. Megan and David were trying to understand the two women, who just kept pointing toward the rear of their yacht.

Suddenly Megan shouted, "There he is, David, there. . . just behind the stern!"

"Megan, get the pole. We'll pull him in," Charlie yelled back to Megan.

"He's trying to swim but he's face down. We'll never reach him with the pole," David responded. He grabbed an inflatable ring, lurched to the side of *Mikatcha* and hurled himself into the water.

"David, no. . . oh Christ!" said Charlie.

"David. *Na. Er mwyn dyn, na*!" screamed Megan.

David went down under the surface of the sea and lifted upwards a few seconds later. As he broke through he saw the white ring drifting ahead of him. He managed to grip the ropes threaded around it, but disappeared under the sea again as a wave crashed over him. He surfaced for a second time and looked up at the woman on the side of *Aunty Betty*. She was screaming and pointing behind David. He turned and saw a body in the water. It took only a few seconds before he reached the man. He swam under the water and up again on the other side. He grabbed the flailing arm and threaded it through the rubber ring. As he did so there were three streaks of lightning and rain began hurtling down. David found that his eyes were watering from exposure to the sea water and he was starting to feel intensely cold. He struggled to clear his vision.

Charlie was shouting from the side of *Mikatcha*. "David, this way, this way. . . come this way!"

David managed to get his arm around the head of the semi-conscious sailor. As he did so they were slammed against the side of *Aunty Betty*. David cried out with pain as his right shoulder took most of the impact. He could hear the woman above, shouting into the evening storms.

Suddenly there was a lull and the seas calmed. David tightened his grip on the man and kicked out towards *Mikatcha*. He could see Megan at the side and then she was joined by Charlie, who was holding out the pole. There were fifteen yards to cover and just when David found it easier to paddle through the water a sudden wave drove them back towards the hull of *Aunty Betty.* He tried to turn his injured shoulder but again it was slammed against the fibreglass. He cried out and went under the water. As he surfaced he flung himself towards the rescued man, who was now moaning and throwing his free arm around.

Again, he locked on to the man and then he kicked out. This time he found the two of them moving towards the extended pole. He managed to attach the hook to the ropes of the rubber ring which was still linked to the injured sailor. Charlie began to hoist the body up the side of the boat but the waves were again crashing against the hull and on two occasions he was forced to let go.

"David!" shouted Charlie. "I need to get a rope. I can't lift you out. Megan's at the wheel so I'm going to drop the pole!"

David was now tiring and was hindered by his throbbing shoulder. They slid back into the water, but Charlie was there again and he hurled a rope which landed on David. He wrapped it around the waist of the rescued man.

"Right, Charlie," he said, "let's try to get him up."

The rain started again and the waves were lifting the two drifting men around the hull of *Mikatcha*. Charlie was beginning to pull on the rope and slowly the victim was inching up the side of the boat, over the rail and onto the deck. Charlie untied the ropes and released the rubber ring. He laid the man on the deck and rushed into the cabin.

"Megan," he instructed, "you look after him. I'll throttle the boat round and then I'll get David."

Megan grabbed a bag from the first of the medical boxes and knelt by the side of the injured man.

Charlie came back a few moments later and threw a rope down to David, who was now struggling to stay afloat. A wave heaved him into the side and his head banged against the hull.

"David, take it!" yelled Charlie.

After two more attempts, David managed to secure the rope around his stomach and slowly Charlie pulled him up and out of the water, over the railing and onto the deck, whereupon David was violently sick.

Justine lay back on the deck of the luxurious motor boat and applied her third application of sun block. The bright Mediterranean sun glared down on her. They had left Monte Carlo harbour an hour earlier.

She watched as the two Spanish girls laughed together. They had been booked by Martin and had been well chosen. Their skimpy bikinis left little to the imagination.

Shortly, the English broker appeared from below with Stephan Andrew. He sat down at the small rectangular table in the centre of the boat. Martin produced two bottles of champagne and commanded the two girls to join them.

"So you will do 2,000,000 shares, Stephan, at 10p."

"Consider it achieved, Martin," replied Stephan.

"Where will the stock go?"

"Middle East, some to India, and my contact in Brazil is taking half a million. It is difficult in England after Pacific Continental but we'll get there." He paused. "You understand I will need to increase my margins. I have some heavy, shall we say, commissions to pay out to the regulators." He drank some champagne and put his hand on the rear of one of the girls. "I will buy at 10 maximum and place probably at around 12.5."

It was a lucrative deal for the Swiss financier. He was buying two million shares at 10p per share, a total of £200,000. He would sell the shares on to other brokers at an average of 12.5p, a total of £250,000. He would make a profit of £50,000. It was the type of transaction he would facilitate on a daily basis.

Stephan stood up, grabbed the hands of both the girls and disappeared down the steps and into the cabin.

Justine came up behind Martin and rubbed her hands over his nipples.

"He's placed the stock?" she asked.

"Deal done," said Martin with a grin.

"Wow, £50,000 profit, Martin."

"I didn't just employ you for your body, Justine. . . And we get 6 percent commission, which is £12,000."

"I thought it was 5 percent, Martin. Cyril Trafford will. . . "

"Cyril will pay it, Justine. He has no choice. He wants the money. That is the price."

Justine stood up and stretched her limbs. Martin followed her with his eyes.

"Pacific Continental? Who are they?" she asked.

"*Were* they," said Martin. "What the press call a Boiler Room," he continued. "They were run by several of my pals. They worked mainly from Spain to avoid the British regulators. They would phone people in England and sell them shares. It was a passport to real wealth."

"That doesn't sound right to me."

"How else do you expect me to pay for the boat?" asked Martin. He put his hands on her thighs. "Or the champagne?" he added as his hands glided upwards.

"Why have you bought in the girls, Martin? I thought you said that Stephan's passion was chess?"

"Yes, chess is his passion. Every man has his weakness, Justine, and our straight-laced Zurich financier has a great big one. It will take both of the girls to satisfy him. Thank God. It's a good way to sell shares you must agree."

"Ah, so he's one of the two-at-a-time brigade," said Justine. "Well, it gives a whole new meaning to the phrase 'Check Mates'!"

The calm of the Mediterranean waters contrasted with the storms earlier in the day in Cardigan Bay. Now they had passed by, the seagulls were in the air again, looking for mackerel and sea bass, and twenty miles down the coast, just outside Aberystwyth harbour, the dolphins were playing through the gentle waves. The clouds had drifted away and the sun was hovering above the western horizon, still high enough in the sky to give clear light and warmth to the occupants of the two boats.

Megan had secured the injured sailor on the deck of *Mikatcha*. He was on his back, having coughed up several pints of sea water. His airways were clear and Megan had managed to wrap him in two grey blankets. A third, smaller bundle was acting as a pillow for his head. He was cold and drifting into semi-consciousness at various times. Megan was massaging his chest and arms and had been able to check his pulse and blood pressure, using the digital equipment she had known was in the first-aid kit. She was quietly talking to him and trying to keep him awake. She felt a surge of encouragement when he was able to tell her the name of his yacht.

Megan looked at David, who was still leaning over the side of the boat. She let him be as he vomited again.

"Here, David," she said, handing him a towel. "Are you sure that you don't need help?"

"You go back to him," said David, indicating Megan's semi-conscious sailor.

Charlie had turned the engine down to idle and was standing amidships so he could talk to the crew of the Aberdovey Lifeboat that had now reached the scene.

"Richard," he shouted, "we're fine here. You take the yacht. The two women are still shouting, so they are ok. You need to check the boy at the back first. Have you called the Sea King helicopter?"

"Charlie, they've just answered another call but they're on their way and are saying they'll be here in fifteen minutes."

Charlie watched as crew member Zoe Wallis managed to climb aboard *Aunty Betty.* She attached a line from the stern of the rescue craft to the front of the yacht. She held it away from the railings until the helmsman of the lifeboat had manoeuvred the lifeboat in front of the stricken vessel and taken up the slack in the line.

She then ran down the deck towards the stern, by-passing the two women and reaching the trembling boy. He was hunched over a rubber ring and crying. As Zoe put her arms around him he cried out, "Dad!". She sat him down and started to talk to him. "My name is Zoe. What's yours?" There was no reply. "He's my son, George," said one of the women, who had moved down to join them.

"George," said Zoe. "Your Dad is on the other boat."

"Is he ok?"

Zoe went to the side and shouted over the water, "Megan, is he all right?"

Megan shouted back, "He's alive but very cold."

At that moment the sound of the helicopter could be heard and, on *Mikatcha*, Charlie was talking to the pilot, who brought his machine within hovering height over the boat. A line fell to the deck and a helmeted airman, dressed all in orange, descended to the deck and went over to Megan's patient. A stretcher was lowered and David caught it and placed it alongside the injured man. Within two minutes the man was secured to the stretcher which rose up towards the open door of the Sea King helicopter, accompanied by the 'dope on the rope', as he was called. As soon as they reached the craft the pilot gained speed and flew off towards the south and Aberystwyth hospital.

Back on *Aunty Betty* Zoe had calmed the two sisters and continued to sit with the small boy. "Your Dad's on his way to hospital, George, so we'll get you to Aberdovey now."

Charlie and the skipper exchanged final words and then the Aberdovey lifeboat began to tow *Aunty Betty* back to the Dovey estuary. George was starting to feel a little better and was telling Zoe about the rescue in the water. "Wow, Zoe, that guy over there saved Dad's life. He was going under. The waves were so high!" Zoe looked over at *Mikatcha.*

Megan had led David into the cabin and was removing his jacket. She gently dried him with a towel and felt the muscles of his right shoulder. David flinched as Megan gave her diagnosis. "Bruising," she said.

"I think it might be broken," said David, grimacing with pain.

The navigational lights were flashing as Charlie picked up the outer buoys and turned the boat towards the harbour. The lifeboat was now five minutes behind them.

Aberdovey was shining brightly in the evening sunlight and the jetty was lit up by a series of flashing blue lights. Charlie throttled back and David and Megan watched as a large crowd of locals and holiday makers began to wave and cheer.

As soon as the lifeboat and *Aunty Betty* were moored, George and the two women were driven away for a medical examination, and to be re-united with George's father.

Zoe and Megan were talking. "How come you were on the lifeboat?" asked Megan.

"I qualified two weeks ago and I was on the Outward Bound

boat in the harbour when the call came. Not a bad start, hey?" She kissed her friend. "Who's superman then?"

They both looked over to the slipway where David was talking to the police and being applauded by the locals.

"Let's meet in the Brit later and I'll tell you everything."

Megan went over to David and pulled him away. "He's exhausted," she said to the police officer and dragged David out of the harbour area.

Within five minutes they were sitting in the bar of the Britannia pub. Megan bought David a pint of bitter and a whisky chaser and a large glass of red wine for herself.

The door opened and Charlie entered. He accepted the pint of bitter that was thrust into his hand and went over to where Megan and David were sitting. Megan stood up and they embraced. Charlie wiped a tear away from her cheek. He hugged her again. As she sat down, David stood. He looked at Charlie. The skipper of *Mikatcha* held out his hand and when David responded he held on for several moments. Not a word was said, but Charlie looked into David's gaze and nodded his approval. He turned and left.

Megan finished her drink and stood up. David joined her and they walked out of the Britannia, past the shops and along Glandovey Terrace. The town was now quiet.

They reached Swn-y-Don and David unlocked the door. He looked around and across the beach towards Cardigan Bay. It was a tranquil evening with a moon glow over the waters. He turned and with his arm wrapped around Megan he gently pushed her into the house. He locked the door behind him.

They climbed the two flights of stairs and went into the main bedroom.

David stood still as Megan undressed him. He winced as she lifted his pullover and shirt over his head. She undid his trousers and let them drop to the floor. She gently rubbed his legs, which were white with cold. She then took his hand and led him into the bathroom.

She opened the doors of the shower and turned the water on, after turning the dial as hot as it would go. She guided David under the water and shut the sliding panels behind her. The water soaked her hair, her top and jeans. She bent down and found the shampoo, which she poured into her hands. She started by washing David's hair. She massaged his scalp. The water and soap ran down his back and his legs. She washed his chest and massaged his shoulders. She wanted to check that the movement was returning to the injured muscles. Her hands travelled down to his thighs and his calves. She then washed his groin area. . . She took the shower head off its bracket and washed him down until all the soap disappeared. She put the spray back and stepped away.

She opened the buttons of her shirt, took it off and removed her bra. She undid the catch at the top of her jeans. She had to push the wet material down her legs. She took off her panties and stood naked in front of David. She let the water run over her glowing skin. She stepped out of the shower and picked up a green bath towel. She pulled David towards her and softly dried their two bodies. She let the towel fall to the floor.

A few minutes later David discovered Megan's second tattoo. As it was in Welsh he did not know what it said.

Chapter Five

Thomas left the hospital car park and returned to Payne Printers. His father's condition had deteriorated. There had been a shortage of staff during the Bank Holiday and he'd been unable to secure any nursing help while he was at his father's bedside. Albert had vomited and Thomas had cleaned it up himself.

He went into his office and closed the door. He took out the *Yellow Pages* and began making a series of telephone calls.

"So you are saying you can take him?" he said. "And, assuming it is prostate cancer, how much do you thin. . . yes I understand that but I am told it is well advanced. . . well, as long as he needs treatment. . . yes, but please give me some idea. . . pardon. . . £5,000. . . a month. . . a week?. . . £5,000 a week. . . and it might be twenty weeks. . . what if I need to take him out?. . . NHS. . . and have you a bed?. . . I need to pay for a private ambulance and – how much? £1,000. . . are you sure? I'll phone you back."

His door opened. "No, not now," he shouted.

"Tom, we need to talk."

Barry Wadd, the financial controller of Payne Printers, sat down in front of the owner. "You don't want to hear this, but Hamilton Brothers have called in the administrators."

"But all their work is for the councils, Barry. That guarantees their payments!" exclaimed Tom.

"Yes, that's the problem. They're all having their budgets frozen and they're not paying their invoices or simply not ordering at all. Bloody government spending cuts." The financial controller paused. "The government is broke, the councils are bankrupt and the banks aren't lending."

"Fucking banks, Barry. Fucking, fucking banks. . . have you spoken to ours?"

"They've agreed to see me on Thursday afternoon."

"Thursday afternoon – for Christ's sake! Today, Barry!"

"I pleaded, Tom, I promise you. Thursday afternoon was the

first time I could get." He looked at Thomas. "And anyway they will say 'No'. We both know that."

A few minutes later Thomas Payne walked out of his office and dialled a number on his mobile phone.

"David. . .Thomas, hello. Many thanks for the documents. . . Can you meet today?"

David explained that he was travelling back from Wales and they agreed to meet in the afternoon. After arriving in Primrose Hill, he changed and began the thirty minute walk towards Oxford Circus and down Regent Street, before turning into Conduit Street. Thomas Payne placed a cup of coffee in front of David at a window table in a café in Berkeley Square.

"David," Thomas said, "You're busy. I'll put it straight to you. My business is running out of money. Can you help me?"

For the next fifteen minutes they discussed the state of Payne Printers, the problem with the bank, the collapse of Hamilton Brothers and the increasing costs of paper and printing inks, which had risen by over 40 percent in the last year.

"And the factoring company won't lend anymore?" asked David. His tone of voice revealed his frustration. The financing of smaller businesses by allowing them to borrow money against the security of their debtors had been an important source of capital. The lenders were becoming more reluctant to offer these facilities.

"The banks are playing a dirty game, David. Three years ago we had a bank overdraft and a factoring facility with a separate company. They were giving us up to 80 percent of invoice value. I can remember that at that time we were owed £100,000 by Hamilton Brothers and the factoring company was advancing us £80,000 against their invoices. It worked well. The charges were high but it gave us cash."

Thomas was expressing his frustration with new banking methods. His original method of obtaining finance by selling his debts to the factoring company was being replaced by more restrictive banking loans.

Thomas drank some coffee. "What time is your meeting?" he asked.

"Keep going. I've got another twenty minutes."

"We also had an overdraft. One day the bank came in and

convinced Barry and me that we should transfer to their factoring company. I remember that my father was at that meeting and was fiercely opposed to the idea. I should have listened to him. We agreed to do what the bank wanted and we transferred. The problems started almost immediately. They imposed charges we hadn't been told about. They cut the value they would give against Hamilton Brothers to 70 percent."

"Surely you held them to account?" asked David.

"David, you cannot get to them. The people at the branches are just clerks. The key decisions are made by people elsewhere. I tried all I could. It didn't stop there. Two years ago they called in our overdraft. £200,000 I had to find. You remember I told you. I cashed in my pension."

David went over to the counter and returned with two more coffees.

"David, these bankers are bloody clever bastards. What they did, effectively, was grab my best security, my debtor book, decided which were the safest options and then put me in a position where I had no choices left."

"Have you tried other banks?" asked David.

"David, forget all this crap you see on the TV and in the newspapers. The banks hate small businesses. It's all a con, this stuff about supporting Britain's enterprises. It's so the chairman gets invited to Downing Street and receives his peerage. This bloke Cameron seems to be throwing them around like confetti. I read the other day that there are now over 800 Lords. The bloody House only seats 300!"

"Ouch," said David. "So, voting Labour are we, Thomas?"

"And it's not just me, David. OK. I'm down so I'm feeling bitter. But I go to these breakfast meetings organised by the Employers' Organisations. You'll hear my opinion time and again."

Thomas picked up his coffee cup but put it down again straight away. "We simply don't matter. I read all I can about the credit crunch. There was an article about this securities bundling. It made a fortune for the bankers. What did they do? They packaged together a load of crappy mortgages and sold them on at a vast profit. They then paid themselves bonuses you can't imagine. So the shit hits the fan. The government bails them out and they disappear into their tropical hideaways."

"I don't think it's quite as simple as that. . ." said David.

"It fucking well is," continued Thomas. "This country has lost the plot. I voted Labour for years. I thought Tony Blair was fantastic. I wasn't sure last time so I voted BNP."

"Gordon Brown dealt with matters quite well, I thought," said David. "The credit crunch, as you call it, was more than just bad mortgages, but some of us are struggling to feel comfortable with Cameron." He paused. "I must go. Thomas, I will think about your situation and phone you."

"Can you help?"

"There's always money available. You want rescue funds. They're expensive and involve some pretty unpleasant people. I'll phone you. Good luck, Thomas."

As he left David turned. "Thomas. Voting BNP. Please, never again. If you want to protest, vote for the Green Party."

"You don't know your printing, David," laughed Thomas. "Our inks are oil based. They don't decompose, so our waste goes to land banks. The Greens hate us printers."

David left the café, walked across the bottom of Berkeley Square, into Curzon Street and back to his office. He went immediately into the front meeting room, where he found Jackson Holmes, Jemma Shah, John Pearman and Margaret Drummond.

"Ah, David, at last," announced Jackson Holmes.

"Is Martin coming?" asked David.

"He's doing what he does best, David. He's raising money for Trafford Discount Stores plc."

"So how much have you raised?" asked John. "I've promised to phone Cyril by six o'clock."

"Well," said Jackson. "Things are going much better. David here had a fantastic meeting with Atlas VCT. Martin spoke to them this morning and they've confirmed their £1,000,000."

Margaret leaped out of her chair and rushed over to David. She threw her arms around him. "I just knew you would do it!" she cried.

"So," continued Jackson. "That means we're around £2,200,000 and I have even better news. Mainstream VCT want to see you for a second time. In fact, Jemma's going to take you there in a few minutes."

"What, now?" asked John. "It's rather late."

"They're staying on especially to see us tonight," replied Jackson.

He looked at Cyril's daughter. "I told you, Margaret, David never fails."

"I must phone Dad," she said and she left the room.

"Have Atlas put it in writing?" asked John.

"Martin only managed to catch Kate Livermore late morning," replied Jackson. "I'm told there is a letter coming."

"Can it be faxed or emailed?" asked John.

"Of course," said Jackson. "Can I suggest, John, you let Jemma take you to Mainstream. Let's go and get the rest of the money."

John and Jemma left the room. David closed the door and sat down at the table.

"Jackson," he said. "That is just about the best news I could have had."

"What is?" asked Jackson.

"Atlas. £1,000,000. I didn't feel great about my meeting with Kate. I wonder what made her invest."

"She hasn't yet. I was playing for time."

"What!?"

"Martin tried to get hold of her but she was in a meeting."

"But you told them. . ."

"Oh grow up, David. I've told you time and again. Think success and it will happen. My job today was to keep their morale up. Martin will get the money. I keep telling you."

"Well, at least Mainstream have said yes," David continued.

"No they haven't," said Jackson. "They've turned it down."

"But Jemma's taking John and Margaret to see them for a second meeting."

"Ah, yes. Jemma's partner works there and I'm paying him £500 to interview them. Why do you think the meeting is in the evening?" laughed Jackson.

"That is foul, Jackson, even for you. It's a sham. This is simply immoral. I don't want to be part of it."

"Sit down, David," said Jackson. "You're beginning to piss me off. We're in difficult times. Our markets have been wrecked by the Americans. Those bastards from NASDAQ come over here bidding for the London Stock Exchange and telling bloody Clara Furze that AIM is a wild west market. What happens? The AIM team start regulating AIM like never before. Rule after rule. We had a great thing going. AIM was the best growth market in the world. We've helped hundreds of companies. There were sixty Chinese companies on AIM. The last three years have been devastating and even now there are more companies leaving than joining."

Jackson paused and grabbed a glass of water. He was now in full swing.

"Clara buggers off to collect her peerage and Monsieur Rolet comes in as chief executive to pick up the pieces. The London Stock Exchange is now number twelve in the world. Just because Clara would not do a deal."

"And then the Americans got their banking wrong and the Fed had to rescue them. And we have to re-build."

"You lied to John and Margaret," said David.

"I didn't lie, David. I bought us time. Martin will raise the money."

Jackson sat down.

"David, let me make two points. You have made a great deal of money out of what we do here. I do, however, sometimes think you are too nice for this game."

David looked at Jackson.

"You lied to my clients," he said.

Megan looked around the concourse at Euston Station. She checked her watch. It was 7:00pm and the weekend commuter rush was coming to an end as the London workers caught their Friday night trains home.

She found herself enveloped in a passionate embrace and she recognised the masculine scent. Her lips met David's. It was the moment she had anticipated with growing excitement. She clung to him. She had wanted this moment ever since the rescue of the sailor from *Aunty Betty* in Cardigan Bay. Later, in the bedroom, he had taken Megan back into a world of belonging that had been lost because of a roadside bomb in Iraq.

Ten minutes later the taxi dropped them off in Primrose Hill.

As soon as they were inside, David grabbed her arm and propelled her up to the first floor. He pushed open the bedroom door and led her in. He stripped off her clothes, undressed and made love to her. At the moment of fulfilment Megan's whole body shuddered as they climaxed at the same time.

"So what time did you say the boys are coming?" asked Megan, as she busied herself in the kitchen. She had found the coffee percolater easily. Every shelf was tidy with labels facing outwards in military rows.

"Josh will be here around 9:30pm," replied David. "Matthew is away tonight but will be joining us for breakfast."

"And who do they think I am?"

"Well, I've told them I'm going to ask you to marry me."

"And do I have any say in the matter?"

"I haven't asked you yet."

They were now in the utility annex, which was dominated by a central wooden table around which all other activities took place.

David was preparing a salmon salad with dressing. He turned up the heat beneath a saucepan full of potatoes.

Megan turned around and there standing in the doorway was a teenager.

"Josh," exclaimed David. His son ran over and hugged his father. "Josh, this is Megan."

Josh glanced at her. "Hi," he said.

They sat down and began eating. Josh was full of his week at boarding school. He talked and talked.

At around 10:30 he announced he was going to bed.

David and Megan settled in the front lounge and listened to The Beach Boys.

"No Miles Davis tonight?" she asked.

"Later," replied David. "This is the greatest group of all time." *God Only Knows* filled the room. "I took the boys to the Millennium Concert in Hyde Park," he said. "Brian Wilson was there. They thought he was great."

"Didn't he stay in bed for ten years?"

"Yes, he did. While he was on drugs. I'm impressed by your knowledge."

"Well," said Megan. "When I was at school we spent three years learning about sheep and then we were allowed to read other books."

"A ddysgon ni cymryd ddim sylw o Saeson twp," she added.

It wasn't true, of course. She had not been taught to ignore stupid Englishmen. She had noticed that David seemed to respond when she spoke Welsh. She was planning to try it out in bed.

David rose to his feet and went over and knelt at the base of Megan's chair.

"I, David, Englishman and resident of Primrose Hill, hereby admit to Megan of Abergynolwyn in Wales, that I am a patronising male."

Megan smiled down at him.

"Guilty as charged," she said.

She took him by the hand and led him upstairs. It was time to talk dirty. In Welsh.

The next morning Matthew had arrived and was sitting at the breakfast table when Megan entered. They looked at each other.

"You must be Megan," said Matthew.

"And you must be Matthew," said Megan.

"Get your coat. We're going out," said Matthew.

They left the house and walked over onto Primrose Hill. There were a few early morning runners but it was otherwise deserted. They walked without speaking until they reached the top of the incline. They sat down on one of the benches and looked out over London.

"You don't want me here, do you, Matthew?" asked Megan.

"I've never seen Dad so happy," he replied. "He's got problems at work – but he always has. Josh and I, we both knew something had happened, and then he told us."

"Told you what?"

"About you. You won the Bells of Aberdovey tennis prize. You're a PE teacher. Your husband was killed in Iraq. . . Dad's potty about you," Matthew paused. "He says he's going to marry you."

Megan looked at the tall, well built, dark-haired man in front of her. He was wearing jeans and a Harlequins rugby shirt.

"Your father's told me about your mother, Matthew. He feels you and Josh. . ."

"Don't talk about my mother."

Megan was shaken by the tone of his voice. Her professional teaching always counselled the avoidance of conflict at moments like this.

"I think I'd better go," she said. "I think you, Josh and your father have some talking to do – "

"He's hitting her."

Megan looked at Matthew in complete amazement. "No. Sorry. I won't go there. Your father would simply not do that."

"Not my Dad. The Frenchman. Maurice bloody le Grande."

"He's hitting your mother?"

Matthew stood up and stared into the North London sky. He watched the planes coming into Heathrow from the west.

Megan sat down beside him. She said nothing.

"We've got to tell Dad," said Matthew.

They started to walk and Matthew told Megan his story. It had all seemed right. His mother had settled well into France and the wedding was lavish. They lived in a village south of Paris. Matthew was not sure what Maurice le Grande did exactly but he seemed to be involved in a number of businesses.

"Two visits ago," said Matthew, "there was a change. Josh wasn't aware of it and, anyway, he was too busy chasing Maurice's daughter. I knew."

He paused and turned to face Megan.

"At Easter I was even more worried. I asked my mother if anything was wrong. She wouldn't say anything. But she couldn't explain the heavy make-up. She was having problems with her eye. She admitted they were going through a difficult patch. I asked her about her face. She said it was nothing."

"Are you sure Matthew? It's dangerous to make assumptions unless you have evidence."

"It was Josh who really found out. Mum kept cuddling him. He's thirteen years old, Megan. It was a bit messed up." Matthew paused again. "Josh told her that he didn't want to be held anymore and she started to cry. Josh told me. I went to see

Mum – I confronted her. He's hitting her. Apparently, he's got 'business worries'."

"And what do you think you should do, Matthew?" asked Megan.

"I don't know," he replied. He looked exhausted suddenly. "We have to talk about it. Me, Dad and Josh."

"And when do you want to talk about it?"

"I think we should go back now. I need to talk to them now."

Matthew half ran back to the house with Megan trailing behind him. David and Josh were sitting at the kitchen table.

"Ah, we wondered where you were. So you two have met?"

Matthew walked round the wooden table and stood by his father.

"Dad. We have to talk."

A look of panic glanced over David's face. "Matthew. You must get to know Megan better before. . ."

"No, it's Mum – Maurice is hitting her."

Megan moved to the door and looked at David.

"I'm leaving, David. I'll get myself to Euston. I'll phone you when I get home. You three need to be alone right now."

Josh rose to his feet and stood next to his brother. They both looked at Megan.

"We know that Dad would like you to stay, Megan. And that's ok with me and Josh."

Emily Bowden took a sip of her cocktail. She looked across the table at her two friends. She stirred the stick around her glass.

"Well, I'm staying there in a few weeks' time so I'll find out," she said.

"How come?" asked Rachael. "Why are you staying with Megan?"

"Mrs Edwards has organised it for me. Mum's not moving into her new home until July so Megan said I can stay with her until my work at Outward Bound begins. Pretty cool."

"So, how do you know so much about this bloke she's got the hots for?"

Emily tried to look a little shy. "If you must know, a couple of nights ago, I slept with Gavin Davis."

"You lucky so-and-so," exclaimed Rhoda, Emily's friend.

"He's gorgeous. How did you pull him? I thought he was marrying Julia stuck-up thing?"

"I'd been to Outward Bound for my interview and one of the helpers, Zoë Wallis, took me to the Britannia. I'll be rooming with her. She told me about last Monday's rescue. It was Megan's bloke who went in to pull out the sailor."

Rachael returned with a bottle of wine and three glasses.

"This is getting interesting," she said.

"Zoë says he's lovely. She had a drink with Megan on Tuesday and apparently it's serious. He bought her that Alpha Romeo she's driving around in. . ."

The girls mulled over this latest gossip.

"So, Gavin. . .?" continued Rachael.

"Yes. . . He was in the Brit. Megan had to leave and he came over. He's such a fitty. He invited me back to his cottage and I went." She rolled her eyes. "We had a fantastic night."

Emily took a large drink of her wine. "Gavin told me it was he and Julia Hetherington who lost to Megan and her man in the Bells of Aberdovey final. His name's David. From London. He's divorced. Megan told me that."

Estyn, the barman, came over and took their glasses away.

"PC Evans is walking around," he said. "I'll bring some orange juice over. He'll be gone soon."

"Seriously, I thought Gavin was going to marry Julia?" said Rhoda.

"She's history," replied Emily.

"So are you seeing him again?" asked Rachael.

Emily smiled.

Martin Van Dijl took out a £20 note, folded it over, pressed the sides and tucked it into the girl's hot pants. She returned to her pole and started gyrating to the music. The stage had a black backcloth and three shining stainless steel props. It was early in the evening and the other two stations were empty.

"Great tits," he said to his guests at the table. "Look at them bounce. And that arse."

"Give her another twenty and she'll take her knickers off," said a voice across the darkened area.

"Business first," ordered Martin. "Right. This fucking

Trafford Discount Stores. Are we getting anywhere, Gary? You're working the VCTs. What's happening?"

"That's the problem, Martin. Nothing. Nothing's happening. They're sitting on their cash. Hamilton Capital has just got a Chinese deal away. £20,000,000. But I'm told it was a good one."

"Justine, what about the private funds?" asked Martin.

"I've offered Albion Risk Capital 6 percent if they'll do £1,000,000. They're thinking about it," she responded.

"We're only getting 5 percent," said Gary. "How does that work?"

"We do a split," said Martin. "And Cyril is going to pay 6 percent. He just doesn't know it yet." Martin laughed out loud. "I've arranged that when the deal is complete in about three months' time a discount broker I know will publish some research. They'll buy £400,000 of shares off Albion at 12p and sell them on at 18p. We get half. About £70,000."

"How do they sell the shares at 18p?" asked Gary

"Because we will have been in the market, buying a few to get the price up, stupid," laughed Martin.

Justine called the waiter over and ordered another vodka and tonic.

"Make it a big one," Martin instructed.

"What I don't understand," said Justine, "is why this is proving so hard. It's a good business. The sector is right. Cyril Trafford is a bastard but bloody good at what he does and little daughter Margaret would take her knickers off in the middle of Oxford Street if Daddy told her to."

"Well, if we don't get it away the business will fail," said Martin and turned to the man on his left. He smiled.

"Now that mention of knickers reminds me. . ."

He called the pole dancer over and, as she leaned over him, tucked a crisp £50 note into her pants. She allowed his hand to follow.

David left St. Pancras International on Sunday morning and arrived in Paris just before lunchtime. He was picked up by his French business associate and they drove in silence to the village of St. Marguerite, thirty kilometres south of the capital.

The car was parked and David walked down the street and

turned up an imposing drive leading towards a small château. He knocked on the front door. There was no reply. He went round the side and reached the rear garden, where he found Michelle sitting by the pool. She stood up and, as she did so, David heard a voice behind him.

"David, mon ami, hello."

David turned and faced Maurice le Grande. He was smoking a cigar and holding a glass.

David smiled. He then drew back his left arm and smashed his closed fist into the face of the Frenchman. Le Grande collapsed to the ground, breaking his glass on a wall and losing his cigar. David reached down, grabbed his jacket lapels and lifted him to his feet. He hit him again, but without the anger of the first blow.

Michelle rushed over to her whimpering husband. She lifted him to his feet and led him back into the house.

David went over to the poolside table, sat down and poured himself a glass of wine. As he was examining the knuckles of his left hand, Michelle returned and took his fingers into her palm.

She laughed nervously, "Just bruising."

"How long, Michelle?" asked David. "How long has he been violent?"

"It's just his way, David. He's had some business worries. He was a large shareholder in a provincial bank which was rescued in October 2009. He lost a lot of money."

David looked at his former wife. "I've arranged for a flat to be available from next Tuesday. It's in Bloomsbury, overlooking the square."

Michelle looked at him and laughed. "Are you mad, David? I'm happy here."

"With him treating you as a punch bag?"

Michelle smiled. "I don't think he'll hit me again. I don't like the fact you punched him David. You were always a bit heroic. . . But I suppose I should be pleased that you still care about me." She smiled. "How are the boys? They must have told you."

"Matthew, yes. They're fine. They were worried about you. I think it best if they stay away for a few weeks."

"I'll come over to see them," said Michelle. "They're at home, are they?"

"Yes. They're with Megan." He realised his mistake immediately.

"Who's Megan?"

The answer to the question was that Megan was somebody David was going to keep well away from his former wife. She would most likely become jealous. She would not be able to help herself. One reason David had not remarried was because he anticipated problems with Michelle and he didn't want to interfere with the access arrangements for the boys, where Michelle had always played fair. The other reason was that David had not met anybody whom he had wanted to marry before.

David stood up and left her question unanswered. He bade farewell to his ex-wife. He was keen to begin the journey home.

At 11:30pm he was collected at King's Cross by Megan and Matthew and taken to the nearest A&E department. Within two hours his hand had been x-rayed and bandaged.

They arrived back at Primrose Hill in the early hours of Monday morning. At 5:00am, after only two hours of sleep, Megan packed her bag and told David she would call a taxi. Her train back to Wales was departing at 5:45am. As she reached for the phone a hand appeared and rested on the receiver.

"I'll take you," said Matthew.

Cyril Trafford sat back in his favourite chair. He looked out of the French window at the beautiful view of the Yorkshire Moors. It was raining.

"Margaret, love, I know I'm loud. Perhaps I should improve my language. Everything I've done in life I've had to fight for and I've more often won. But I'm telling you, something is wrong. I hate the City but I know how those bastards operate. Pay 'em fees and they're anybody's. Ours is a good deal. Look at John's latest analysis. Of our fifty-two shops only three are down. The top ten are up over 15 percent."

Cyril paused and savoured his glass of whisky. Since his wife had died he spent more time on his own. He lived for when his only daughter visited him.

"Dad," said Margaret. "We trust David and he's saying that the recovery is only just taking place. I spoke to him yesterday and he told me the feeling is that retail sales are collapsing because people are running out of money."

"Fair enough, but we are doing well. It makes our performance even better. I have a hunch that he is not the problem. Trust me, Margaret. I can smell an issue. Something is wrong. They'll regret trying it on with Cyril Trafford."

Thomas Payne sat down and faced Martin Van Dijl.

"I want my money back," said Thomas. "£30,000. Now."

"It's not as easy as that," replied Martin. "We've bought you shares in the placing. You've signed the legal document. The money is with the registrars and can't be touched. You said you wanted to invest in Trafford Discount Stores. That is what we have done for you, Thomas. You'll thank me. It's a great investment. You're an astute man. They'll go to £50,000. I give you my word."

"Fucking sell them!" said Thomas. "Today, now. Buy the fucking things yourself. I want my money back!"

Martin pressed a button underneath the right hand side of his desk. A tall, well dressed man entered.

"Archie, Mr Payne was just leaving."

Martin looked at Thomas.

"I'm sorry, Mr Payne. I can't help you. You have signed the form. There's nothing I can do. I promise you it's a good investment. You'll make lots of profit."

Thomas stormed out of the office without a backwards look.

David arrived at Swn-y-don on Friday evening at eleven o'clock.

Megan had prepared pasta for supper, which they ate in the dining room before moving upstairs to the lounge. David put on a Mahler symphony.

"Miles out, Gustav in," said Megan.

David thought about acknowledging her musical knowledge, but remembered the barbed Welsh sheep remark just in time.

They talked about their weeks and then, a little unexpectedly, Megan asked David a question.

"Tell me about the City, David."

"What about the City?"

"Why do you earn so much money?"

"I'm good at what I do."

"No doubts on that score," said Megan. "But what I mean

is. . . well. . . everybody I know works hard. Farming round here is tough. As a PE teacher I give everything I've got. I'm not complaining. I'm paid well enough. But you said you're getting a £200,000 fee for this Trafford Discount Stores business. How does that work?"

"Hell, Megan," said David, "it's a bit late for this type of chat. But I will tell you something. I make a good living, yes, but I am not the one making the real money."

"Who is then?"

"There are two groups. The advisers who organise the transaction. They, if you like, are the policemen. They ensure that the documentation is legal and all the rules are met. For that they get fees and bonuses. But it is the sponsors who raise the money from investors who really earn the money. Would you like to know about the three card trick? It's how the sponsors work."

"The three card trick," mused Megan, as she stood up to pour a brandy into David's glass. Mahler crescendoed into his second movement.

"It works like this: a sponsor forms a company. He and perhaps three or four business associates put in some initial capital. It's usually £50,000, because that's the minimum amount you need for a plc."

"What's a plc?"

"Public Limited Company. You must be a plc to join a public stock market. The point is that they buy shares in the plc at 0.1p per share."

"No. Can't understand that."

"The shareholders own the company. They will each put in £12,500 in shares at 0.1p each, so each of them owns 25 percent of the company. Each has 12,500,000 shares at 0.1p per share."

"So what does the company do?"

"Good question," said David. "At this point they find a business. Something like a diamond mine in Zambia. They negotiate the drilling rights. They calculate they need £250,000 to buy the rights and start drilling. They raise that money privately at 1.0p per share. They do this by issuing 25,000,000 shares at 1.0p per share. This means that the four original sponsors hold shares worth £125,000 each – a gain of £112,500 each."

"What, so they get all that money just for identifying a mine in Zambia?" she exclaimed.

"They're being paid for their special skills."

"Crap," replied Megan. "Or would you like that in Welsh?"

"Hey, you asked the question. I'm not here to defend capital markets."

"Ok, sorry. Carry on."

"So, now the fun begins. As soon as the drilling produces any sort of results they start issuing research notes. These are FSA-regulated brokers' notes."

"FSA?"

"Financial Services Authority."

"Hang on. Aren't they the bunch who caused the Northern Rock disaster?"

"Holy Mother of Mary!" cried David. "There has to be a system of regulation. They're like Ofsted for banks. Let's stick to the point. The brokers issue research notes and get the financial public relations people to start getting the press to mention the mine. They then announce they're going to float the mine on the AIM. At 4p per share."

"What?! Is that a joke?"

"It doesn't stop there, Megan. The market doesn't like it if the sponsors sell shares at that point. The officials at AIM might get sniffy. What happens is, they raise, quite legitimately, say, £1,000,000, perhaps £2,000,000, to get the mine working. Once the money is raised and the shares are listed, the PR machine really starts working. The financial press are really worked on. Lunches, dinners, weekends away. They may even fly them to Zambia to show them the mine."

David stood up and changed the CD, putting on Mahler's second symphony. He poured another drink for Megan and for himself.

"By now the share price will be rising up to perhaps 10p and beyond. As there's a demand for stock, the sponsors start selling and their objective is to clear their holding."

"So, let me get this right," said Megan. "The sponsor puts in £12,500 for 12,500,000 shares which he sells for £1,250,000."

"Great. Good maths. Yes," said David, "and it's completely legitimate."

"And that's the City?"

"It's one small part of the City."

"I'm going to bed," Megan said. Under her breath, she added, "*Diolch i Duw am Cymru*." Thank heavens for Wales.

David was now polishing his Mahler CD.

Chapter Six

Megan was quick to apologise as she realised she had inflicted unintentional pain. David was standing by her side shaking his left hand vigorously. They were walking together down the Roman Road, which runs from the eastern end of Aberdovey down the side of the Dyfi estuary to Machynlleth, and she had become so absorbed in their conversation that she had forgotten her partner's self-inflicted injury, and had grabbed his left hand as she slipped on one of the uneven rocks.

"Megan," said David, "do you think they missed something on the x-ray? I'm sure there's a broken bone."

Megan raised her eyes to the skies. She was beginning to understand the personality of the man standing beside her. She adored his adventurous attitude. His rescue of the sailor in Cardigan Bay was now part of the folklore of Aberdovey. She had sat and watched in growing admiration as he had led Matthew and Josh through an intimate family discussion about Matthew's fears that his mother was being physically abused by her French husband. She could see David was relishing the chance to strengthen his relationship with his sons. He made Matthew go over his suspicions again and again. "Did you see a black eye?" and "Did your mother admit to being hit?"

But not even Megan could have foreseen the events of that Sunday in France. She had gone to bed on Saturday evening after they had shared the day together, unsure about what David had decided. The three of them knew a decision had been made but never imagined the solution was the dramatic crossing of the Channel, the dash to Paris and the car ride to St. Marguerite. Even as she and Matthew waited at the hospital on Sunday evening and into Monday morning, nothing could have prepared her for the quietly told story as David related events at the home of Maurice and Michelle le Grande. She had watched Matthew's eyes light up as he asked David yet again to tell him about the moment he had hit the Frenchman.

Megan had pondered David's relationship with Michelle

on a number of occasions. She accepted the sex angle, not least because she was the beneficiary. She had spent an evening at her cottage the previous week adding up the number of men she had slept with. She decided to discount the teenage fumbles and for most of her late teenage years and early twenties she was devoted to Rhys. Their sex life had been fairly average, but somehow it had not mattered. There were two university relationships, the second of which was interrupted by Rhys appearing at the campus, worried that he had not heard from her. She loved that.

But the years following the death of her husband had been messy. Gavin Davis was typical of several brief escapades, and her two month affair with the husband of the business studies teacher at Dolgellau High School was a disaster which had ended following a humiliating meeting in Gillian Edwards' study. What had affected her was not the lecture she received from the headteacher, but her inability to respond to the question about the morality of messing about with somebody else's marriage.

Following the sea rescue, she had been swept away into a magical heaven of sexuality. From that first experience after the hot shower and their initial and hesitant moments of love-making, she had lost herself in an avalanche of fulfilment. No man in her experience had told her she would experience three orgasms. She remembered as he had whispered in her ear – she could not believe that she would enjoy the dirty talk. She remembered the ecstasy of the ultimate act of penetration and the sensation as her internal juices poured down and mixed with his.

She had not questioned whether it would be as good a second or a third time. On each occasion David worked with sensitivity to ensure she was satisfied. The first time he went between her legs with his mouth would remain with her forever.

Her reverie was interrupted. "Look, Megan," said David. "I told you that my hand is swelling up. Do you think I should get a second opinion?"

Megan decided on her course of action.

"Stop being a wuss, David. There's nothing wrong with your hand."

"Oh."

Low tide had been one hour earlier, just an hour after the

sunlight had started to brighten the wide expanse of the estuary. Birdsong was everywhere and somehow the whole fauna was stirring as the tidal waters began to wash over the sands.

"Megan," asked David. "Why is that chap jumping up and down?"

Megan looked across the central part of the estuary and, on one of the sandbanks, a man was throwing his arms up in the air. As he landed on the sands he jumped up again as high as he could.

"You guess."

"He needs help?"

"I don't think so."

"He's training for the Welsh marathon."

"Unlikely."

"Right," said David. "Time to turn on the intellectual power. Let's be logical. There is a man in the middle of the Dovey estuary jumping up and down. I don't know why."

"What equipment has he got?"

David peered across the incoming waters. "A bucket," he answered.

"Correct."

"He's an out-of-work window cleaner."

"He's a fisherman!"

"Jumping up and down to catch flying fish – of which I can see none. . ."

"He's cockling, David," chuckled Megan.

"Is he now?"

"Yes, he's only got about half an hour left before he'll have to come back to the rocks for safety. What they do is jump up and down on the sand to make the cockles and mussels underneath think that the tidal waters are coming in. The fish then come to the surface and the fisherman has his catch."

"And you and I have our paella," said David.

"I'm sure if we wait he'll be pleased to take your money," agreed Megan.

Thomas Payne had been at the hospital throughout the night and had held onto his father's hand the entire time. He noticed that his skin felt cold and he was watching the monitor at the side of the bed. His pulse was becoming erratic and he felt a sense of relief when the nurse and a doctor appeared at the bedside. He left the ward for a few minutes and was then ushered back by the nurse.

"Mr Payne, I am Dr Zawaldi. I'm the duty doctor."

Thomas shook the offered hand and nodded to the doctor. Before he could ask any questions he was given the news he feared.

"We are so sorry, Mr Payne, but your father has only a few days left, perhaps even less than that. We are starting to give him morphine so he will not be in pain."

Thomas looked down at his father. "Can't you operate?" he asked.

"No," replied Dr Zawaldi. "He went to see his doctor far too late. He must have been in great difficulty and pain. The cancer is quite developed."

"Prostate cancer?" asked Thomas.

"And the rest," stated Dr Zawaldi. "Our tests show it has spread considerably."

"A few days?" asked Thomas.

"At best," said the doctor, as he moved away to another patient.

Thomas sat down at the side of the bed and took his father's hand. His mother had died many years earlier and he was an only child. There was a brother somewhere. Thomas was the only real friend Albert had left, apart from his ex-army drinking mates at the pub.

There was a groan and Albert opened his eyes and looked at Thomas.

"Get me out of here, son," he pleaded.

Justine Hathaway enjoyed the sense of real warmth as she disembarked from the aircraft at Nice Airport.

"Shall we get the helicopter straight away?" she asked.

Having received an affirmative answer she led the way and within minutes they were flying out to sea and landing at Monte Carlo. The taxi ride to the Ritz Hotel took twenty minutes and Justine enjoyed travelling along parts of the motor racing circuit.

They booked in at the hotel and went up three floors before being shown into their bedroom. Justine never lost the sense of luxury as she gazed around the room. There were two bedrooms and two bathrooms. She opened the bottle of champagne and read the note of welcome. This was the lifestyle she coveted. She would never forget being evicted from the family home when her father lost his job. Whatever it took she would never again want for money and what it could buy.

"Do you want a glass?" she asked.

Martin had already changed and was lounging on the sofa wearing a towelling robe.

"Thanks," he said, taking the glass from Justine and using his other hand to stroke her inside thigh.

Justine disappeared into one of the rooms and then into a bathroom. Martin made two phone calls. She reappeared fifteen minutes later wearing a tee shirt and thong. She stretched out on the larger of the two chairs.

"Tell me, Martin," she said. "I just don't understand. You're making no real effort on Trafford Discount Stores. Why not? Jackson is a good client of ours and David tries so hard."

"Rensburg's a wanker," said Martin.

"No, he's not," said Justine. "He's straight and hard working. He's worried to death about the deal."

"Justine," said Martin. "Just think about it. Cyril Trafford thinks he's God. A small time discount shop owner and he acts as though he's Richard Branson. There are always clues. Come on, the finance director is his daughter. It's a joke. She will do anything he asks."

"No," said Justine, "she's quite sturdy. She. . ."

Martin interrupted. "Justine, what Cyril wants Cyril will get. Look at that share sale. The other directors should never have allowed it. I had a real problem with several of the shareholders. Don't forget we did the original fundraising. He was totally out of order to sell shares when he knew trading was poor."

"It was legal and the non-executive directors approved it," said Justine.

"Bollocks. The two non-execs are wankers. One is his old army sergeant and the other is a drunken land owner," slurred

Martin. This happened now and again, when Martin became suddenly affected by alcohol even after drinking a modest amount. Justine thought he should see a doctor but dared not suggest it.

"So why does Park Avenue allow these things to happen? They are the AIM Nomad. It is their job to control the company," said Justine.

"Money," said Martin. "Or, rather, fees. You see, Justine, the Nomads are the workhorses. It's the brokers who make the money."

"Which we do by raising money – which is why you're such a clever man."

"Actually, I am rather good. I saw Kate Livermore last night. She's in for a million," said Martin.

Justine tensed. "Kate doesn't like you. We know that. So why see her? I thought David had her covered. Isn't she known to be loyal to her clients?"

"Kate needs their investment to prosper. Her fund already has several million invested so she cannot allow it to fail.

Martin paused. "Fucking fund managers. I was born in the East End with nothing, Justine. Everything I have done I have achieved for myself. Kate Livermore! Sodding Daddy has been chairman of the Stock Exchange, she goes to Oxford and walks into the City."

Martin stood up and poured another two glasses of champagne, one of which he handed to Justine. He noticed that she had rubbed her skin with oil.

"But what really gets up my nose, Justine," he continued, "is the way they earn their money." His voice assumed a mock public school cadence. "Let's form a fund. Oh goodie, we will call it Atlas VCT. And I will have a salary of £300,000."

"That, Justine, is what gets me," he went on. "Before there is any performance they are paid fucking thousands. Me – every penny I earn is from my own efforts."

"Quite a lot of them did lose their jobs over the last three years," commented Justine.

"Yeah, but did you see the pay-offs? All the focus was on the bankers. But the City is not stupid. There was the government rescuing everybody and the bastards had it all stitched up with their exit contracts. Me, Justine, I haven't got a contract."

"You do have a lot of money, though, Martin," smiled Justine. "And you will have even more when we've raised the money for Trafford Discount Stores."

"I'll fucking get it," said Martin. "Now, get over here."

Justine moved over to the sofa and listened as Martin whispered in her ear. She was appalled.

"No, Martin. That's really obscene. Can't we just have regular sex, just for once?"

Gillian Edwards was pleased her office had been given a spring clean. As she showed her guest through the door and to the offered seat, she felt a glow of confidence.

Ieuan Jones AM was proud of his title. He was an Assembly Member, elected by the voters of his constituency. He put his briefcase to one side and accepted the cup of tea which was being offered to him by the headteacher's secretary. He seemed rather pleased that there were biscuits provided on the tray.

"Mr Jones," said Gillian, "you are, of course, welcome. Megan Williams will be here in a few minutes. Are you going to tell her or would you like me to explain the position?"

"Mrs Edwards, I think I should."

"That's fine, Mr Jones. I just have one concern. You are saying there are three people being interviewed. Megan is a mature woman and she will understand the situation. But I worry she may get. . . er. . . shall we say, disappointed."

Ieuan Jones nodded. "That's a fair point, Mrs Edwards. I think it is down to me to convey to Mrs Williams the achievement in being chosen at this stage."

The telephone on Gillian's desk rang and a few moments later the secretary showed Megan into the room.

"Megan," said Gillian, "this is Mr Ieuan Jones, the Assembly Member for Children, Education and Teaching in the Welsh Government. Mr Jones has travelled up from Cardiff to visit us."

Megan looked a little perplexed but accepted the offered hand and then sat down opposite the visitor.

"Actually, Mrs Williams," said Ieuan, "in the National Assembly, although we can now call ourselves the government, we are referred to as cabinet members, and my full title is Minister for Children, Education, Lifelong Learning and Skills."

Megan radiated a smile. "You're the Assembly Member for Ceredigion, aren't you? I think you were elected by the additional member route?"

"Very good," patronised the minister. "You know your politics. There are sixty Assembly Members of whom forty are directly elected and twenty by, as you say, the additional member system. It's really proportional representation. With all this talk in Westminster about voting systems, we are ahead of England. That was the way I was elected in 2007." He glanced at Gillian Edwards and then back to Megan. "You are a Labour voter, I trust?"

Gillian coughed. "Megan, Mr Jones is here on official business. . ."

"Yes, I am," said Megan. "In fact, I have been a member for the last eight years. It is marvellous that Carwyn secured us such a good result and effective control in the Assembly in the elections."

"Megan," interrupted Gillian. "Mr Jones is here to talk to you about a possible career move."

Megan raised her eyebrows.

"Megan," continued the AM. "Mrs Edwards has nominated you for a new position, which is immensely important. The Assembly has allocated an amount out of its development budget to focus on the Olympics. You will be hearing about it shortly. The former leader, Richard Morgan, is holding a press conference in two days' time."

Ieuan poured a second cup of tea and took a bourbon biscuit, which he demolished with two bites and some rapid munching. Megan never took her eyes away from his face.

"We want winners, Megan. You are a winner. You played hockey for Wales. Your teams here win. Mrs Edwards says you are very driven."

"What is the position, Mr Jones?" asked Megan.

"It's a bold move," replied Ieaun Jones. "It's my idea. There will be an independent cross-party committee chaired by Mr Morgan. As you know he has retired from active politics but I have persuaded him to come back for this project. You will report directly to one of my colleagues but I will be over-seeing the development."

"It sounds exciting, Mr Jones," said Megan.

"It came to me as I was walking around my local lake. We need to be visionary, I thought. Something radical. That's why voters elect people like me, Megan."

Megan continued to hold his gaze.

"There are three candidates, Megan. I have interviewed the first two and you are the third."

He went on.

"Megan, the contract is a four years' secondment. You will be paid your present salary plus 20 percent. You will be reimbursed all your expenses and there will be a bonus payment which we have yet to work out. At the end of your contract your job here will be open to you." The minister paused. "You may see the school as your base, although we will expect to see you in Cardiff regularly." He indicated the teapot was empty and Mrs Edwards picked up the phone.

"I shall want a weekly report," he said.

The door opened and the secretary came in to collect the tea trays. "And some more biscuits," said Gillian.

"The interviews are next Thursday," the minister said, "in Cardiff."

He smiled. "Now, Megan, you want to know what the position is, don't you? Well, we are going to create the role of a roving ambassador to spot talent. We want Welsh winners at the Olympics. In our schools there are, hidden away, perhaps three or four real gems. I've looked at the system. The Welsh educational structure is one of the best in the world, but it inevitably has to deal with everybody. Here at Dolgellau you are responsible for. . ." – he looked down at his papers now on the desk – "over 120 pupils." He paused as the door opened and a fresh pot of tea was placed on the desk. He picked up a biscuit. "Somewhere there will be a winner we have not yet identified."

"But," spluttered Megan, "it's not that easy. I'm with these girls all day long. I can see ability. I see it all the time. But saying to a girl 'Hey, you are a Welsh winner' – that is something totally different. They're growing up. They're faced with examinations and university entrance. And some of them are far more interested in boys and. . ." She paused. "The Games are next year, Mr Jones. I can't achieve what you want in that time."

Ieuan Jones coughed as the third bourbon biscuit stuck in his throat.

"But, Megan, you have not said that they are not there. The winners."

Megan looked at Gillian and then at the minister. "They are out there, minister. Your vision is brilliant. The question is – how to find them?"

"We want to add to our success in 2008," Ieuan replied. "Wales, Megan, is on the move. We have had an Ashes Test Match at the SWALEC Stadium here in Cardiff for the first time and the Ryder Cup at Celtic Manor in 2010."

"I thought we did well in the Olympics, minister," said Megan. "We had five medal winners, and I was applauding with the rest of Wales for Nicole Cooke and Geraint Thomas when they won their gold medals."

"Yes," he said. "Two golds was a good result, even though they were for cycling."

"Actually, minister, it was three. Tom James won a gold in the coxless fours."

"Yes, yes, rowing," said Ieuan, irritably. "But, Megan, we want athletes like Colin Jackson and Berwyn Price. Where is the next Lynn Davies? We want to hear the Olympic Stadium roar as Welsh athletes win gold."

"Minister, I need time to think. The Olympics are next year. Of course I want the job but my initial reaction, and please minister, Mrs Edwards, please, I am not being negative, but. . . it. . . it's so little time. . . to find these people. . ."

"You have not listened carefully, Megan," replied Ieuan. "I have referred to the Olympics. I have not mentioned London or 2012."

Megan looked from one to the other.

"I'm sorry, I'm lost," she said.

"I am a man of vision," he beamed. "We want you to follow through all that happens leading up to the London Olympics and to prepare a plan that prepares Welsh winners for 2016."

"Oh," said Megan, "well, that is unbelievable, minister, it's brilliant." She paused. "Wow, so. . . Brazil."

"Yes, just think, trips to Rio de Janeiro. . ." smiled the minister. He gathered himself. "And that, Megan, is what the interview panel wants to hear from you on Thursday. Your ideas. How you are going to do it."

He handed her a sheet of paper. "Here is a summary of the position, but you will be able to agree the final specification with my colleague."

"Thursday," said Megan. "That's in two days' time."

"Yes," said the minister, smiling at Gillian.

"And what if I decide not to apply?" asked Megan

Ieuan looked at her. "I don't think that is likely, is it, Megan?"

"No," she replied. "No. I'll be there. Three candidates you said?"

"Three," he confirmed.

"Megan. *Ti'n ddigon da*?" she said to herself. But even as she asked herself whether she was good enough, she was planning the defeat of the other two candidates. She would get this job.

Michelle le Grande landed at Heathrow airport and took a taxi to central London. She spotted her sons and hugged Josh close to her as Matthew took her case. They approached the reception desk at the Westbury Hotel in Conduit Street. She instructed the porter to take the case to her room and mother and sons went into the lounge and ordered afternoon tea.

"Right, Josh. You first. I want to hear all your news," said Michelle.

As Josh gushed with details of the under-fifteens cricket team, fights and the confiscation of his mobile phone, Matthew looked at his mother's face. There was less make-up and none of the signs he feared.

The tea arrived and Josh decided to concentrate on the sandwiches, which he thought were too small.

Matthew told his mother about his success in the first year examinations but concentrated more on his thesis on the 2008-2010 banking crisis, which had earned special praise from his tutor.

"I have to thank Dad," he said. "He knows his stuff. He

told me to research the Secondary Banking Crisis in 1974 and compare the two. I did and it worked."

"So what were the main points?"

"You're interested?"

"Definitely."

"There were two key issues," said Matthew. "In 1974 the Bank of England was in charge. During the late 1960s there was the growth of what they called secondary banks. They made the mistake of borrowing short and lending long. In 1974 one went bust and all the others started to collapse. The Governor of the Bank of England called the chairmen of the main banks and told them they were going to put £200,000,000 each into what was called the Lifeboat. They did and the crisis was averted. But the stock market was still suspicious and so the Governor called in the Head of Prudential Assurance and told him to start buying shares in the stock market. He did and the stock market recovered. End of crisis."

Matthew paused as a second plate of sandwiches was served by the Polish waitress.

"I was born in 1966 so I can't remember it," said Michelle. "Go on, Matthew. This crisis?"

"Same problem really. The collapse of confidence in the banking system and no credit. But this time the real difference was that throughout 2008-2010 there was confusion about who was in charge." Matthew paused. "I'm sure you don't want all the detail."

"No. Go on, Matthew. Josh, please don't eat any more of the sandwiches. I really am interested."

"Right," Matthew continued. "The Governor of the Bank of England found he was arguing with the Head of the FSA, that's the Financial Services Authority, and then the EU officials tried to get involved. In the end it was Gordon Brown, then the prime minister, who showed the necessary leadership."

"So," asked Michelle, "what did your tutor say?"

"He was chuffed. He wants me to do well."

"And your father?"

"Dad made a real effort. He read the whole thing and did some research for me." He paused. "You know Dad. We spent more time arguing about leadership than we did about the crisis itself."

The afternoon drifted on and Josh became restless. As the two sons prepared to leave, Michelle held Matthew's arm and spoke quietly to him.

"Matthew," she said. "Please tell your father that I'm fine and everything is going better. You're going to find out anyway, but Maurice has had a bit of a breakdown. Nothing to worry about, and he and I are working things out. We're selling the house and moving back into Paris. We'll be living in Maurice's flat."

"You need to tell Dad yourself," said Matthew.

"Yes, I know. I will. What he did, in a funny way, meant something to me, Matthew."

"Pity you left him, Mum."

Matthew noticed that Josh was through the revolving doors and turned to leave the hotel.

"Matthew," said his mother. "Who is this Megan?"

"Megan, Megan, slow down for Christ's sake," pleaded David.

They had been on the phone for twenty minutes, as Megan told David about the meeting earlier that day and her plans for the presentation at the interview.

"Thursday morning. You are being interviewed on Thursday morning?" interrupted David.

"I'm staying in Cardiff on Wednesday evening," she answered. "I'm being interviewed at 9:30am on Thursday morning."

"It's all a bit rushed."

"I've not thought about that," replied Megan. "Mrs Edwards has confided to me that she was a week late sending in a reply to the minister's letter."

"Email me your hotel details."

"You're coming?" she asked. "But what about your work? You've only got a few days to finish the Trafford. . ."

"Just email me, Megan."

David left West London on Wednesday afternoon, following a row with the chairman of Park Avenue Capital. Traffic on the M4, once he was past Reading, was travelling freely and he began to enjoy the Wiltshire countryside. He tuned into Classic

FM. He paid the fee, crossed over the bridges into Wales and thirty minutes later his SatNav guided him off the motorway, into Cardiff, and to the Holiday Inn hotel.

He phoned Megan from the car and she met him in reception. Together they went up five floors, closed the door of the room and went to bed.

Later that evening room service arrived and, as they enjoyed Welsh lamb served on a bed of mashed potato, Megan went through her presentation.

"Are you using a PowerPoint?" asked David.

"No. I've been told I can't. I have ten minutes."

"Do you know who's on the interview panel?" asked David.

Megan smiled. "Mrs Edwards has done some digging. She's spent the last two days fussing over me. Anyway, there are, she thinks, seven of them. Certainly the former leader, Richard Morgan, is chairing it, because Mr Jones told me. Mrs Edwards says she suspects all the Party leaders will be there. That's another four."

"Are you sure?" said David. "It sounds a bit heavy."

"They're really going to splash this," said Megan. "The search for Olympic winners."

They pushed the meal table to one side and Megan went to open a bottle of wine.

"No," said David. "No alcohol." He took out a pad of paper and looked at Megan.

"What are you planning to wear?" he asked.

Megan disappeared into the bedroom and a few minutes later she came out wearing a light green two piece suit. She had tied her hair with a scarf.

"No scarf," said David. She took it off and shook her hair. "Fantastic," said David.

Megan went back into the bedroom and came out in casual clothes.

"Right," said David. "Let's hear it."

Fifteen minutes later David put down his pad and looked at Megan. "That," he said, "was not so good."

Megan stared at him. "I've got a few hours to go and you wreck my self-confidence. Thanks."

"You have twelve hours to get this job."

"Can I go to bed, please?" Megan said, crossly.

"No."

"David, that's the best I can do. I am me. I'm Welsh. I love sport. I love my country. That is what I want to convey. Me! Megan Williams from Abergynolwyn."

"Megan, they have already decided about you or else you would not be there. Mrs Edwards will have told them all that stuff. Think, Megan. Why are they sitting there? What do they really want to hear?"

"I don't know, David. I don't bloody know," Megan said. She felt deflated.

"They want to identify potential Olympic winners. They want to find the person who can deliver that. You can bet your last Welsh leek that the other two candidates will take exactly the path you are proposing."

David returned to his briefcase. "They want winners. Let's give them winners. Matthew has spent the morning with his mates. Here is their list of the greatest Welsh sporting heroes."

Megan took the list: Gareth Edwards, Lynn Davies, Joe Calzaghe, John Toshack, Terry Griffiths, Jonathan Davies, Ian Rush, Mervyn Davies, Cliff Morgan.

"We could do with some women," said Megan.

"Who?" said David.

"How about Tanni Grey-Thompson?"

"Who?"

"She's one of the greatest disabled athletes in the world, David. She has won, I think, about sixteen Paralympics medals and the London Marathon six times."

"And she's Welsh?"

"Born in Cardiff."

"Add her to the list."

"Now," David said, "here's the pad. Let's start structuring a winning presentation. You are going to give them Welsh winners and then you are going to convince them you can find the Olympic gold medallists."

An hour later the basis of the presentation was complete. Megan gave her first full rehearsal; ten minutes of Welsh winners, what makes a winner, and what she would do to find them herself. The last line was pure David. "*You are here today to find a winner. I will find mine. Have you found yours?"* Megan swallowed hard. Would this line impress the judges or lose her the job?

By midnight David had made Megan repeat the presentation five times.

Early the next morning Megan and David were sitting in the annex to Committee Room 14 in the National Assembly. As Ieuan Jones entered, David kissed her and left the room.

The minister shook hands with the three candidates. He explained that each would be asked to make a presentation of no more than ten minutes. "Now," he said, "there will be only one successful candidate and it will be my job to tell you the result. The committee will be making an immediate decision. Please stay in here and when the selection is made I shall come out here and ask the successful candidate to come back in. I will write to the other two and send you your expenses."

All three candidates made their presentations.

At 10:30 Daffyd Morgan was called back into the room.

Daffyd leaped to his feet and rushed after the minister.

Megan looked at Sandra Wilson, who was furious. "They were always going to choose a man," she blurted. "Anyway, I'm too English," she said, "I don't know why I was chosen in the first place."

Megan stood up and left the room. She went down the corridor and into the reception area. She met David's eyes and walked up to him.

"You did your best, Megan," he said. "You did so well to be selected for interview. I'm really proud of you."

"Let's just go home, please, David," said Megan.

David picked up his briefcase. He put his arm around her shoulder and they began to leave the building. A small dark-haired woman came rushing up to them.

"Mrs Williams – it is Mrs Williams, isn't it? I'm Mr Jones' secretary. I saw you through the door. Where are you going?"

"Mr Jones said he would send me my expenses," said Megan.

"Mrs Williams, what are you talking about? The committee are expecting you. You've been selected. Come on."

Megan looked at David, astonished. The small woman pulled at her arm.

"Go, Megan!" shouted David, as the two women rushed off.

They were met by Ieuan Jones. "I'm so sorry. I thought that Daffyd had. . ."

"He was a good candidate," said the minister. "So much so he has been offered a position in my department to link more schools with the Welsh Football Association."

He smiled. "However, Mrs Williams, the members were unanimous in their choice. They all want you to become our Olympic flame."

Megan returned into the committee room and was re-introduced to the other seven panel members. She shook hands with each of them.

As she stood in front of the former first minister, Richard Morgan took her hand and smiled, "And where, young lady, did you get that line from?"

"Which line, minister?"

"I will find mine. Will you find yours?"

Albert Payne died at 3:22am. Thomas had been called to the hospital during the evening of the night before. He had been delayed following the termination of his credit lines by two of the three suppliers used by Payne Printers.

The nurse had called the doctor a few minutes earlier as his father's breathing became shallow. She was now disconnecting the tubes and drawing the sheet up to his chin.

"I'm sorry," said the doctor, before leaving.

"I'll come back in the morning," said Thomas to the nurse. "Thank you for what you have done." The nurse looked surprised on hearing his words.

He looked down at his father and then gazed around the ward. He simply could not accept that his father had died in these circumstances.

Chapter Seven

Megan opened the door of her cottage and stared in complete amazement.

"*Duw*!" she exclaimed.

She then realised she was wearing only a thin nightdress and wrapped her arms protectively around herself.

Matthew looked at her and smiled. Josh was looking at the car parked outside the home.

"Matthew. . . Josh. . . what are you. . .?" stammered Megan.

"Well, seeing as you're going to marry our Dad, we thought we'd better come and inspect you," said Matthew.

"Have you got any food?" asked Josh.

She ushered them in and they settled down at the kitchen table, and before long Megan had prepared breakfast. They helped move four bouquets of flowers which Megan had put in buckets of water.

"Dad told us about your new job," said Matthew. "He was so pleased. Well done anyway. I wondered why he had us researching Welsh sporting heroes."

"So you found Abergynolwyn ok?" said Megan.

"Dad told us the directions," said Matthew.

"So he knows you are here?" asked Megan.

"He was all for it. I phoned him from Tywyn. Anyway, you know what's going on. You were on the phone with him yesterday for nearly an hour. He told you he's with Jackson Holmes all day today. His deal has suddenly taken off. He's working this weekend. He says they're completing on Tuesday."

"What's 'completing'?" asked Josh.

"Not sure, Josh. I think it's when they get their fees. Dad seems really chuffed, " answered Matthew.

"So you think he's happy?" asked Megan.

"Dad's always ok," said Josh. He paused from buttering his toast. "We're staying over. I've brought my things."

"Er, what Josh is trying to say, Megan, is may we please stay tonight?" asked Matthew.

Megan consented and took the two of them upstairs into the second bedroom. She suggested Matthew slept in there and Josh used the sofa in the lounge.

"So, apart from inspecting me, what else would you like to do?" asked Megan.

Matthew produced a hand-written list:

1. *Drive in Alpha Romeo*
2. *Swn-y-Don*
3. *Golf club*
4. *Mikatcha*
5. *Pub*
6. *Pharaohs*
7. *Dolgellau High School*
8. *Pub*
9. *Fish and chip shop*
10. *Crabbing (Josh)*

Megan laughed. "Ok guys," she said, "it's going to be a lovely day weather-wise, so get changed and we'll be off."

"Dad has insured the car for me," said Matthew

Megan raised her eyebrows. "Has he?" she acknowledged. She phoned David and Matthew heard her laughing. She let him know the boys had arrived safely and that she was missing him.

They left Abergynolwyn with Matthew driving, Josh in the passenger seat and Megan in the back. She was wearing a white top, white jeans and sandals. Her hair streamed out as Matthew accelerated out towards Tywyn. They cut around the back streets and were soon travelling towards Aberdovey, past the cemetery, alongside the golf course and into the town. Matthew parked the car opposite the houses in Glandovey Terrace, they crossed the road and Megan opened the front door to Swn-y-Don.

"God, why are you selling it?" asked Matthew. "It's a great house." He'd forgotten his promise to his father not to mention the proposed sale.

"Is it for sale?" asked Megan.

"Shit," said Matthew. "You're not supposed to know. Dad's buying a house that's for sale on the hillside. . . It's behind the garage. He's offered £850,000 for it. Sorry. He told me not to tell you. It's meant to be a surprise!"

Megan spent some moments digesting this latest piece of news.

"Right," she said. "Let's go down to the harbour. We've probably missed Charlie, but we'll go and see."

They left the house, crossed the road and walked the 200 yards to the jetty. There, moored up to the pier, was *Mikatcha.* Megan looked around and spied Charlie talking to the Harbour Master. She went over and Charlie gave her a big hug.

"Congratulations, Megan," he said. "We're all so proud of you. My Megan saw it on television. Just to let you know, I'm available for advising on boat trips to Brazil."

She laughed and introduced Matthew and Josh, explaining their connection with David. Megan asked if Charlie would take them out in the evening.

"We can go out now," said Charlie. "My party's cancelled on me. Not their fault. They've been stranded in Portugal by that airline that's gone bust."

Thirty minutes later *Mikatcha* was heading out into Cardigan Bay. Neither Matthew nor Josh ever left Charlie's side. Megan climbed the metal steps and went aloft, sitting on a chair on top of the cabin.

She became lost in her thoughts. The adrenalin of last Thursday's events was still with her and the ovation she had received at Friday morning's assembly at Dolgellau High School had reduced her to tears. Later in the morning she had received two telephone calls, one from Ieuan Jones and the other from Richard Morgan. Following the press conference at lunchtime her mobile had not stopped. She looked back at Aberdovey and the house for sale on the hill. "£850,000," she mused.

Down below, Matthew and Josh wanted to know the full story of the rescue of *Aunty Betty.* Charlie told it as it had happened.

Matthew looked at Charlie. "Wow, Dad could have died," he said.

"Unlikely," replied Charlie.

"Yes, but he might have drowned," continued Matthew.

"I've never lost anybody and I never will, Matthew," said Charlie.

They arrived back in the harbour, thanked Charlie and,

against Megan's better wishes, went to the Britannia. Matthew handed Megan the keys to the car and ordered drinks. He started on a pint of lager. Megan and Josh had soft drinks.

The door of the lounge bar opened and in came Emily Bowden and Rachael Hodge. They saw Megan straight away and rushed up to her.

"Mrs Williams, it's you!" exclaimed Emily. "We're so proud of you. It was on the television!"

Megan smiled and introduced Matthew and Josh before going to the bar. The girls played safe and ordered glasses of fresh orange juice. Megan bought them their drinks and, when she returned to the table, found that Emily had moved round to sit by Matthew. Josh had managed to edge his way to the fruit machine where he happily occupied himself, as well as watching the cricket on the television.

Rachael wanted to hear about Megan's interview and Emily wanted to hear about Matthew. She fired questions at him. They ranged from London, to music, to tweeting, to drinking and back to London.

Josh came back from the bar with another ginger beer and three packets of crisps. Rachael had exhausted the topic of Megan's new job.

Emily had now undone the top button of her shirt and Rachael sensed she did not stand a chance. Emily continually ran her hand through her blonde hair and by crossing her legs had managed to make her skirt ride to her upper thigh. She positioned her right hand on Matthew's knee.

After half an hour or so, as they were getting ready to leave, Matthew turned to Megan.

"Er. . . Megan, I hope you don't mind, but the girls have offered to take us to Cader Idris. We'll see you tonight."

"Will Josh be all right Matthew? It's quite a walk to the top of that mountain and you need proper equipment, even on a day like today," said Megan.

"He always comes with me. He'll be safe, I promise you." Matthew smiled at Megan. "Anyway, I don't think climbing mountains is quite what they had in mind."

They were gone and so Megan returned to her cottage. She

tried David on both his numbers but was unable to contact him.

At 6:30 in the evening Matthew and Josh returned. Matthew said he was off for the evening and would be back in the morning. He gave Megan no opportunity to question his announcement, but she knew where he would be staying. Josh raided the fridge and then settled in front of the television.

Megan checked him and left her mobile phone number on a piece of paper which she placed on top of the TV. She left the house, got into the Alpha Romeo and drove out onto the Aberdovey Road, where she slowed just before the bridge, turning right into the wide avenue leading to the railway station. There were still holiday makers around, playing pitch and putt, bowls and tennis. Megan watched briefly as a teenage girl demonstrated a classy tennis serve which sped past her angered father. Megan thought briefly about her new job.

She turned and walked slowly to the corner and looked up at the hill which dominated the landscape leading into the town. In the centre, with its own plot, was a white house with modernised Georgian windows. It was surrounded by beech, oak and willow trees. Megan thought it had six bedrooms. She could see the balcony, deserted for now. She thought ahead and imagined herself and David in a few weeks' time, sharing an evening bottle of wine and a seafood cocktail.

She went back to her car and, on an impulse, decided to walk through the dunes to the seaward side of the golf course. She soon became lost in her thoughts.

It was all happening so fast, but Megan was enjoying herself. She felt excited about getting back to Josh and seeing Matthew in the morning – although she anticipated that Emily Bowden might have worn him out.

David spent the early hours of Sunday morning running around Primrose Hill and thinking about Barack Obama or, more specifically, the American economy. Economic evidence from the American authorities had suggested the beginnings of a recovery from social and financial meltdown. House prices were stabilising. Sales of new cars were surging due to the success of the scrappage scheme. Exports were improving and energy costs had levelled out. But now the level of government borrowing had become the issue. "And yet," thought David, "the Middle East, China and much of the Far East hold their currency reserves in dollars." He wondered if the Middle and Far East could allow the West to fail. In Europe the Eurozone was under pressure as Greece collapsed and other countries, including Italy, came under pressure.

David compared this with the desperate efforts of the Coalition Government, who had been battling with the ever-increasing financial demands of the banking sector. The official term was 'quantitative easing'. David's summary was 'good money after bad'. He liked David Cameron, but had his doubts. The economy needed revitalising. There were supposed to be massive cuts in spending but the official figures showed that this was simply not happening. "Where," David wondered "will growth come from?"

Later in the day he was meeting Jackson at Park Avenue Capital.

His plans were coming together. He would be completing the Trafford Discount Stores transaction tomorrow. He was confident his offer for the house on the hill in Aberdovey would be accepted and, anyway, he was willing to pay more if required. He had spoken by telephone to Jackson during the previous evening and they had provisionally agreed a parting of the ways. David had been surprised at the financial settlement, which gave him what he wanted.

And David was in love with Megan.

Megan replaced the receiver on the telephone, frowned, poured herself a glass of red wine and went through the back door of her cottage into the small sloping garden, which had a river flowing past the lower boundary. She lay down on a sun lounger and took off her bikini top. She decided to move round by ten degrees so that for the next two hours she could benefit fully from the afternoon sunshine. She smothered herself with suntan cream, had another drink of wine and lay back.

She had reassured David on the phone that Matthew and Josh had left for the return journey to London. "I'll leave them to tell you the details but they seem to have enjoyed themselves," she reported. "I feel well and truly inspected." She did not say that she suspected Matthew had more than enjoyed himself.

It was nearing the longest day of the year and the sun was very hot on her skin. Megan was only too aware of the dangers of exposure to prolonged periods of direct sunshine, not least because the Health and Safety Manual commissioned by Dolgellau High School contained a whole chapter on the subject. Whatever she said and taught, it was always the pictures of skin cancer which had the most profound effect on her audience. One in particular, of a seventeen-year-old fair-haired girl on a 'before' and 'after' basis, had been known to cause several girls to retire rather quickly to the toilets.

Megan was a blonde with medium length hair, which she allowed to lie naturally without much interference. Her skin reflected her upbringing along the West Wales coastal region and her love of the outdoor life. She had virtually no blemishes and considered her tattoos artistic features. Well, one of them. She loved her Welsh dragon, but slightly regretted the second drawing, which was on her lower buttock and said '*cariad croeso*' across a heart – the result of a drunken night out in Cardiff some years earlier.

Megan smiled to herself as she wondered whether David realised that when he was exploring her body he was greeted at the top of her leg with 'welcome lover'.

She ran her hands over her skin. In recent weeks she had lost over eight pounds in weight, partly as a result of her decision to cut down on alcohol, but she had also joined in additional training sessions at the Academy and resumed her daily runs around the village. She was in love and somehow food seemed less important.

She went over in her mind time and again the interview at the National Assembly. She was now certain she was in love with David, and the visit of his two sons had brought her real pride. But, more than anything, it was David's role in preparing her for the presentation to the Committee that had made her realise that she had found someone special. His willingness to travel to Cardiff in the middle of what she knew was a demanding week for him; his thinking through of the content (she learnt afterwards that Sandra Wilson had the best CV of the three candidates and had managed to ruin her chances by spending fifteen minutes talking about herself and never taking her eyes off Richard Morgan). Slowly the sun grew hotter still and Megan raised the umbrella. She lay back and went slowly to sleep. She dreamed about a house on the hill with six bedrooms, a modern kitchen, a secluded garden and views right across Cardigan Bay.

Jackson Holmes tapped the side of his water glass with his pen and suggested to the now attentive occupants of the board room at Park Avenue Capital that the meeting should begin. He waited for Cyril to express himself, but the chairman of Trafford Discount Stores was strangely quiet.

"Ladies and gentlemen, may I welcome our valued and respected clients, Trafford Discount Stores and, in particular, their brilliant chairman, Cyril Trafford."

There was a pause and Justine clapped her hands. Martin glared at her.

"Ladies and gentlemen, may I now offer the floor to David Rensburg."

"He'll be fucking playing 'Jerusalem' before long," Cyril thought to himself.

Margaret Drummond beamed across the table. David blushed.

John Pearman was calculating the value of his share options. He winked at Jemma Shah. Julian Bearing was assiduously writing the Minutes.

"At ten o'clock this morning," said David, rather pompously Jemma Shah thought, "the registrars for Trafford Discount Stores plc reported the following position. They have received, cleared funds totalling £4,200,000. The list of Placees is here and I now present this list to this meeting. You will read that Atlas VCT came in for £1,000,000 and Martin has secured the rest from five investor groups. The funds, less the costs, will be transferred to the company within the next few days."

"Where's fucking Mainstream on this list?" asked Cyril. "I spent an evening presenting to the bastards."

Jemma gulped and grabbed at a glass of water.

"They decided they are a little too committed elsewhere," interjected Jackson.

"An announcement will be released through the London Stock Exchange at around two o'clock this afternoon," concluded David.

"We need a Board Meeting to allot the shares," said the solicitor. Julian Bearing carried on writing.

"Yes, yes," continued Jackson "Can I. . ."

"Right," said Cyril, "you fucking wankers. These fucking costs. We are going through them line by line. We have raised £4.2 million and we get a balance of £2.8 million. Fucking costs total fucking £1.4 million."

"It's the market rate," said Martin. "There is a financial recession. You should be thanking me."

Cyril looked at the broker.

"Fucking market rate, my arse!" he yelled. "It is you fucking advisers, accountants, lawyers, public relations and the bloody rest. Bill after bill. It starts with the fucking government and permeates all through this Satanic City."

"Cyril," said Martin, "to use your language, you have no fucking choice. Pay the fees and go and expand your business."

Cyril looked at the broker and then at Margaret; next he glared at John Pearman and finally he settled on David.

"Fuck the lot of you," he said, and walked out of the building to his car. His chauffeur took him back to his hotel where he went to the bar and ordered a large malt whisky.

He stayed at the bar until his daughter arrived. They had dinner together and, at a little after ten o'clock, Cyril Trafford kissed his daughter Margaret for the last time.

At around three o'clock in the early hours of the next morning he died in his sleep. It did not matter what the post mortem would subsequently say.

He was exhausted. He was lonely and, finally, he was beaten by the system.

At eleven o'clock on the Wednesday morning an announcement was made through the London Stock Exchange that Cyril Trafford, the founder and chairman of Trafford Discount Stores, had died. Trading in the shares of the company was suspended pending clarification of the situation.

David held both her hands and sighed. The deep lines across

Margaret's forehead told their own story. Tears flooded down her face.

"When did you say your husband will be arriving?" asked David.

"He's on his way. He'll be arriving at King's Cross in about an hour."

He released her hands and poured her another glass of wine.

"I'm going on, David." Margaret banged her glass on the table. "We have the money. Well, we have what is left after Mr sodding Martin Van Dijl has taken his share. Why did you allow this to happen, David?"

Now was not the time for explanations. David lifted his glass.

"Is the business in good shape?" he asked

"Doing well. Eighty-three percent up from when we last raised money. We can now open another four branches. My real worry is John."

"John Pearman?"

"He is unsettled. His work is fine and he controls the company effectively. But – and I can't be sure – I think he and his wife may have money problems. He left a credit card demand notice on his desk and one of the clerks passed it to me. When I gave it to him, he laughed and said he would add it to the collection."

"You'll need to find a chairman to replace your father. The Stock Exchange will want reassurance that the Board of Directors is being properly led. It won't be easy to find the right person," said David.

"I'll bury Dad first and then I'll look for one." Margaret looked at David. "David. What do you know about Martin Van Dijl? What I mean is, what do you *really* know about him? I find him unsettling. He's creepy. That woman Justine is scared of him."

"Forget him, Margaret. You have the money. Put all that has happened out of your mind. I'll worry about things here. Go and say goodbye to your father. He was a great man."

"He's dead, David. He had a heart attack. But it's not that simple. Who gave him that heart attack?"

"He lived life to the full, Margaret. This is going nowhere."

"Remember his last words in the meeting. I was looking at him. 'Fucking advisers', he said. And, David, he was looking at Martin Van Dijl when he said it."

"Well," said Martin, "that makes life rather easier." He watched as the girl wrapped herself around the pole and stretched her legs out towards him.

"What does?" asked Justine.

"Trafford snuffing it."

"Martin, he only died yesterday. Even for you that is gross."

His expression darkened and he grabbed her arm. "What do you mean 'even for me'?" he snarled.

"Please, Martin, let go. I'm sorry. It's just that it seems wrong to talk about him like that." She rubbed her bruised limb.

The waiter hovered and took away a further order for the three of them. "And make hers a large one even though she's bollocking me!" shouted Martin.

A second girl appeared on the stage and Martin's attention turned to her black thighs.

"Beautiful," he said and started to wave a £20 note in the air. She was playing hard to get, edging her way over to him. The currency disappeared into the usual place. She gave him a smile which suggested there could be more to follow.

"Where's Gary?" asked Justine.

"Sacked him," replied Martin. "He can't sell."

The dancers were now accelerating their movements and Martin's attention was darting from one to the other.

"She," he announced, "is very fuckable."

"Martin, you will get us thrown out," hissed Justine.

"What, from my own club?" he laughed.

"Excuse me?"

"Not that it's any of your business, but I bought it two weeks ago. Sex sells. Even in a fucking recession people will pay for sex." Martin laughed. "I had a meeting with the local authority. This toffee-nosed bastard told me 'we are going to have lap-dancing clubs re-classified as sex encounter establishments.'"

Justine joined in his laughter.

"So, how was Zurich?" asked the third drinker.

Martin was now watching the one dancer. He was mesmerised by the white outfit on her black body, which glowed as she started to sweat.

"Great, Stephan is with us."

Justine waited until the waiter had put the drinks in front of them. She lifted her glass and thought carefully. Her arm was throbbing.

"I'm lost," she said. "With us where?"

The first girl had now moved away from the pole and removed her top.

"I'll leave Jackson to explain it," said Martin.

Jackson Holmes turned his attention from the stage and looked at Justine.

"We thought several weeks ago that Trafford Discount Stores was in trouble. It's easy to think of fundraising as a sort of tick-box exercise. But it's not. You can do all the checking in the world but you sense a sniff. In this case we became concerned about Cyril Trafford. He has always been loud and crude but of late he has been showing increased tension."

"So?" asked Justine.

Jackson paused and then continued. "It's silly and I've seen it before. It is the obvious that is missed. But think about it. Cyril knows, or knew, that there is a deep recession. The banks are closed for lending. He also knew that David and Martin rarely, if ever, fail to raise the money.

We found out he had a private doctor in Glasgow. We paid him a lot of money. We were delayed because this doctor had principles. We then found out that he had debts. He told us Cyril would be lucky to live another six months. Blood pressure, diabetes and the rest."

He refreshed himself with his pint of lager.

"What we needed was for Cyril to live long enough for Martin to secure the funds."

"Why?" asked Justine.

"Price," said Martin. "At 12p they are very cheap. And all our friends have them."

"But. . . er. . . you said you think Margaret Drummond is a weak link. When we were assessing the situation. That's what you said, Martin. You said she'll be running the company."

"That's the key point," replied Jackson, "and yesterday I spent a long time with our lawyers putting the final pieces together."

"What pieces?" said Justine.

"We will be requisitioning a General Meeting. We'll get control of the company and put our own management team in."

"But that doesn't seem right. What about Margaret. . .?"
Martin slapped her across the face.

A week later the two executive directors of Trafford Discount Stores plc found themselves sitting in the reception area on the second floor of Tower Bridge House. Margaret looked out of the window into St. Katharine's Dock. The June sun was streaming in from the east. She watched the moored wooden sailing boats, *Adieu* and *Ardwina*, both immaculately varnished, rock gently on the water. In the foreground was a row of City Owner motor boats. Two were for sale. The whole area was alive, even during the recession, with busy coffee bars, tourists and residents, some of whom had purchased their Docklands' home with 100 percent mortgages five years earlier, at the top of the market boom.

Margaret looked at David. She then moved her gaze to her right where John Pearman was studying a pile of papers.

They were shown into a meeting room. Nick Billings introduced himself and two other members of the law firm.

Margaret surprised the other people present. She spoke in a subdued and tense voice.

"I've not buried my father yet," she said.

Nick chose his words carefully.

"Mrs Drummond, not one of us in this room wants this meeting to be taking place. I suggest I quickly summarise the position for you and then you can make your decisions."

Margaret glanced at David, who nodded his head. He wanted Margaret to trust his legal friend. He knew at this point in time his anger over the betrayal by Jackson and his broker associate had to be shelved. This was now a legal situation and Nick was a good corporate finance lawyer.

"Mrs Drummond, my firm has been introduced in a private capacity by David Rensburg. We know David well. We have been asked to advise the Directors of Trafford Discount Stores plc on the consequences of the receipt by all the shareholders of a notice calling for a General Meeting."

Nick paused as he took a sip of water.

"As you know a General Meeting can be called by shareholders representing 10 percent or more of the issued share capital. The General Meeting has been requisitioned by shareholders who own 17 percent of the stock. For the sake of clarity, in our opinion the General Meeting has been called correctly."

"But they know my father has just died. They must realise I'm very busy?"

Nick looked over his dark-framed glasses.

"That is almost certainly why they have called it now."

"The General Meeting notice contains a number of resolutions. In effect, they want to take control of the company by replacing the Board of Directors, with the exception of John Pearman."

Margaret looked at her chief executive.

He coughed. "They spoke to me three days ago, Margaret. I felt it was in our best interests to go along with them."

Margaret just stared at her fellow Board member.

Nick interrupted. "It's a usual move, Mrs Drummond. It's you they want to get rid of. They'll appoint new directors and John will effectively be out-voted on the new Board. It will give comfort to the shareholders that the chief executive is staying on."

"So this is all about me?" said Margaret.

"I wish it were otherwise," answered Nick, "but yes."

"So what happens now?" asked Margaret.

"The General Meeting will take place in due course. They have chosen to have it at the London Hilton in Park Lane. They have proposed that an independent chairman of the meeting is appointed. Their suggestion is a lawyer we all know and we'll not oppose this."

"But what happens?" repeated Margaret.

The corporate finance lawyer frowned.

"As I said, the Board is obliged to convene the General Meeting which will have to be held within a matter of weeks." He paused thoughtfully. "Each resolution to remove a director and to appoint a replacement will be put to the meeting and, if there are more than 50 percent of shareholders in favour, it will be passed."

"But will all shareholders turn up?" asked Margaret.

"They will rely on proxies. Effectively, each shareholder can, if they wish, vote by post. Providing the registrars, who will be at the meeting, have received sufficient forms by the closing date, the chairman will have to allow the vote to take account of the proxies received."

"And who wins?" asked Margaret.

"I'm going to ask my colleague, Nathan Miller, to try to answer that question," said Nick.

Nathan looked up from his file.

"We've only had forty-eight hours on this. We're revising our calculations all the time." He looked to his left and at Amanda James, who smiled at Margaret.

"We are working very hard for you, Mrs Drummond," she said.

"The latest estimate we have," continued Nathan Miller, "and we are awaiting the latest report from the registrars, is that there are 80,222,228 shares in issue. There are 52,306,109 shares held in nominee names, including those shares controlled by Martin Van Dijl. If we add all the shares we feel confident about, in the sense we know who the underlying owners are, we calculate that they have around 38 percent of the votes. Obviously the family control around 20 percent. That is you and your father. Then there are about 20,000,000 shares in the hands of private investors. Martin Van Dijl's people will be phoning these people up to persuade them to vote for the resolutions. All they need is 50 percent plus one to succeed."

"Just remind me of how nominees work?" said Margaret.

Nick explained. "You can choose to hold your shares in a nominee name. It is quite usual. Many stockbrokers like their clients to have their shares registered in the nominee name of the firm. It makes selling easier. Most institutions hold their shares in nominee names. It can be used to disguise who the real owner is. But we can issue a notice and the nominee then has to reveal the true owner."

"So," said David, "it sounds to me that the 20,000,000 shares are key to the outcome, Nick."

"In all probability," replied Nick.

"If I may say something," said Nathan. "We obviously have a great deal of experience in these matters. There are two private shareholdings that stand out. Do you know who Arnold Matthews is, Mrs Drummond?"

"He's my godfather."

"Great," said Nathan, "then he will be for us. And who is Alice Kaye Kimmins? She has 4 percent. It's a big holding."

"I've never heard of her," replied Margaret.

"So, to summarise," said Nick, "we need to get to work. It's going to be close."

"And I may lose my company," said Margaret.

"Probably not. With the family shares and John Pearman's 2 percent, I think we're safe," replied Nick.

John Pearman, the chief executive, stood up.

"You're going to find out soon enough so I might as well get it over with." He looked at Margaret. "Sorry, Margaret, business is business. I shall be voting with Martin Van Dijl."

Margaret looked in complete amazement at her colleague of twelve years.

"I suggest you do not say anything, Margaret," said John Pearman. "I'm sorry that this is happening now. I wanted them to wait until after the funeral bu. . . well, I have to think about the future and my family."

"If my father were here now, John, you'd have just disappeared through that window."

"Thank you for saying that, Margaret. It makes me feel better because it convinces me of my position. You and your father have taken me for granted for too long. I have made Trafford Discount Stores. It was me who worked out how to survive the recession. You two just took everybody else for granted. Martin Van Dijl values me."

"He's bought you, hasn't he?" said Margaret. "How much, John?"

John looked at his former colleague.

"That's all you know, isn't it Margaret? Just like your father. You think everything is about money."

John Pearman picked up his file and left the meeting room.

Nathan crossed out a figure on his list. Amanda James, the assistant solicitor, nodded in agreement and recast the voting lists. She already knew, along with her colleague Nathan, that it was going to be very close.

David could not stop Megan talking over the phone. The cause of her excitement was Prince Charles' recent visit to Aberdovey.

Megan had watched the events in the harbour with colleagues from the Outward Bound School. The children of Aberdovey School had sung a song for the Prince.

But it was the reason for his visit that took Megan's interest. The Prince had officially launched the new Time and Tide Bell, which was to be installed later in the year underneath the jetty.

The bell was one of twelve such installations around coastal Britain. They had been crafted by the sculptor, Marcus Vergette.

"David," enthused Megan, "it was wonderful. The bell is for all of us – The Bells of Aberdovey."

She had researched the project carefully and used the material in several of her classes at Dolgellau High School and with the kids from Outward Bound. The purpose was to make a permanent installation of the Time and Tide Bell at the high tide mark at various sites around the United Kingdom.

The first had been installed in July 2009 at Appledore in Devon, the second in the Outer Hebrides, the third at Trinity Buoy Wharf, in the Docklands, and the fourth in Aberdovey.

"David," continued Megan, "the idea is that as the seas rise at high tide the clapper strikes the bell. The movement of the waves creates a varying, gentle, musical pattern."

"Are you reading this stuff?" asked David.

"Yes. I downloaded it from the internet," replied Megan. "But listen, David. The thinking is that as global warming increases, the periods of bell strikes will become more frequent and, as the bell becomes submerged, the pitch will vary."

"September you said?"

"Yes."

"I think we should be there for the installation." He laughed. "Actually, of course we'll be there. We'll be living there by then."

Justine reeled away as the fist landed on her chest. She was knocked backwards and fell over the sofa positioned in the bay window of the luxury flat on the 14th floor of Seldom Tower, overlooking the Docklands.

She was, however, focusing on the leather belt which Martin had removed from his trousers and which he had wrapped around his fist.

"You never say 'no' to me, you slut!" he shouted. "You get

back in that bedroom and let me watch you use this fucking vibrator!"

Justine looked around and reached for a beer glass left on the table from the night before. She picked it up and lunged at her attacker. As she did so she slipped and the glass in her hand hit the corner of the bay window wall, smashed and a piece embedded itself in Martin's arm. There was an immediate flow of blood.

Justine ran away from him, into the passage and out through the front door. She ran down the stairs, all fourteen floors, and out into the courtyard. She realised she was wearing very little clothing. She had no money, no credit cards – but she did have her mobile phone clipped onto her shorts.

She pressed 'names'. By now she was weeping and could not see the print. She pressed the green button and almost immediately a voice answered.

"David Rensburg." And again. "David Rensburg, hello?"

"David, it's me. . . Justine."

David held the phone closer to his ear. "Justine?. . . Justine who?"

"Justine Hathaway, you know – with Martin Van Dijl."

"Ah, Justine, yes. You never usually phone me."

"I need help."

"I don't understand, Justine. Where's Martin? You usually stay with him, don't you?"

"Where are you?"

"I'm sitting on a park bench in Primrose Hill," replied David. He had been thinking about the Bells of Aberdovey and Megan's excitement over this new Tide and Tide Bell. Somehow the bells were drawing them together. . .

Justine pleaded with David to fetch her.

"Justine, call the police or an ambulance. You need proper help. Do it now."

"David, please! Please, come and get me!" she cried.

Within half an hour and following a rapid car drive across London to the Docklands, David had found her and taken her back to his home. She asked if she could have a bath and David found some clothes in the spare room. She refused his offer of a private doctor but did take some pain killers.

When she had settled back into the lounge, David handed her a large gin and tonic. She began talking almost immediately and told of the loan she had taken from Martin and how she had been his mistress since. "He has a wife in Woking and he goes home quite often. He expects me to be available whenever he calls."

"We work together and most of the time Martin is fine."

"You've always seemed happy together," said David.

"We have been," said Justine, "but about six months ago he started asking for some. . . shall we say. . . outrageous things. One night I arrived about ten o'clock and he had hired a girl who he wanted in bed with us."

She took a large gulp of her gin and tonic and continued, telling David how three months ago Martin had wanted to whip her and, when she refused, had slapped her.

"Even now I can't understand why he changed so quickly. I know men like three in a bed so I didn't think much of it. Funnily enough, after that we seemed to become closer for several weeks. . . But then he started watching more porn on TV – you know, the sex channels – he liked this lesbian one the best and he would want me to watch him masturbate."

"Justine. I want to help," said David. "But I think I've heard enough. . ."

"But then he brought out this whip. He wanted to whip my buttocks."

"Ok. I'm either taking you to the police, to the hospital or to your home," said David. "Which is it?"

"He's always sorry afterwards," she said.

"What are you going to do?" asked David.

"I don't know."

Thomas collected the ashes of his father from the undertaker and drove down to Bexhill, near to Hastings, on the south coast of England. As he walked along the pebble beach he recalled childhood holidays and his mother and father being silly.

He walked to the water's edge and slowly poured the ashes into the sea.

He returned to his car and drove home to North London, where he tried to work out how he could avoid the repossession order issued by the Building Society.

On Thursday, two days after their meeting, David shook hands with Jackson Holmes. It had been agreed that David would leave Park Avenue Capital with a payoff of £2,000,000. Both sides agreed that for tax purposes it was a redundancy situation. He would work for a further four weeks and then his contract would be terminated.

As they stood on the door step fronting Curzon Street, Jackson said a few irrelevant things and then said to David that perhaps he was too decent for corporate finance work.

David turned to Jackson and stared into his face.

"Are you behind the Trafford EGM, Jackson?" he asked.

"It's for the best, David. Margaret will be out of her depth. I always do the best for the shareholders. Martin has put a good team together."

"If you win the vote," said David.

"Martin rarely gets it wrong. It will be close but it's in the bag, as they say. . ." Jackson adjusted his silk tie and straightened the lapels of his jacket.

"David, I can only repeat what I said – you are better off out of corporate finance. Leave the dirty work to people like Martin."

"If I ever meet Martin Van Dijl again you may see another side to me," said David.

He slowly walked away from the offices of Park Avenue Capital and hailed a taxi to take him to Primrose Hill.

He was never to return.

PART TWO

Will the Bells Ring?

Chapter Eight

David arrived in Aberdovey on the Friday night at around 10:00pm. Megan was out at the front of Swn-y-Don waiting for him. As he parked his car she rushed over the road and hugged him.

"*Rwy'n dy garu*, David," she said and she meant every word. She really was in love with him.

They went together into the house and settled peacefully in the lounge rather than rushing up to the bedroom. Megan had prepared a seafood cocktail, containing crab, shrimp and prawns, for each of them and opened a bottle of champagne, which she poured carefully into the glasses she had placed on the central wooden table.

She was unable to contain her excitement.

"I've had a letter from the minister," she said, and handed David a brown business envelope from which he took a series of papers held together by a paperclip.

"It confirms the terms of my position," said Megan, "and is a detailed job description. It all sounds great, so organised. . . The last sheet I have to sign and send back. I start on 5 September."

"Maybe I should check everything through tomorrow?" asked David. "Would you mind?"

"I'd like that," replied Megan. She stood up and poured more champagne into David's glass. He was sitting in his favourite seat in the bay window of the lounge.

"So, how are you going to find these Welsh winners?" asked David.

"The main thrust of what was said to me, mainly by Mr Morgan," gushed Megan, "is that I'm free to watch the whole of the preparations leading up to the London Olympics next year and then structure my 2016 plan. I have to deliver it six months after the end of the London games." She took a breath. "But I want to do much more. I've done some research on Rio de Janeiro. It's going to be very hot for the athletes. . ."

"You are getting ahead," said David, amused.

He looked at Megan. Her eyes were sparkling and she was alive with expectation. She was somehow holding herself more authoritatively. She was also perhaps the most beautiful woman David had ever seen in his life.

"And in Wales?" asked David. "What's your plan?"

"I'll not waste time on the obvious," replied Megan, "such as writing to all schools and sports organisations. It's set out in the job description. They had given the position and the methodology much more thought than was clear from what the minister said."

She was now reclining on the sofa and had tucked her legs beneath her. "When I read everything this morning it was fantastic, David," she smiled. "I was so chuffed personally, because I succeeded in getting the job. But today it dawned on me what an opportunity I've been given. Professionally." She looked intensely at her partner. "I want to find those winners."

"Monday is the first week of July," continued Megan. "I have two months before I start work and I'll be finishing at the High School in two weeks' time, although Gillian Edwards has said I can concentrate on my new work almost immediately."

Megan stretched her legs over the end of the sofa. "I've decided that if I'm to succeed I must be able to recognise a winner when I meet one. It's not like my work at the school or even Outward Bound. Much of the time I'm having to focus on examination results and some of my success in sport has been because you win hockey tournaments by putting teams together. You come across individual talent and we have several young tennis players who might progress. I've managed to advance a number of the girls to national levels – but that's not quite the same as finding Olympic gold medalists."

David wanted Megan to talk on without interruption.

"What I'm going to do is try to understand what is different about a winner. I'm going to study winners – Lewis Hamilton, Andy Murray, Wayne Rooney. How did they seem to come from nowhere to become world beaters?"

"All good Welshmen," said David.

"Mock if you wish," said Megan. "I'm arranging to see all the Welsh medallists from the last Olympics." She stood up and went and sat at David's feet. "David, please think about it. Is finding a winner a checklist? If somebody ticks ten boxes have I found a champion? I'm not so sure. If I'm going to succeed I've decided I'll have to develop an inner sense. I must be able to know." She paused. "I'm rambling but I know what I mean." She laughed. "It was Matthew to the rescue!"

"What's Matthew got to do with it?" asked David.

"He's emailed me the list of Welsh champions that you had him prepare. I've already ordered their books. Most of them have written autobiographies. I want to learn everything I can from them."

David put his hands on Megan's shoulders. "Time to open another bottle, I think," he said.

When Megan returned to the lounge she noticed that David was fiddling with the CD player.

"Listen to this, Megs," he said. "It's from *The Sound of Music*."

"Megs!" she exclaimed. "Where has that come from?"

"Megs," said David. "I think it's going to be my name for you from now on."

"I'm Megan, David. Nobody calls me 'Megs'."

"Exactly," said David. "Nobody except me."

Megan considered. "Megs," she repeated. "Perhaps."

"Listen to the music, Megs," instructed David.

Megan lay back and heard again, "Megs". Oh yes, she would live with that.

She then applied herself to the recording.

"David, *The Sound of Music* is by Julie Andrews. It's about 500 years old!"

"Not quite, Megs, but you're heading in the right direction," continued David. "Who's singing this?"

Following an orchestral introduction a baritone voice filled the lounge:

Climb every mountain, search high and low
Follow every byway, every path you know

Megan found the sound enchanting and dragged David over to the sofa, where she wrapped herself around him.

Climb every mountain, ford every stream,

Follow every rainbow, 'til you find your dream!
A dream that will need
All the love you can give,
Every day of your life
For as long as you live.
The baritone returned and the song reached its conclusion.
Climb every mountain, ford every stream,
Follow every rainbow, 'til you find your dream!

David pressed the remote control and played the track again.
"Who was that?" he asked.
"Deep South in America," said Megan. "Motown."
David was just about to congratulate her when he again remembered the Welsh sheep comment.
"But who?" he asked.
"No idea," said Megan.
"The Four Tops," said David.
"I doubt if I was even born when they were singing," said Megan.
"You were," said David, "they were touring up until the mid '90s. The lead singer, Levi Stubbs, died in 2007. It was his voice that you just heard."
"Miles Davis, Mahler, the Beach Boys and now the Four Tops. You have varied musical tastes."
"I like sounds," said David. "I always envy those people who seem so knowledgeable. Me - I read CD cover notes and pretend I'm an expert. The Levi Stubbs CD came from a Woolworth's moment."
"A Woolworth's moment?" repeated Megan.
"When Michelle and I were raising the family we went through periods of having very little money. On a Friday evening on the way home I would allow myself five pounds. I would have a beer and go into Woolworth's. They've gone bust now, of course, but back then they sold cheap CDs and over the years I've found a number of brilliant tracks. Never the full CD, of course, because otherwise they wouldn't be cheap. But every so often you come across a gem and that one from the Four Tops is an example."

They cleared away the glasses and then climbed the two floors to the bedroom.

A few minutes later Megan and David made love with an intensity and passion neither had ever known before.

The following morning Megan had agreed to walk to the golf club at 12 noon to meet with David. Gareth Williams wanted to discuss business matters and had suggested he and David tee off at eight o'clock.

David confided to Megan that his game was a little rusty, but when Gareth calls. . .

When she had dressed and gone down to the kitchen she found a book and a note from David on the table.

'Please read this. Love. David x'

She picked up the book and read the cover.

'The Downwave: Surviving the Second Great Depression.'

The author was Robert Beckman. Megan turned over and read the blurb on the back.

> *This is what happens in* The Downwave – *whole countries go bankrupt, banks large and small go bust. Companies crash, whole industries disappear, and millions lose their jobs. House prices tumble. Building Societies shake, office blocks become unsalable, land values slide, and share prices slump. People live differently, think differently, wear different clothes, watch different films, hum different songs, and see sex differently. History shows it will happen – and can happen. Can you cope? This book shows you how to survive in a world turned upside down. Ignore it at your peril. It could change your life.*

It was published in 1985.

Megan made herself a cup of coffee and then went out of the house, across the car park and into the sand dunes, where she settled down. The sun was high in the summer sky. She creamed herself and adjusted her bikini top. She started to read *The Downwave.*

Justine Hathaway looked down at her legs. She saw that rivulets of blood were streaming down the insides of her thighs. She lifted her nightdress and cried out in horror.

She staggered over to the phone.

She dialed 999.

Two and a half hours later Justine came around from the operation. A nurse held her hand and a doctor told her gently that she would never be able to bear children.

Megan met David at lunchtime and listened as he described his round of golf and his defeat at the hands of Gareth. They had a salad at the club.

After lunch they left, walking through the sand dunes and onto the beach. David began to tell Megan about the incident earlier in the week.

"So, out the blue, this Justine Hathaway phones you up and you go and rescue her in East London?" asked Megan.

"Yes," said David. "She was very distressed. She'd been attacked by Martin Van Dijl. I'm not completely clear what he did but it sounded pretty bad."

"Should you have taken her to hospital?"

"I tried, Megan. She would not go. She said the police would get involved and that couldn't happen."

"So what did happen?"

"She seemed to recover and while I was taking a phone call in the study she just went. I saw a taxi outside. I've phoned her several times but her mobile's been off."

Megan looked thoughtful. "Are Matthew and Josh aware of this?" she asked.

"No. They're both away. Josh is staying over with someone and Matthew is somewhere else. To be honest, I don't know where."

Megan reflected further. "Did you clear up, David? Did you notice anything in the bathroom?"

"I had to wipe up some blood, yes. . ."

They walked back to the sea front and to Swn-y-Don where they changed into their beachwear. By mid-afternoon, and protected by suntan cream, they began the walk to Tywyn. As they reached the headland of the estuary and began the turn towards the northern hills, they hit low tide and found firm sand on which to walk.

"I like the hemline theory," said Megan.

"You've read it!" exclaimed David.

"Selectively," said Megan. "It's not that long and I enjoyed it. He was spot on with his predictions as far as I can work out. Just about everything he wrote, over twenty-five years ago, has just happened."

"Absolutely," said David. "In fairness to Beckman, globalisation and the internet have advanced more than he could have known, but his basic point is that the world moves in forty year cycles."

"So do you agree with the hemline theory?" asked Megan, chuckling but stopping abruptly. "David, get out of that pool! Weever fish. I have warned you."

David jumped out of the water left by the outgoing tide. "Thanks," he said.

He moved back to Megan's side. "It has merit," he said. "Moral standards decline as society grows richer and more decadent. Beckman used the rise in a girl's skirt to make the point. Perhaps today you might focus on the availability of pornography on TV. It's the same thing."

"So, are we decadent David? I'm quite happy for my skirt to rise."

"Beckman was an American economist. This was his first book and he spent the rest of his life trying to repeat it. He became notorious through his London radio show, where he ended up using his dog to pick share tips. He scattered the names of shares on pieces of paper and put them on the studio floor. Whichever one the dog stood on was his share tip of the day. The dog actually outperformed the stock market."

Megan turned to the Cardigan Bay waves and rushed into the water. She went out thirty yards and then swam along as David continued walking. She rejoined him half a mile further towards Tywyn. David was looking at the sandbags on the side of the twelfth green which, earlier in the day, he had played with Gareth. Today there was no wind and David's nine iron shot had landed his ball within a foot of the flag.

Megan shook her hair and wiped the water off her skin.

"So why have I read *The Downwave* this morning?"

David stopped and turned to face Megan.

"Because, Megs, I have decided how I want my life to go."

The floodgates opened as David told Megan about his talk with Jackson Holmes.

"I've had enough." He stopped and explained the calling of the shareholders' meeting and the effect on Margaret Drummond and Trafford Discount Stores. He told Megan that his last act would be to sort the matter out and defeat the attempt to oust Margaret.

"Jackson kept saying to me that I was too moral for corporate finance. But he made one point that I could not argue – I've made a lot of money."

David splashed some water over Megan and continued by explaining that they had agreed a payoff of £2,000,000.

"*Duw*!" exclaimed Megan.

"I'm selling Jackson my 30 percent of the partnership. I'm supposed to work on briefly but I've decided not to go back. I'm finished with London, Megs."

They had now reached the rocks built around two large pipes which carried the rainwater from the hills into Cardigan Bay. They sat down and David handed Megan a banana. She threw the peel into the water and watched as it disappeared out to sea.

"So where does Robert Beckman fit into this?" she asked.

"Bob, to his friends," said David. "I re-read his book on Tuesday evening and I stayed up half the night. It was like a flash of inspiration, Megs. You know last night when we were talking about music. About knowing a little about things. I don't know anything about jazz. I just read the cover notes and pretend I do. But I do know about finance. It's my trade."

He put his hands on Megan's shoulders and looked into her face.

"I'm going to write a book. I'm going to write about the importance to a modern democratic society of an efficient capital raising system. Do you remember last year when Vince Cable told the banks to lend to small businesses?" Megan did not know who Vince Cable was but decided to let David speak on. "Of course, it never happened but what it really showed was a breakdown of the system."

David stood up. "Megs, I know that system and I know how it can work better. That will be my book."

Megan looked out to sea. "*The Upwave* by David Rensburg," she said.

They began the return walk to Aberdovey.

"So where are you going to write this book?" asked Megan.

"Mainly here in Aberdovey," replied David. "Matthew has told you that I've bought a house for us. I'm collecting the keys tomorrow morning so I can show you. I'm keeping Primrose Hill because I will need to spend time in London and the boys want to stay there."

"The house you are buying," said Megan, "who's going to live there?"

"We are."

He stopped and took a box from his pocket. He opened it and placed on the fourth finger of Megan's left hand a diamond-encrusted engagement ring.

He held Megan gently in his arms and kissed her.

"David?" asked Megan, wiping her eyes, "have you just asked me to marry you?"

As they continued walking on the sands Megan turned again to David.

"This hemline theory. My skirt rises as I want more sex?"

"Well, that's a loose translation of it," said David.

"Well, my skirt's pretty high right now," said Megan, as they hurried back to Swn-y-Don.

The following morning David had responded with some surprise to an instruction from Megan. He appeared at the front door of Swn-y-Don wearing a dark suit, white shirt and a sombre red tie.

They both got into the Alpha Romeo and Megan drove out of Aberdovey, through Tywyn and turned right on the road to Talyllyn lake. After twenty minutes they arrived at the village of Abergynolwyn. David had been to Megan's cottage twice before, but he realised she had driven past the lane and parked instead outside a row of small terraced stone and slate-built houses. She took a key out of her pocket, unlocked a front door and went into a front room.

"Mam, it's Megan," she shouted.

From out of the back a small, white-haired woman appeared. She was dressed all in black and around her shoulders was a shawl. Megan went up to her and kissed her cheeks.

"Shall we have a cup of tea, Mam," she said, and led her into the back kitchen. They reappeared with a tray of tea and a plate of biscuits.

Mrs Williams sat down on a chair and looked at David.

"My Rhys would be thirty-five now," she said. "How old are you?"

"I'm thirty-nine, Mrs Williams," replied David.

"Mam. My name is Mam."

Megan leaned over towards David. "She's asking you to call her Mam," she said.

"He was about your size. Stand up."

David stood up.

"He was just a little taller and broader."

"We're going to take you to church, Mam," said Megan.

The three worshippers left the house and walked down the road to the chapel where they joined the other villagers. David rather enjoyed the service and relished the bible-thumping sermon on the sinfulness of modern life. He agreed in principle, provided the vicar could exempt two million pound payoffs.

"I tell you, brethren," the preacher roared, "in our modern society, greed and the pleasures of the flesh have overtaken family, community and the church!"

There were rumblings of approval from within the church.

"God gave us sex to reproduce our children. We are the only animal on this planet which uses sexual intercourse for pleasure. It is WRONG, brethren, and a sin. I tell you, those who practise these outrageous and anti-Christian pleasures will face a future of eternal damnation!"

When the collection plate came round David put in a twenty pound note in a futile effort to avoid the satanic punishment he had realised he was due.

After the service the vicar and a number of villagers disappeared to the local pub. Megan and David walked either side of Mrs Williams, who put her arms around each of their elbows.

They arrived at the house and, once they were in, Megan made a pot of tea.

Megan poured, served and then looked at her mother-in-law.

"Mam," she said. "I'm going to marry David."

Mrs Williams looked first at Megan and then at David.

She got up from the chair, her face reflecting her arthritic pain. She walked slowly over to David and kissed his face. She moved to Megan who had stood up. They hugged each other in a long embrace.

"God bless the two of you," she said.

She sat down slowly and looked again at David.

"You're a good man," she said quietly. "My Rhys was a good man too."

David stood up and pulled up a chair which he placed at her side. He sat down and took her hand in his.

"Now, Mam, I want you to tell me all about Abergynolwyn," he said.

Megan watched and breathed a sigh of relief. As Mam told David about the early days of the mining communities and the building of the railways Megan found that she was playing with her engagement ring.

As they drove back into Aberdovey David realised he had missed the agreed appointment with the estate agent. He telephoned their office in Tywyn using his BlackBerry and, when he obtained a recorded message saying they were out with clients, he sent them an email.

He suggested to Megan that she park the car in the station road. They then crossed the road by the grocery stores and climbed the hill two thirds of the way to the top. The 'For Sale' notice was leaning slightly over, having been buffeted by the wind over the six months the house had been on the market. It was vacant and they spent an hour peering through windows and doorways. David said it had six bedrooms, two lounges, a breakfast room, a dining room, a study and a conservatory. The space behind was poorly cultivated and would, David informed Megan, be ideal for the swimming pool. The back garden sloped upwards over four tiers. Back to the west side there were two stone built garages.

Megan agreed to collect the keys on Monday and have a look inside. It was hardly necessary. She was already in love with her new home.

They walked back to Aberdovey, under the bridge, along Glandovey Terrace, past the afternoon queue at the fish and chip shop and to Medina's at the rear of the chemist shop, where they had an early afternoon pot of tea and Welsh cakes.

By three o'clock they were installed in a sand dune 200 yards north of the wooden walkway which led from the caravan park behind the fire station and the beach. Megan wore a new white bikini and asked David to cream her back. She lay front down on her towel.

David sat up and watched the activities taking place in the estuary. There were families on the beach, people walking pets, boats coming in and out from the sea, a yacht race and three jet skiers whose waves would lash against the estuary banks.

Megan lifted her head.

"David," she said. "*The Upwave* by David Rensburg – why should I read it?"

"Why did you enjoy *The Downwave*?"

"It was well written. I liked its central thesis. I could relate it to me. I felt I learned something. It was funny in places and daring in others."

"Wait for my book," laughed David. "It will improve on all those features."

"But finance, capitalism, whatever you were saying yesterday. How am I interested in that?"

"Well, Mrs Williams, sorry, Mrs Rensburg to be, you have hit the nail on the head. When I re-read Beckman's book, it made me realise how, over the last four years of the recession, the press, and the financial press in particular, have struggled to explain country and global finances. But Beckman did it and so will I."

David lay down beside Megan. "Let me give you one example. At one point in 2008 the Treasury, also known as Gordon Brown enterprises, put £37 billion into the banking system. Since then, of course, billions more has gone in. The press announced a collapse of our financial system. The public gained an impression of Gordon Brown standing by a printing press pumping out £100,000 notes."

David paused and drank some water. "What is £37 billion?"

Megan failed to give an answer.

"What is £1,000?"

"Not far short of half my take home salary. A good holiday. An extension to my cottage. A sum to put away for a rainy day."

"Do you have a credit card?" asked David.

"Yes. Just one. MasterCard with Abbey or Santander or whatever they call themselves. They have my mortgage and they wrote and offered me a card."

"What's your credit limit?" asked David.

Megan sat up. "Hey, do you know what? They gave me a £3,000 limit."

"Do you use it?"

"Only occasionally."

"What's interesting, Megan, is that everything we have just talked about you have been able to relate to. In other words, if you can understand a financial matter or term at a personal level you feel comfortable."

"Agreed. But I've lost your theme."

"Right. Let's value the government.

"Do let's."

David ploughed on, undisturbed by the hooter signaling the start of the last boat race of the day. "As you earn a salary, what is the government's salary?"

"Pass."

"Tax," said David. "The government's main right is that of taxing. Nobody can take it away from them. In 2010 it raised £630 billion in taxes. That is about £3,000 per head of population."

"Ok," said Megan. "The government taxes us."

"Now, you can argue that the tax revenue is a return on capital assets."

"What assets?" asked Megan.

"What the government owns," replied David. "It's a difficult concept but I can show you it another way. Let's go back to your finances."

"That I can understand. I'm broke."

"So is the government. But let's imagine you have a Building Society account with £10,000 in it."

"This I could enjoy."

"At the moment the interest you would earn on your savings would be about 3 percent. That works out to £300 per year."

"That I can understand. It's not much is it, David?"

"Ok Megs. What you can do is use the same thinking to work out what the Government is worth."

"Can you?"

"Yes. The Government receives £630 billion in a year. As you earned £300 so the national treasury gets that sum of money."

"Where from?"

"Taxes, VAT, inheritance duty, the extra you pay on fuel and so on."

"Go on."

"£630 billion represents 3 percent from your example. Right, so 100 percent is £10,500 billion."

"Is it?"

David beamed. "The point is that £37 billion, which they have injected into the banks as a percentage of £10,500 billion, isn't that much."

"David," said Megan. "I think we are in the back of CD covers territory. I'm not sure you really understand what you're saying."

"I read the argument in the *Financial Times* last week. I was just trying it out."

"What time are you leaving for London?"

"No later than six."

No more words were needed as they packed their towels. But then Megan spoke.

"David," she said, "Can you email me a summary of the article you read? I intend to help you with your book and I've not understood a bloody word of what you've been talking about."

On that Sunday evening Megan wrote a letter to David, which she posted the next morning.

Afon Cottage
Abergynolwyn
Gwynedd
Cymru

My Darling David,

There are so many words I could use to express my feelings at this moment and love, affection, devotion and respect would be leading contenders.

When Rhys was killed I felt guilty that I was alive. Mam often asks 'Why Rhys?' and I have felt the same way. For a number of years I have lived as well as I could and my love of sport and my teaching role have sustained me.

In some ways I have friends and yet at times I am alone. I have never been a girly type really. As for male friends, Rhys and I were together for so long and since his death it has been. . . messy.

That is, until you came into my life. I heard you through the walls of the changing room. My creased tennis dress and my weight. But Gareth said that I was gorgeous. I lived on that and wanted to get back to what I knew I could be.

Now I am going to marry you. I cannot rationalise the last few months. . . Where have you come from? Have I more to learn about you? I do know that you are a man who can get hurt and is, at times, searching for things.

Well David. You now have Mam (!), you have Matthew and Josh, and you have a partner who will be devoting her life to your happiness. I will always be there for you, come what may.

Fondest love,
Megs xxx

Margaret Drummond looked out the window of Tower Bridge House and noticed that a third cruiser had been put up for sale.

She turned to David.

The receptionist asked that they move into the meeting room. They were greeted by Nick Billings. Nathan Miller and Amanda James were sitting at the table, studiously checking a column of figures.

The solicitor offered coffee and biscuits and then came straight to the point.

"Mrs Drummond, the General Meeting is on Friday 15 July. We have eleven days left. It's very tight."

"Tight?" asked Margaret.

Nick looked at Nathan.

"As far as we can be sure," he said, and he turned and glanced at Amanda James, who nodded in agreement, "we think that they have a certain 48 percent of the votes. This means the small shareholders hold the balance."

"Mrs Drummond," asked Amanda, "are you sure you do not know who Alice Kimmins is? Alice Kaye Kimmins. She lives in Meifod in Wales. We've phoned her twice but she's refusing to talk to us."

David looked at Nick.

"Meifod is just outside Welshpool. It's just across from the border with Shropshire. I pass through it on my way to Aberdovey. I'll go and see her."

"Ok, but no pressure, David. You must not in any way give her grounds for complaint."

"And what do you think Martin Van Dijl is doing?" said David.

"David?" asked Megan. "Why do I have to go to. . . where. . . Meifod?"

"You're a woman," replied David.

Megan refrained from the obvious reply. She was aware that David was in a serious frame of mind.

"A woman," she repeated.

"This Alice Kimmins – she may not even know she owns the shares. She might have inherited them. She gets all these phone calls from London. She may be scared. My hope is that she will find you reassuring."

An hour later they arrived at the village of Meifod, on the western edge of Welshpool, in the county of Montgomeryshire. They quickly found a small farmhouse where they were met by three barking dogs.

Thirty minutes later they were leaving. Alice Kaye Kimmins had refused to talk to them.

As they drove away Megan snapped.

"You played that wrong, David. Mr 'Big I am' from the City. Shareholder value. I thought I was going to play a part?"

"Megan," said David, "do you really think you could have done any better? She is just not interested. Funny, her shares are worth about £400,000. She didn't seem to care."

"So what happens now?"

"Margaret Drummond is going to lose her business. She has buried her father and she will almost certainly be voted off the Board."

"And do you care?"

"Yes," replied David, "I care. That bastard Martin Van Dijl."

Megan looked at David

"Yes," she said. "It really does matter to you, doesn't it?"

Matthew put a coke down for Josh and drank from his pint of lager.

"So Joshy boy," he said, "Dad's really fallen for her – Megan."

"She's ok," said Josh.

"Different to Mum?"

"Very," laughed Josh.

The chairman of the General Meeting of Trafford Discount Stores called the meeting to order. The first floor meeting room of the Hilton in Park Lane contained fourteen people.

He eventually reached the voting and the Change of Directors item. The registrars confirmed the proxies received. David had calculated there were three shareholders in the room he did not know.

He was cross because Megan was not replying to his text messages.

He held Margaret Drummond by the hand.

"I'm so sorry, Margaret," he whispered.

"Resolution Two. The removal of Margaret Drummond as a Director of the company," said the chairman. "We have proxies for 49 percent and so we have a show of hands. All in favour please."

The three shareholders raised their hands.

"Those against, please."

Margaret Drummond raised her hand. She was alone.

"I therefore declare. . ."

The door at the back of the room opened. Through it entered Megan, together with Alice Kaye Kimmins.

"I wish to vote," said Alice Kimmins, in a confident voice.

Martin Van Dijl leaped up out of his chair. Jackson Holmes looked angry. Stephan Andrew frowned.

"She fucking can't vote. She's too late. You called the meeting to start on time. Finish the vote!" shouted the red-faced broker.

The chairman looked at Nick Billings.

"Sit down, Mr Van Dijl," he said, and he then emphasised his request, "Mr Van Dijl, SIT DOWN."

Jackson put his hand on Van Dijl's shoulder and pressed downwards.

The chairman of the meeting looked towards the newcomer.

"Can you please confirm that you are a shareholder in Trafford Discount Stores plc?"

Alice walked to the front of the meeting and handed over a share certificate. The chairman looked at it and handed it to the registrar, who confirmed it was in order and entered her in the register of attendees.

The chairman invited Alice to take a seat.

"Miss Kimmins," said the chairman.

"Mrs," she corrected.

"I'm so sorry. Mrs Kimmins. You have not heard the previous comments I have made. I must tell you that your vote will decide the resolution which calls for a change of Directors. I must ask you. Has any pressure been brought to bear on you over this matter?"

"Yes it has," said Alice.

"And are you able to say by whom?" asked the chairman, looking at Megan.

"I've received five phone calls from a man who said he was acting in the best interests of the company. He advised me not to vote."

"Advised you?" asked the chairman.

"He said I would be making a mistake if I attended this meeting," she responded.

"Mrs Kimmins," the chairman continued, "I must ask you – do you understand the importance of your vote? You will determine whether or not there is a change of Directors."

"In that case, there will be no change of Directors," announced Alice.

"You're sure that is the right decision?" asked the chairman.

Nick Billings glared at him.

"Margaret Drummond will lead Trafford Discount Stores," she said quietly.

Alice paused and looked at Margaret.

"You are my sister," she said. "Cyril Trafford was my father. My mother was his secretary for many years. He paid my mother off and I was brought up in Wales. He came to see me every birthday. He never missed one."

Stephan Andrew turned to Martin Van Dijl.

"I am not very happy with you, Martin," he said.

Megan left Euston with Alice, from where they would return to Wales. She and Margaret Drummond were to meet for several days together the following week.

David had hugged Megan till she hurt.

"Tell me again," he insisted. "You went back to Meifod. . . What did you say to her?"

Megan looked at David.

"As you said yourself, David. I am a woman."

At around 9:00pm on the same day David decided to go for a walk on Primrose Hill. At the last minute he decided to leave his BlackBerry on the hall table. He was exhausted. This was the start of a new beginning. He chose to relive the day's events. He wanted to think about Megan.

Was he already changing his way of life? He was never away from his phone and any return to the house meant listening to his landline answerphone. But Megan was travelling and he wanted to reflect upon how he was really feeling. She had worked out that the cover of confidence was just that. In itself that was exciting, because he had confided in Megan more than anybody else in his life.

He walked around Primrose Hill and so began to relax that, at the bottom of the slope, he cut across into Regent's Park and walked towards St. John's Wood. He didn't return home until around 11:30pm. It was dark outside.

He played answerphone messages from Megan, Matthew

and Margaret Drummond. He poured himself a brandy and listened to some Chopin.

He went to bed at 1:00am.

That same evening Martin Van Dijl also thought he was alone. He sat on the balcony of his flat until just after half past nine, when he moved inside. He rubbed his arm. The throbbing reminded him of Justine's attack. He was planning his next strategic move on Trafford Discount Stores. They had given him four weeks to come up with a new strategy to remove Margaret Drummond.

After making a phone call Martin sat in silence, wondering whether the agency would be able to secure a girl for him at short notice.

He heard a noise and shouted out, "Justine, is that you?" He was losing his senses. Justine would not be coming back.

Far too late he realised that there was a gun pointing at his head.

"You won't use that," he laughed. "You haven't got the guts."

"You really are a piece of shit," said a voice.

"So shoot me," said Martin.

The bullet hit him in the centre of the forehead. He was dead before he hit the floor. The assassin removed a pair of rubber gloves and placed the gun in Martin's right hand, wrapping the fingers around it. "Bastard," he said.

Martin Van Dijl's body gave a last convulsion as the air left his diaphragm.

The room was now empty as the telephone switched to answerphone.

"Mr Van Dijl, the Mayfair Agency. Grace Donald is on her way to you. She's only eighteen and this is her third assignment. Please be kind to her."

Chapter Nine

Detective Sergeant Sarah Rudd looked at her watch and wondered how her message, sent by text, had gone down with her husband. They had planned to take their three children to France for the day. It was a favourite recreational event which they all enjoyed hugely. Nick was a headmaster but had started his career as a French teacher. They had planned to go to St. Omer, about ninety minutes from Calais. They would visit the local supermarket, where their children delighted in following the French shoppers up and down the rows of shelves. They would put in their baskets exactly what the French residents bought for themselves. At the beginning of July the weather was near perfect and, although it would be busy, school holidays were still two weeks away. Sarah wanted to top up on her cheeses and she knew that Nick would be buying red wines.

"Nothing short of a murder will stop me," she had told Nick. "I'll be home at eleven o'clock. A few hours sleep and we will be off for the day."

DS Rudd shut the door of the bedroom and told Grace Donald to stop blubbering. She waited while the young woman wiped her eyes.

"You're a prostitute?" she said.

Grace regained her composure and rubbed her face with paper tissues. She looked at the thirty-two-year-old policewoman.

"I prefer the job description 'escort'," she said. She was pretty, perhaps five foot four, ginger hair cut short and bright green eyes. She was wearing a white top and skirt.

"You get paid by men for sex. That's being a prostitute," said DS Rudd. "Yes or no?"

Grace flared. "If it matters to you, 'yes'," she said defiantly.

"What matters to me, young lady, is that you are in the 14th floor flat of a man who has just been murdered."

"But I found him," cried Grace, standing up. "You surely

don't think. . . I phoned 999 immediately! Please, I don't want to be here."

DS Rudd indicated to Grace that she should sit down.

"How old are you, Grace?" she asked.

"Twenty-one. Twenty-one and five months." She had added three years to impress the police officer.

"And how long have you been working as a prostitute?"

"This is my third time."

"Where were you born?"

Grace quickly told her story. She had been born in Aberdeen and went to Edinburgh University, where she graduated in media studies. She had heard from a friend in London, at a time when she could not find work north of the border, of an opportunity in London, in Mayfair. She had met the owner and had been impressed by the care she was offered. She had been given a full medical and the opportunity to meet other women working for the agency. She was taught basic self-defence and advised on the various types of men she would meet. She was paid £300 an hour. She knew the client was charged well over £1,500 an hour. She was free to refuse to do anything she did not want to do.

"Was the murdered man, Martin Van Dijl, your first client?"

"No," Grace replied. "My third. The first was an old man who asked me to take off my clothes and spent half an hour looking at me before falling asleep."

"And the second?"

"If you don't mind I'll pass on that."

"I do mind. Please answer the question, Grace."

"I had to go to Kensington. To a hotel. He was a regular client from the Middle East. He. . . er. . . had some strange ideas."

"And what were you told about tonight's assignment?"

"I was at home in Camden. I share with a friend from university. I thought I was out of luck. Friday nights are when we are told to be prepared to work at short notice. Obviously men get horny after a Friday night drink. The weekends are when I have been told to expect to earn well. There's not so much work around at the moment, according to the other girls. Anyway, the agency phoned and offered me this job."

"What did they tell you about the client?" asked DS Rudd.

"I didn't have to take the assignment. They said he was becoming a regular and there had been problems. He likes us to do certain things. . . you know."

"No, I don't," the detective replied. "What things are you talking about?"

"He tried to whip a girl and he uses. . . instruments."

"And you still came?"

Grace looked at DS Rudd. "£300 is £300," she said.

Within twenty minutes DS Rudd had completed her questions. She took Grace through her arrival at the flat: the open door, finding the body in the lounge, what she had touched and her call to the emergency services. She took her address and mobile phone number and the details of the agency.

She led her out into the lounge and called over a police constable.

"It's past midnight. Can you take her home please?"

As she was leaving, DS Rudd opened a pocket and took out a card. She took Grace aside.

"You're playing a dangerous game, Grace. Get a proper job before you get hurt. Here's my card with my mobile phone number. I've written it across the top of the card as well. If you ever need me, twenty-four hours a day, you phone me. Do you understand?"

Grace nodded and left with PC George Benning. She would be back in her flat in Camden Town within forty minutes.

DS Rudd went over to a man of about fifty. He had greying hair and looked tired.

"I don't think Martin Van Dijl was a church-going person," she said.

Detective Chief Superintendent Anthony Johnson nodded.

"They've found a lot of pornography in the study. I've given permission for the computer to be taken away. There are drugs in the bathroom. Looks like cocaine. Ah, Doctor Marples. How good of you to come."

"Very straightforward, Chief Superintendent. Healthy male, aged about forty, one shot to the top of the head from about ten yards. The gun was placed in the right hand after death occurred. Time of death: about two hours ago. He has an injury high up on his left arm. It is a day or two old. Probably a cut made by glass or something sharp. He was injecting." The doctor paused and wiped his forehead. "He had masturbated earlier in the evening."

"You can tell all that from a brief examination?" exclaimed the DCS.

"His penis has some bruising. He held it too tightly as he relieved himself," replied the doctor. "You can remove the body. Good night."

A second officer in a white protective suit came over. "Ma'am, sir. Nothing. No dabs anywhere we reckon except for his. We have another set in the bathroom but we think they're at least a week old."

"What about the gun?" asked Sarah Rudd.

"Nothing, ma'am. Probably bought in a South London pub. No prints. We'll give it the works in the laboratory."

"Professional kill?"

"No, ma'am. Probably not. In fact, ma'am, definitely not. The attempt to put the gun in the hand was amateurish and to leave the gun was strange."

"In what way?"

"Ma'am, you're the detective, but I would say this was a crime of passion. I don't think the killer had killed before and, by leaving the gun, is suggesting he has no intention of killing again."

"Or her," said DS Rudd.

"Sorry, ma'am. Of course. It could well be a woman."

At that point a second policewoman appeared.

"Ma'am, nothing. Four of us have knocked at every door in this block and either side. We'll have to repeat it in the morning. We've only spoken to about half the residents. Some just would not answer."

"Security cameras?" asked DCS Johnson.

"Sir, there are eight in all. The caretaker has to speak to his bosses in the morning to enable us to get the tapes. He did say he thought four of them aren't working."

"They came here, shot him and left," said DS Rudd. "They knew him and he knew them. He had the door open for the girl. The killer just walked in."

"I'm not sure," said Tony Johnson. "Time of death was

10:30pm and the girl didn't arrive until 11:00pm. Would he leave his door open all that time?"

"He was expecting somebody else?" asked Sarah Rudd.

"We're checking his mobile calls. I'm going home. We'll catch up in the morning."

"Goodnight, sir," said DS Rudd.

She stayed for another hour looking closely in each room, reading correspondence, puzzling that there were so few photographs, looking at what she thought were a number of expensive paintings, and ending up in the larger bedroom. She looked under the bed and picked up an item the scene of crime officers had missed. She stared at the vibrator.

"Hmm, I don't think you were a very nice man, Mr Van Dijl," she said to herself.

Megan and David had been talking for over fifty minutes.

David wanted to ensure that Megan had arrived home safely. They went over the events of the previous day one more time.

"I left her at Welshpool," said Megan. "She was being collected by a friend."

"Did you learn much more about Alice Kimmins?" asked David.

"She talked mostly about Cyril Trafford," replied Megan. "Her mother had thought that Cyril would divorce and marry her. She did say the phone calls from London had scared her."

"Martin Van Dijl. . ." said David, "and now he's dead."

"So, tell me again, David. Jemma phoned you?"

"Early this morning. The police had visited her. They had traced her from his mobile phone numbers. He was murdered last night."

"So who would have done it?" asked Megan.

"I have thought about it once or twice myself," replied David.

At eleven o'clock on the Saturday morning DS Rudd and PC Billing arrived at the Fulham flat of Justine Hathaway. She checked their identification and let them in. They accepted her offer to make a pot of tea.

"You know why we are here?" asked DS Rudd.

"Yes. Martin Van Dijl. I had a call from the office this morning," replied Justine.

"Do you mind if the officer looks around your flat? We don't have a search warrant," said DS Rudd.

"Go ahead," agreed Justine.

"Do you have a gun in the flat?" asked the policewoman.

Justine looked surprised at the question. "No," she answered.

"Martin Van Dijl phoned you here last night at 8:37pm. True?"

Sarah Rudd paused as a text message arrived on her mobile phone.

"We all love you. Hurry home. Nick."

"Yes," replied Justine.

"What did he want?"

"He said he was sorry and would I go and see him."

"Sorry about what?"

"Excuse me, I need a drink," said Justine. She went over to the cocktail cupboard and poured herself a large vodka and tonic. She returned to her seat. She told the detective about the events at Martin's flat, his violence and her escape by injuring his arm, her phone call to David Rensburg and how he had collected her and taken her home.

The detective concentrated on why Martin had phoned her.

"I ended up in hospital. We have had a relationship. He wanted me to go round so he could say how sorry he was."

"Why did he not come here?"

"He'd been drinking."

"How did he hurt you?"

"It was a sex thing that went wrong," said Justine. She took out her handkerchief and wiped her eyes. "The inside of my vagina was torn and I had to have a hysterectomy."

"But that is GBH, Justine. Did you go to the police?"

PC Billing returned and was told to go outside.

"The hospital wanted to call the police but I refused," said Justine.

"So how could you have gone round to his flat? It is a long drive or a difficult tube journey for someone in your condition."

"I had no intention of going. In fact, I've not been out of the flat since I got back from the hospital. I didn't want him to know that."

"But you must have thought of revenge?"

"I loved him," said Justine. "We had some wonderful times together. I just thought he was going through a stage in his life. I should have done what he asked me to do. It was my fault."

DS Rudd looked at the pale, distressed girl. She stood up.

"I may have to come back, Justine. Have you got someone to look after you?"

"My mother is arriving from Greece this afternoon. I'm going back with her as soon as I can travel."

"I will need to speak to your doctor, Justine, and I want details of your hospital ward."

Justine walked slowly over towards a table and wrote on a piece of paper.

"That is my doctor and here is the hospital card," she said, handing over the items.

"Please do not leave the country without phoning me first. Here is my card," instructed the detective.

DS Rudd then left the flat and got into the waiting police car.

"Nothing, ma'am," reported the police constable. "A rather ordinary flat. No personality. I checked the shoes as you asked. There were eleven pairs of outdoor shoes and two pairs of trainers. It is difficult to say. It was dry last night. Somehow I don't think she had been out, ma'am."

"No," said Sarah. "Nor do I."

Jackson Holmes invited DCS Johnson and DS Rudd to take seats at the board room table of Park Avenue Capital.

"You are aware that Martin Van Dijl was murdered last night?" said the DCS.

"Yes, of course," said Jackson. "I had a call from his office and it was on the local news."

"We found a number of papers in Mr Van Dijl's flat referring to Park Avenue Capital and your number is frequently on his mobile phone. There were four text messages in the last two days. You knew Martin Van Dijl well?"

Jackson gave a lucid and fluent explanation of the business relationship between the two firms. He went into detail about the Trafford Discount Stores aborted transaction. He volunteered that he had developed a friendship beyond business with the murdered man.

"So did he have any enemies?" asked DS Rudd.

"Martin was aggressive by nature," replied Jackson. "He was a dynamic salesman and abhorred failure. But at this moment I cannot think of anyone who might have wanted him dead."

"Where were you last night, Mr Holmes, between the hours of 9:30pm and 11:30pm?" asked DS Rudd.

"I was here."

"All night?"

"We were working until around midnight. There's a deadline on a transaction we're hoping to finish on Tuesday."

"We?" asked the detective.

"There were several of the team here. Most had gone by 8:00pm, but Jemma Shah stayed on. She's my office manager. She left around ten o'clock. I decided to sleep here. There's a flat on the top floor."

DS Rudd and DCS Johnson continued the questioning.

"Do you know Justine Hathaway?" Sarah Rudd asked.

"I thought you would want to discuss her," Jackson replied.

The story he told was consistent with the information already in the possession of the police.

"And you were friends with a man like that?"

"I was upset when I heard what had happened to Justine," said Jackson, "but she was a golddigger and Martin gave her a lifestyle she would not have lived elsewhere. I think it was only in the last few weeks that Martin developed. . . more extreme tastes."

Sarah Rudd looked at Jackson. "You knew there was a Mrs Van Dijl in Woking?"

"Of course. Martin never hid it," replied Jackson.

As they left the building and waited for their car in Curzon Street, Sarah Rudd sent a text message.

"Home in one hour. How about Chessington Zoo?"

DCS Johnson looked around at his bleary-eyed group of colleagues. Several had clearly enjoyed the previous day of rest. He called the room to order and asked DS Rudd to summarise the Martin Van Dijl murder case.

"Martin Van Dijl was 39 years of age and lived at Flat 4/14 off Selsdon Towers in Docklands. He was murdered at around 10:30pm last Friday evening. He had booked a prostitute. She arrived at around eleven o'clock and found the body. We have checked her out. She is clear. He was shot once through the head from about ten yards. The gun was left in his right hand. We are still examining it but we are getting little of importance. The gun had not been fired for at least two years."

DS Rudd paused and took a sip of water from the glass on the table in front of her. She moved her papers around.

"Martin Van Dijl lived a double life, in that he had a wife and two children who live in Woking. I went to see them yesterday afternoon. His wife knew all about his London existence but she receives generous house-keeping and Martin went home every week. His mother lives round the corner from his wife and had nothing but praise for her son. We think there is no possibility that any of them were involved."

She again drank some water.

"Martin worked in the City of London as a discount broker. A discount broker is a stockbroker who specialises in buying blocks of shares and selling them on to private individuals, often at huge profits."

"He appears to have been very successful. He was liked by his staff, although they considered him ruthless. Several of the female staff mentioned his personal habits."

"He co-habited at various times with Justine Hathaway, who worked in his office. Two weeks ago he put her in hospital after some unpleasant sex games. She is going to Greece shortly with her mother. We are satisfied she was not involved, although so far she is the only person with a motive."

"On Friday evening Martin Van Dijl had phoned Justine and asked her to go round to his flat. Although she did not say 'no', she had no intention of going. Martin left the door of his flat open for her, we think, which allowed the murderer to just walk in. We think that Martin was sitting down when the shot was fired. There was no struggle. Almost certainly he knew the person who shot him."

"No struggle at all, ma'am?" asked a detective.

"No, Jeremy, none. He knew the murderer. There's really no doubt on that."

Sarah paused. She then picked up her narrative.

"Extensive interviewing of the flat owners has produced nothing. People round there keep themselves to themselves. The cameras are inconclusive. Thank you to those of you who worked yesterday. It is appreciated.

"We have spent the time available to us considering the sex angle. Grace Donald, the prostitute who found the body, was only on her third job. She is only eighteen – although she told us otherwise. She is desperately young. We have eliminated her."

"There was pornography throughout the flat and he was on cocaine, we think. But the doctor thinks more social than regular. It's just a feeling, but I don't think this was anything to do with sex."

DS Rudd took another drink of water and then continued.

"We have a lot of work to do today on his business dealings. The interview with Jackson Holmes of Park Avenue Capital was helpful but didn't give us any leads. We will have to interview all his staff and all his associates.

"He travelled extensively around Europe, so we're beginning to try to trace his main contacts. But it's not easy because he was quite secretive about what he did. Justine Hathaway really didn't know much about his life when she was not there."

"I want your views, but first, there is something strange about this murder. Just consider this: *He was not expecting trouble because we think he had left the door of the flat open.* He thought Justine Hathaway was coming and yet he ordered a prostitute."

"Was he confused? The pathology report says there was alcohol and cocaine in his blood but not in any great measure. *He had no self defence in the flat. No gun, no stick, no knife. This was not a man in fear.* We can't be sure but we think somebody walked in and shot him as he sat on the sofa. He did not lunge forward. We think he knew the person."

"Add that up and we think somebody he knew killed him and he was not expecting it. So we have a murderer who acted out of character. The fact they left the gun suggests they have no intention of murdering again."

"But, frankly, at this stage we have no idea who did it."

DS Rudd sat down and DCS Johnson rose. He allowed a general discussion to develop and then allocated responsibilities for the rest of the day.

He and Sarah Rudd returned to his office.

"I want this cleared up quickly, Sarah. It's all over the papers. The press are calling it 'the City prostitute murder'. God knows where they got that from. The Financial Services Authority has been on. They are worried about the publicity. They've been monitoring Martin Van Dijl for some months. I'm seeing them later."

DS Rudd stood up.

"Find him and find him quickly please, Sarah."

"Or 'her', sir," she replied.

Stephan Andrew moved his bishop three white spaces and smiled at his opponent. He knew that it was check mate in three moves' time.

"He's dead," said the other man.

"Convenient," replied Stephan. "I was never completely sure about his plans. I felt Margaret Drummond proved herself to be tough. She'll follow Cyril Trafford well. We will hold on to our investment."

"Do they know who shot Martin?" asked the dark figure.

"No," responded Stephan. He smiled to himself. "No, they do not know, according to my police sources," he continued.

He responded to his opponent's next move by moving a pawn forward.

"But I'll miss him. He was a personable man and he did know how to sell shares. I must tell you, though, the British markets are not so attractive. Their recession is bad. It is hard to find fair value. I spoke to Beijing yesterday. They're saying they'll be looking at Hong Kong, which has recovered, of course, and South America."

Stephan Andrew's opponent knocked his queen over in submission and left the office to enjoy the midday Swiss air.

The financier remained behind. He picked up his phone and tried to reach Jackson Holmes.

DS Rudd knew that it was a waste of time but still she decided to revisit Justine Hathaway. She had phoned to let her know she was coming and was now sitting in the flat drinking afternoon tea. Justine explained that her mother was shopping in the West End and they were leaving for Greece in two days' time. She gave the detective her mother's address and phone number.

"Justine," said Sarah, "you knew Martin Van Dijl better than most. We think we now have a picture of him, but we can't find anybody who really had a motive to kill him."

"Apart from me," said Justine.

"You had every reason to kill him but we both know that you didn't."

"You are sure it was somebody he knew?"

"All the evidence says so. As a detective you develop a sixth sense, and as you enter a murder scene you know almost immediately what has happened. Martin Van Dijl was sitting down in a relaxed way and somebody shot him. There was no struggle." She paused. "How well do you know his European connections? We have come across several references to a Stephan Andrew, either in Zurich or Rome. . ."

"Martin did some business in Europe, but mostly he worked in London. Stephan Andrew is a nice man. I speak mostly to him in Zurich. He couldn't have killed Martin. I am sure of that because, when Martin phoned me that evening, he asked me if I knew when Stephan was coming over again."

"So there's nobody you can think of who might have had a motive? What about you? Was he protective?"

"Yes. He cared about me and he cared about his wife. They both seemed to like the arrangement they had. He went home once or twice a week. He never bad-mouthed her."

"Did you not feel guilty, Justine? Another man's wife?"

"It's a fair question. But no. I can't explain why not. Perhaps because the two worlds were so separate. . . London has that effect on people."

Matthew looked at his father.

"So you're going to marry her, Dad?" he asked.

David went on to tell his son about the events at the weekend and his decision to sell out of Park Avenue Capital and begin a new life in Aberdovey. He explained about Megan's new position and the house they would be buying. He even told Matthew that he would be writing a book.

"I want to look at money, Matthew. In corporate finance we gain a terrific insight into the mind of the businessman. I will try to explain, in terms people can understand, the role money plays in their lives. They say one third of marriage splits are a result of money problems."

"The Dummies Guide to Money," said Matthew.

"In a way," replied his father, "but what I really want to do is explain money in human terms. As an example, Gordon Brown's golden rules which applied for ten years. How many people really understand a statement like '40% of GDP'?"

Matthew poured his father a second beer and sat down in the front lounge of the house in Primrose Hill.

"Megan – you're sure? It's been a bit quick and she's nothing like you. Don't get me wrong, Dad. . . it's just we're a little surprised at how fast it's all moving."

"So what did you think when you went to inspect her?" asked David.

"Dad, she's great. . ."

"So what's the issue, Matt?"

"It's just – you've got it wrong once and it's very sudden. It's as simple as that. Josh and I. . . We don't want you to get hurt."

"Has your mother discussed this with you?"

"She's aware of Megan, yes, and she phoned me last week. You going to France and belting Monsieur le Grande seems to have had an effect on her. She asked me how you were and she wanted to know all about Megan."

"I still think you are hedging, Matt. There's something you're not telling me."

"Ok. Mum thinks Megan is purely a. . . god, this is embarrassing. . . an. . . er, sex thing. Mum says you were always er. . . randy. . . and she thinks you have fallen for the sex."

"And what do you think, Matt?" smiled David.

"Dad. She's stunning. But, she seems special too. My instinct is that you've got it right."

"Thanks, Matthew. I appreciate that. You realise I have been thinking through exactly the same questions? Last Friday evening I walked alone for two hours going over and over in my mind whether I've made the right decision. The move to Aberdovey – is Megan an excuse? After your mother and I divorced. . . I knew depression, which lasted several years. I was lonely."

"So, are you sure, Dad?"

"The answer, Matt, is Megan. There can never be anybody else for me. She's something special. She has also been alone and she suffered horribly when her husband was killed. Both of us know what we want and, put simply, we have found it."

"Zoe, it's been too long!" exclaimed Megan.

She hugged her friend, went over to the bar of the Britannia and returned with two large glasses of red wine.

"So, Zoe, tell me all about Outward Bound," said Megan.

"They're missing you, Megan. You've cancelled several classes. But, to more important matters. . . the ring!"

Megan put her left hand on the table, allowing Zoe to examine the engagement ring.

"Wow," she said.

Megan smiled. "I have no idea how much it cost but knowing David. . ."

"Now, I want to hear it all again," said Zoe. "You were walking along the beach at low tide and suddenly, out of the blue, he produced a ring. Right?"

"We were talking about the house he's trying to buy. He seemed to have it all planned. That is David, I suppose. There was no flowery stuff. He just put the ring on my finger. It was incredibly romantic in a way."

"How did he know your size?" asked Zoe. "Does it fit properly?"

"He's rather smart, that Mr Rensburg. He'd bought me an eternity ring in New Bond Street in Mayfair. It wasn't that expensive. When we went in I half wondered whether it was leading to an engagement ring."

"You were disappointed?"

"Perhaps," said Megan. "Half of me was saying it's all too rushed. Yet when he didn't mention an engagement ring I felt a pang."

They each drank some wine. The Brittania was quiet due to the beautiful July weather. There had been so many overcast weather patterns swirling around Cardigan Bay in recent weeks that the sunshine brought everybody out onto the beaches and into the water.

"Emily Bowden, is she settling in with you?" asked Megan.

"She's great. She's in my room now, although she has to go back to the Academy occasionally. She's a bit unfit. I gather her PE teacher has had her mind on other things."

They laughed together.

"So, Megan, this David bloke. You're sure?" asked Zoe.

Megan looked at her friend.

"Is anyone ever totally sure, Zoe? When I was with Rhys I spent a period wondering what life might be elsewhere." Megan took a drink of her wine.

"I'm not one of these falling in love types, Zoe. David just walked into my life when I wasn't looking, and the rest, as they say. . ."

"So you're as certain as you can be?"

"Yes. I have only one thought and that I can do nothing about. You see, I don't think you ever know until you are tested. So far, for David and me. . . it has been an. . . adventure. When Rhys was killed my world shattered. I know David and I will be tested. Don't know how. But when it happens we will get through it."

Megan jumped up and collected the two empty glasses.

"Hell, Zoe," she cried. "I'm getting introspective. Let's go for walk."

They walked out of the Britannia, into Market Square and up the hill towards the Aberdovey Hill Village. At the top they took a path which meandered amongst the houses and cottages. As they walked round a bend between two concrete walls a swarm of butterflies surrounded them.

They waved their arms and, as quickly as the butterflies came, they went.

"Painted ladies," said Zoe. "You can tell from the orange and black. They've been brought over by the winds from France."

Zoe looked at her friend.

"Megan," she said, "I cannot imagine anybody not being happy here."

DCS Johnson looked at DS Rudd. He was fond of her.

"So, Sarah, you have no ideas? " he asked, pouring them both a cup of tea.

"No, sir. There is only one obvious suspect and that is Justine Hathaway. But, she did not do it, sir. I've spoken to the surgeon who operated on her. Her insides were a mess. The surgeon thought that even a woman bent on revenge would not be able to find sufficient strength to make the journey, get to the 14th floor, pull the trigger, put the gun in his hand and leave to get back home."

Sarah drank some tea.

"Added to that, sir, she's not revengeful. She loved him and does not actually blame him for her injuries. If she is acting, well, it's Kate Winslet at her best, sir."

"And his wife?"

"Absolutely nothing. She may be worse off because it's thought he wasn't as wealthy as it might seem. We're beginning to understand that this last deal he was working on was a bit of a make or break for him. He'd bought a lap dancing club and borrowed heavily on it."

"But he mixed in some unpleasant circles, I gather?"

"Yes, sir, but he was popular. He was generous, so his staff say. Ruthless, yes, but that is their game. Discount brokerage is pretty shitty, sir."

"Your next move, Sarah?" asked the DCS.

"I'm taking a day off, sir, and I'm going to walk the Cotswolds with my husband."

"Good idea," Johnson agreed.

There was a knock at the door of the office and the DCS's secretary entered.

"Sorry, sir. Can the Soco officer see you and Detective Sergeant Rudd? It's important."

Sergeant John Allaway entered the office and seemed breathless.

"We have him, sir, ma'am. It's unbelievable, but we've got a minute DNA on the trigger of the gun. I've had it checked by the head of the laboratory. There is absolutely no doubt. It's totally admissible."

"You said 'he'?" asked DS Rudd.

"We have a match."

"So who killed Martin Van Dijl?" asked the DCS.

"David Rensburg of Primrose Hill, London NW1, Sir."

Chapter Ten

At around 9:20 on the morning of Wednesday 15 July, a police car drew up outside David Rensburg's Primrose Hill home. He had been in his study since late dawn. Earlier, he had completed a four mile run around Regent's Park, showered and changed. He'd rubbed cream into his left calf muscle where he'd felt a slight pull.

DS Rudd and PC Ian Williams walked slowly up the short path leading to the front door. It was answered almost immediately. The two police officers were allowed in and gave an explanation to justify their presence.

DS Rudd detailed the background of the murder of Martin Van Dijl and asked David to explain where he had been from the hours of 9:30pm to 11:30pm the previous Friday evening. The two police officers listened intensely to his response.

"So, Mr Rensburg," said DS Rudd, "let me understand you correctly. Today is Wednesday. Five days ago, in other words, last Friday evening, at around 9:30pm you walked out of this house, across into Primrose Hill, up to the top of the hill, down the path in the centre, across Prince Albert Road and into Regent's Park. You walked round Regent's Park for two hours and then you came home – home being here in Primrose Hill." She stopped as David's BlackBerry began to ring.

"No, please answer it," said the detective.

David spoke for a few moments and then put the phone down.

"As I was saying," continued DS Rudd, "you spent two hours not exactly sure where you were. You met nobody. You spoke to no-one. You can't remember seeing anybody. You recall there was a cloudless sky and that the moon was giving clear visibility. But you saw nobody you can remember. There was nobody at home before you left or when you arrived back."

"No. As I said," explained David, "Josh is at boarding school and Matthew was away for two nights. I now know he'd gone back to Wales to see a girl he'd met there."

"Can you tell us her name?" asked Sarah Rudd.

"Yes. I can. But why should Matthew be involved?" said David.

"Mr Rensburg, this is a murder enquiry. Last Friday night Martin Van Dijl was killed between the hours of 9:30pm and 11:30pm. We know that you were involved with him professionally and that the transaction you were working on had become the subject of a dispute. We know what happened at the Hilton Hotel. We've heard from Justine Hathaway that you came to her help. You had every reason to dislike Martin Van Dijl."

David was struggling. The two police officers had been in his front room for over an hour. They had explained that he was free to ask them to leave whenever he wished. He could phone his solicitor. He was trying to co-operate but his story was getting weaker.

"I can tell you where I was," continued David. "I was walking around Regent's Park. I'm at a major turning point in my life and a lot has happened to me over the past few weeks. I wanted to think."

"Think about what?" asked the detective.

David sighed and said he was going into the kitchen to make some more coffee. He returned a few minutes later and put the tray down on the table. Sarah stood and poured out three cups of black liquid. As she did so, David's BlackBerry rang and he took a quick call. He then sat down opposite the police officers.

"I've decided to leave London and move to a coastal village in West Wales called Aberdovey. I'm marrying a woman called Megan Williams. These two factors are the result of a series of events which have taken place over the last few weeks."

David paused and looked at DS Rudd. "It will be my second marriage," he continued, "and my son Matthew had questioned me about my motives. He made me think deeply. Last Friday evening I was here on my own and I decided to go for a walk and think things through. Megan is. . . she is the most beautiful and wonderful woman I have ever met. It's her second time too. She's a widow. Her husband was killed in Iraq. We want to make our lives together."

"Is Matthew against you marrying Megan?" asked DS Rudd.

"He and Josh are all for it. In fact over the last few weeks we've become closer, particularly since. . ." he paused.

"Since what, Mr Rensburg?" asked PC Williams. Sarah glared at him.

"It's about my ex-wife. We've worked hard to ensure that Matthew and Josh have had equal access to us both. They enjoy their trips to France, but recently there's been an issue. . ."

"You're referring to this Megan woman?" said DS Rudd.

"No," said David. "Michelle has been asking about her. But this was about what was happening in France. Matthew and Josh became concerned that, well, to put it bluntly, it seemed that Michelle's husband had been hitting her."

David told them about the events leading up to his cross channel trip to France, his confrontation with Maurice le Grande and the admiration it produced in his sons.

"So you hit this man?" said DS Rudd.

"He was physically abusing my ex-wife. My sons were disturbed. I had to do something, obviously."

"So you punched him. Did you give him any opportunity to explain his actions? Were you certain he was doing what your sons thought? Had your ex-wife contacted you and asked for help?"

"I regretted hitting him twice," said David. He realised immediately that he had not needed to make this admission. He was beginning to feel confused.

"You hit him twice?" said DS Rudd, looking at the agitated man opposite her.

"It's not like it sounds," pleaded David. "Michelle is my ex-wife. She's the mother of my two boys. Matthew was upset by his last two visits to France. Josh, who is younger, had noticed a change in his mother's behaviour. I thought Michelle was in trouble. I had to do something. I suppose that when I arrived at St. Marguerite I was worked up. But I was also right. My visit sorted out what was going on. Michelle has visited London and seen the boys. She and Maurice are still together and they are working out their problems. I was right to do what I did."

"So, who are you thinking of hitting today, Mr Rensburg?" asked the police constable.

"Now you hold on!" flared David. "You arrived this morning unannounced. I've co-operated with you. I've not phoned my lawyer. I'm being honest. I'll continue to answer your questions, but don't penalise me for being truthful."

"Did you reach the mosque?" asked DS Rudd. "Excuse me?" said David. "What mosque?"

"Last Friday night you walked round Regent's Park. You would have passed the London Central Mosque on the west side, off Park Road – the A41 into London if that helps, Mr Rensburg. Do you remember passing it?"

"Yes. No. I'm sorry. I can't remember," said David. "I can't recall the mosque, although I know it well. . . One thing I do remember – I think I reflected on cricket as I neared Lord's."

"Why did you think about cricket, Mr Rensburg?" asked the police sergeant. "I thought you were agonising over your Welsh girlfriend."

"She's not my girlfriend. We are engaged to be married. I was thinking briefing about cricket because Megan and I are going to live in Wales and. . . no, I'm sorry but I now can't remember why I was thinking about cricket."

"Did you stop and talk to anyone?" DS Rudd went on.

"At 10:30 at night?"

"Do you own a gun?"

"No."

"Have you ever owned a gun?"

"No."

At this point his BlackBerry rang. He took the call and returned five minutes later.

"You must live on your BlueBerry," said DS Rudd.

"It's called a BlackBerry," said David. He laughed. "Megan's trying to get me off it, but it's become a way of life. When I move to Aberdovey I think it will have to go."

"You always have it with you?" continued the detective.

"Yes. In Corporate Finance your clients expect you to be available all the time."

"So how many calls did you receive when you were walking around Regent's Park?" asked Sarah Rudd.

David instantly realised the problem hurtling towards him.

"Actually, I did not have it with me," he said quietly.

"And how many calls did you miss?" she continued.

"There were. . ." He picked up the BlackBerry and scrolled

down to 'Missed Calls'. It took him a few moments to find last Friday's list. "There were three," he said.

"Who from?" asked the police officer.

"Matthew. . . er. . . Megan. . . and, er. . . Justine Hathaway," he replied.

"Now, wouldn't it have been helpful if you had followed your usual habit and carried your phone with you. One confirmed call and we could leave you alone," said DS Rudd.

"Well, I didn't," said David defiantly. "I wanted to reflect. I wanted to be alone. Some days all the communication is overwhelming. There seems no escape. I wanted to think about Megan."

"You were kind to Justine Hathaway. You collected her from Selsdon Towers, she stayed with you, you showed her great kindness," said Sarah Rudd. "What did you think of what Martin Van Dijl did to her?"

"It was a strange series of events," said David. "Out of the blue I get this call saying she needs help. I know Justine, but not that well. She is efficient in her work. At Park Avenue Capital we have Jemma Shah and the two are rather similar. You wonder what you would do without them. It happened quite quickly. I collected Justine, brought her home here. Of course at that point I did not know of her injuries. She had refused an offer to take her to hospital. She sat where you are and poured her heart out. Then she went back to her flat the next day and only later did she go to hospital."

"So I repeat my question, Mr Rensburg. What did you think of what Martin Van Dijl did to her?"

"I don't know," said David. "I disliked the way Martin Van Dijl treated her, of course."

"And when you heard of the severity of her injuries, what did you think then?" asked DS Rudd. "Do you understand that she cannot have children?"

David sighed. "I did not murder Martin Van Dijl," he said.

Neil Levy exploded. He had agreed to see his client at short notice. They were together in his offices at Red Lion Square in Holborn, between the City and the West End.

"You what!?" he exclaimed. "You should have phoned me!"

"Neil," stuttered David, "it was all so sudden. I opened the front door and there were two policemen. They were polite and asked if they could come in. They said they would leave whenever I wished."

"So it seems, from what you say, that you could not account for where you were when Martin Van Dijl was murdered. Where were you?" asked the solicitor.

"I've told you. I was walking around Regent's Park, thinking about Megan."

"She must be quite a girl."

"And they focused on two other issues. I didn't take my BlackBerry with me, which I had to admit was unusual, and they reasoned correctly that I had been upset by events affecting Justine Hathaway."

"So who did kill Martin Van Dijl?"

"Good question. I've phoned Jackson Holmes, who was probably closest to him in my circle, and he said everyone is baffled. He was quite popular because he was lavish with his money. Jackson said I had as good a reason as anyone, apart from Justine Hathaway who was too ill to do it."

"And you do not have a gun?"

"No," replied David.

"It'll be an outsider. Somebody he had upset," summarised the solicitor.

"Jackson said," continued David, "that it was almost certainly somebody well known to Martin. The police had told him that."

"Everybody has secrets," said the solicitor. "In a week's time the real murderer will have come forward or been found. Seen it before. Just relax, David. Now we need to review your exit contract from Park Avenue Capital and my partner wants to talk to you about your house purchase in Aberdovey."

Neil poured two cups of coffee and looked at his client. "Call me at once if they come back," he instructed.

"So what do you think I should do?" asked Megan

"Dad has told me not to tell you," said Matthew, "but he's had a shit of a day." Matthew checked the power supply in his mobile phone. "He was with the police this morning and then he saw his solicitor. He's just sitting in the lounge tonight."

"Should I come up, Matthew? I can get time off school."

"No. That would be nice, but I think Dad wants to work this out for himself. Why not phone him and see if he decides to tell you."

Megan put her phone down and a few minutes later called David.

"I knew he would phone you," he said. "I suppose I was hoping he would."

"David, get real. You did not kill Martin whatever-his-name-is. The police are clutching at straws. End of story."

"Megan, I felt guilty. It's silly. They were so disbelieving. How can anybody walk round Regent's Park and not remember anything? I cannot recall seeing anybody."

"That's because you weren't looking for anybody," said Megan. "It's quite easily done." She paused. "The story about Justine Hathaway. The way she phoned you. Her injuries. Your concern for her. Did the police press you on that?"

"I gather she was still too weak to kill him herself, although she surely had good reason to shoot him. He tore her insides out. They were trying to say it gave me a motive and apparently one of the staff at Park Avenue told the police I had said threatening things about Martin, which is quite possible. But as I said to Detective Sergeant Rudd – that is a million miles away from actually killing somebody."

"You've seen your solicitor?"

"Yes. Neil is very good. He's taken control of matters."

"And what did the police say they were going to do?"

"They just left."

"Mae rhywbeth yn anhygoel o'I le 'ma," mused Megan. She was right. Something was very wrong.

Earlier on Wednesday afternoon the two detectives investigating the murder of Martin Van Dijl met at Paddington Green Police Station.

"Well, sir," said DS Rudd, "I have met with the head of the forensic laboratory and there is no doubt at all. David Rensburg was involved in a car crash two years ago, along the Marylebone Road and, although he was driving, he was innocent of any charge. There were all sorts of problems with the other driver.

He tested positive and was later convicted. In the course of the police attendance David's DNA was taken. The DNA from the murder weapon matches. Absolutely no doubt. The gun was the one used to shoot Martin Van Dijl."

"So, he wiped it clean and made an amateurish attempt to make it look like suicide," said DCS Johnson. "He missed the trigger."

"A small part of it, sir," continued Sarah. "He can't account for his movements during the hours of 9:30pm to 11:30pm when he says he was in Regent's Park. He did not take his phone with him. He had a motive, in that Martin Van Dijl was involved in a controversial business transaction which had caused David some personal difficulties."

"And Sarah," interrupted Tony Johnson, "There was this strange business with Justine Hathaway. The way she phoned him. They say they did not know each other that well and yet his was a number on the names' list on her mobile."

"It was the seventh name, sir, and she did not have a long list. I questioned her about this and she said that she didn't use the list that much. She retained numbers she knew Martin Van Dijl might ask for, which is why Jackson Holmes was the first. I think on the night she phoned David she was in stress and scrolled down to his name without realising."

"Are you defending him?" asked Detective Johnson.

"I know what you are going to say, sir, but David is not a murderer. He might do something more emotional – I'm thinking of his trip to France to whack his ex-wife's husband – but the victim here was murdered in cold blood. It's not something I think David would do."

"And you can explain all the issues, can you, Sarah?"

"I know, sir. Go with the evidence."

"Exactly," said the DCS.

On Friday morning, at 6:00am, DS Rudd, together with a team of six police officers, knocked on the front door of a house in Primrose Hill.

David was cautioned and taken to Paddington Green Police Station. At 9:00am he was joined by his solicitor, Neil Levy, and at 9:30am the police began their taped interview. DS Rudd was joined by PC Angela Manning.

The detective sergeant started with background information and then concentrated on David's work at Park Avenue Capital. She asked question after question about the work of a corporate finance department. She wanted every term define: AIM, the Alternative Investment Market – part of the London Stock Exchange; a Nomad, a nominated adviser – the professional who helps companies join the market.

She went into the Trafford Discount Stores transaction in great detail and had difficulty in understanding the relationship between David Rensburg, as the AIM Nomad, and Martin Van Dijl, as the AIM broker. She could not understand why David had been to see Kate Livermore at Atlas VCT when Martin Van Dijl was responsible for raising the funds.

She insisted on understanding the new terms: the broker – the firm that raises money; a VCT, a venture capital trust – a fund that takes in money from investors and lends it to growing businesses.

She wanted to understand the events leading up to the General Meeting held by Trafford Discount Stores. She insisted on covering, several times, the evidence from the Park Avenue Capital staff, one of whom said that she had heard David make threatening remarks about the murdered man.

Neil Levy interrupted on several occasions with certain points on which he wanted clarification. In particular, he managed to get the police to admit that they were not putting much emphasis on the reported remarks which David purportedly said. He also would not allow the police to question David further on the General Meeting, which he felt was outside the scope of their questioning of his client.

Sarah then spent a long time trying to understand the Justine Hathaway incident. How well did David know her? Why did she phone him? Why did David take her to his house? What were his feelings when he understood the extent of her internal injuries?

Neil refused to allow his client to answer the questions about David's feelings for Justine. He became angry when DS Rudd asked David if he had become excited at the thought of Justine Hathaway using a vibrator.

They had a break at 11:30am and David and his solicitor were allowed to leave the police station. They walked around the adjoining streets, David lost in thought. The interview started again at 12:30pm. DS Rudd then began a long session on the hours of 9:30pm to 11:30pm on the evening of the murder. A large scale map of Regent's Park was produced and David was left floundering as he was unable to say, with any conviction, where he had walked. Had he seen anybody he knew? Could he remember when he had reached Lord's Cricket Ground?

At this point, Neil said it was up to the police to disprove his client's version of events.

"Mr Rensburg," asked DS Rudd, "do you own a gun?"

Having received a negative reply she asked whether David had ever owned a gun. David replied that in the whole of his life he had never had a gun, fired a gun, loaded a gun or wanted a gun.

DS Rudd took out of the drawer of the desk in front of her a plastic bag with a gun inside.

"Mr Rensburg," she asked, "do you recognise this gun?"

"No," said David. "I have never seen it before."

"Mr Rensburg. I am not satisfied you have looked at the weapon I am showing you."

"I don't need to," replied David. "I know I have never seen that gun before because I can't remember ever seeing or holding a real gun in my entire life."

"Can you explain, then, why we have found your DNA on the trigger?" asked DS Rudd.

David looked at the police officer in complete amazement.

"You've made a mistake," he said. "How can you be sure it's my DNA?"

"You had a car crash in the Marylebone Road two years ago, Mr Rensburg," said the detective.

"But I was the innocent party – you can't use a sample taken on that occasion!" he shouted.

"We can," she replied. "We think you wiped the gun clean, but you missed a small area on the trigger which is where we found the DNA that matches yours."

"That proves nothing, Detective Sergeant Rudd," said Neil Levy.

"It shows that your client is not telling the truth, Mr Levy. You may want a word with him. We will leave the room for a few moments." She and PC Manning stood up and left the interview room.

Megan did not know what to do. David was not answering her calls. The home telephone number was continually on answer-phone. Matthew's mobile phone was switched off.

She was baffled by her conversation with David.

The interview recommenced at 2:00pm. Sandwiches and coffee were brought into the interview room.

DS Rudd switched tactics and asked David to explain his trip to France and his attack on his ex-wife's husband. She wanted to know why David had hit Maurice le Grande twice.

This led to a discussion about David's health. The detectives had picked up from staff at Park Avenue Capital that David was beginning to refer to the stress of the job. DS Rudd was soon into David's recent medical. David admitted that he had recently been given a prescription for high blood pressure.

Suddenly Sarah Rudd switched again to the walk around Regent's Park and tried to understand why David had not taken his BlackBerry with him. DS Rudd went back the previous seven days and David was unable to remember a period of more than an hour when he did not have his phone with him.

The detective then began asking about Megan Williams. David became defensive and angry. He did not want Megan involved.

"But she is involved," said DS Rudd. "Of your own admission you were walking around Regent's Park thinking about her."

Neil Levy started to become restless and it was agreed that the interview would stop at that point and recommence at 9:00am the next morning. David was to stay in custody overnight and his solicitor chose not to oppose this. He secretly felt it was the best place for him.

At nine o'clock that evening DS Rudd assembled together with six police officers at the north east corner of Primrose Hill.

One of the younger police constables commented that Primrose Hill was the highest point in North London, but the mood was sombre and his observation was ignored by the others.

"Right," said DS Rudd, "here is the photograph of David

Rensburg. He is six foot two inches tall, weighs 177 pounds. He has black hair with a touch of grey. He was wearing sea-blue trousers and an open shirt and pullover, both light blue in colour. He says he left home, which is just down the hill to your left, crossed into here and then walked down the hill over Prince Albert Road and into Regent's Park. He seems unable to remember where he went in the Park, although we think he walked in the direction of Lord's Cricket Ground because he can remember thinking about cricket."

Sarah Rudd handed out the photographs, together with boards and writing pads.

"We think we're most likely to find somebody who might have seen him leaving Primrose Hill or coming back around 11:30pm. Here is the map of the area and you will see that I have positioned each of you at the various entrances. If you find somebody who thinks they remember him radio me and I'll come down. Don't leave your stations at any point because I want to cover the area for the whole two hours." She smiled. "I've arranged for some refreshments to be brought round to you at 10:15pm."

The six police officers left the group and went to their allotted positions. They began to stop local people, asking if they recognised the man in the photograph.

The first call came through to DS Rudd at 10:05pm and she quickly drove to the south of Primrose Hill. PC Liam Lamb was with an elderly man who lived in St. John's Wood. He walked every evening at around 10:00pm, but not always along Prince Albert Road. Last week he had decided to go into the park. He thought he remembered seeing a man who looked like David Rensburg.

"What was the weather like last Thursday?" asked DS Rudd.

"It was raining," said the local resident.

"And you must have been pleased that England won the Test Match," continued the police officer.

"It was a wonderful win," said the man. "Good old England."

Sarah thanked him and said she would be in touch. Her husband had been rather upset that England had lost.

During the evening there were only three more possible sightings. One was discounted, as DS Rudd realised the man was drunk. A younger woman was a real possibility until she admitted she had argued with her boyfriend earlier in the evening and had been crying. She thought the man was six foot four inches. The final potential witness said he was certain he had seen David. He gave Sarah Rudd his name and address and said, as he was in a hurry, he would attend the police station in the morning, despite DS Rudd's efforts to hold him. The name and address were false and the next day the man never showed up.

At 9:00am the next morning DCS Anthony Johnson and PC Monica Welsh conducted the next stage of the interview.

Tony Johnson was much more aggressive and quickly clashed with Neil Levy, who would not allow a single point to go unquestioned. Again the issues were threefold: David's inability to prove that he was walking in Regent's Park when Martin Van Dijl was shot – including a fierce debate over David's decision not to take his BlackBerry – David's hatred of the murdered man which was endorsed by Martin's treatment of Justine Hathaway, and David's DNA on the murder weapon.

Coffee was brought in at 11:00am and the interview was continued until 12 noon.

David was allowed to go out with Neil over lunch.

In the office Tony Johnson discussed the situation with the newly arrived Sarah Rudd.

"Nothing last night, Sarah?" asked the DCS.

"No, sir. The problem is," continued Sarah, "that we can't prove he was in the flat. The traffic cameras were not on at that time, assuming he drove his car, and the Home Watch TV cameras, the ones that were working, show nothing. The house to house has not even found anybody who saw the prostitute arrive."

"And we have no other suspect?"

"No, sir. The DNA on the gun will, of course, virtually rule out anybody else."

"But you still don't think he did it, Sarah?"

"I've spent quite a lot of time with him now, sir. His home, his story, his stress and this new woman in his life. I don't think he's a murderer."

"What about the incident where he drove to France and hit his ex-wife's husband. Was that not the action of an aggressive man?

Sarah drank some coffee and nibbled a sandwich.

"You see, sir, that for me proves he did not commit murder. David is a passionate man. When he talks about his sons or this Megan woman there is a pride, and I think his actions in hitting this Frenchman were symptomatic of his sense of right and wrong. His ex-wife was being hit. He rode to her rescue. A bit theatrical, I agree, but he's that type of man."

"Which is why, Detective Sergeant Rudd, he was angered by what happened to Justine Hathaway, and by her injuries which were inflicted by a man he already hated. I think you need to do your job, Sarah," concluded the DCS.

Margaret Drummond was surprised to receive a phone call from Zurich. It took her a few minutes to understand that it was Stephan Andrew. She confirmed that she knew about the murder of Martin Van Dijl and she understood that Stephan controlled 12 percent of the shares of Trafford Discount Stores plc.

"I also appreciate, Mr Andrew, that you voted for my dismissal at the meeting," she said.

"You are angry with me," said the Swiss financier.

"Well, you are – were – with Martin Van Dijl," replied Margaret.

"That is correct, Mrs Drummond. I wish to apologise. I like your business but I'd been taken in by Martin. He wanted control."

"Why?"

"Because your shares are significantly under-valued. Park Avenue Capital were wrong to allow the shares to be sold to the public at 12p. On your profit projections your shares are worth at least 25p. You are weathering the recession brilliantly."

"So, Mr Andrew, why did Park Avenue. . . ?"

"Look no further," interrupted Stephan, "than the relationship between Jackson Holmes and Martin Van Dijl. Jackson is wealthy. Public school educated. Well connected. He used David Rensburg as a front of respectability. Behind the scenes there were some rather questionable practices."

"Which you supported, Mr Andrew," said Margaret.

"Actually, not so, Mrs Drummond. We avoided many of their deals. We've always liked your business. Your father was a great man."

"What's the purpose of your call, Mr Andrew?"

"I want you to trust me."

"You want to make money from our shares."

"Of course. But you will need some help. I have some ideas. Would you like to hear them?"

"I will give you another three minutes, Mr Andrew."

"You should appoint Nick Billings to act for the company on all matters. We were impressed by him. You should ask him to come here to Zurich. We'll open up all our books to him and allow whatever checks he wishes. Then you can trust us."

There was a pause and Margaret heard the sound of a glass being placed down.

"You should pension off John Pearman. He needs time away. Pay him off. You should be appointed chief executive. You'll need a finance director. A London recruitment company will be paid by us to find you the right person."

Again Stephan paused, but on this occasion he wanted to ensure that he had Margaret's attention.

"Do I have any more of my three minutes left?" he asked.

Margaret laughed and told him to continue.

"You must replace the non-executive directors, but that can come later."

There was another pause and Margaret thought she sensed an intake of breath.

"If you do all these things, Mrs Drummond, we will make available to Trafford Discount Stores an unsecured credit line of €10 million."

"Why?" she asked.

"We want you to have fifty branches opened by the end of 2014. Mrs Drummond, forget what you read in your press. The British economy will recover strongly. The Treasury can sort out your debt by continuing their cost cutting and selling off your assets. It's already being planned."

"I'll think carefully about what you're proposing. Please email Nick Billings a record of everything you've just said."

In the weeks ahead Margaret was to remember this exact moment as the moment she knew that the burial of her father was completed. For a reason even she could not rationalise, she thought about making a hairdresser's appointment. She would go shopping in Mayfair and buy some business outfits. She was heading towards being the chief executive of a quoted business. For some almost illogical reason she had decided that with Stephan Andrew behind her she could not fail. She wanted to look the part.

"Of course," Stephan continued, "it will be sent within twenty-four hours. And there is one final point, Mrs Drummond."

"Oh. I thought we had finished, Mr Andrew."

"You'll need a chairman. It's an important position as far as the London markets are concerned."

"We would like you to ask David Rensburg," he continued. "He has an excellent reputation in the City and in Europe. And you have seen his loyalty to you."

At 3:00pm DS Rudd and PC Alan Jones returned to the interview room and apologised to Neil Levy for the delay in the resumption of the interview.

"I think this has gone on long enough," stated the solicitor. "Your case against my client is simply too weak for this to continue."

"Quite the opposite, Mr Levy," said DS Rudd. "Our case is watertight."

"So," interrupted the solicitor, "who had sight of my client at the murder scene? Have you photographic evidence to show my client's car in the vicinity of Selsdon Towers? Which neighbour noticed my client in the block of flats?"

DS Rudd moved her chair and faced the solicitor.

"Your client cannot explain where he was on the night of the murder. Mr Rensburg says he was in Regent's Park. Last night myself and six police officers spent two hours from 9:30pm to 11:30pm asking people if they had seen your client. We did not receive one lead we could rely on."

Sarah took in some deep breaths.

"Mr Rensburg, you are not denying that you disliked the murdered man and you have confirmed that you made threatening comments about him to the staff of Park Avenue Capital. In slightly strange circumstances, you became involved in Justine Hathaway's injuries and you did not like what Martin Van Dijl had done to her. You cannot explain why you were not carrying your BlackBerry in Regent's Park."

Sarah looked again at Neil Levy.

"What your client has also failed to answer is the fact that we found DNA on the trigger of the murder weapon. The murderer had thought he had wiped the weapon clean. He missed a small but vital part. We have checked this evidence very carefully. Of course, the DNA could have been on the gun before the killing but you, Mr Rensburg, say you have never seen this gun."

The detective took a drink of water.

"We are also aware that you were under stress. We have spoken to your doctor who confirmed that he was treating you for high blood pressure. During the last few weeks you yourself admit that you have been under tension. The injuries to Justine Hathaway proved too much. You snapped, Mr Rensburg, and you killed Martin Van Dijl."

"So, charge my client, Detective Sergeant Rudd," challenged the solicitor.

DS Sarah Rudd looked firstly at Neil Levy and then across the table to David Rensburg.

"Mr Rensburg," she said, "this morning, at his request, I returned to the offices of Park Avenue Capital and met with Jackson Holmes. He said that he wanted to report the events at the GM. For the record GM means General Meeting and it was held at the Hilton, Park Lane, last Friday, the day of the murder of Martin Van Dijl."

She paused and drank some water.

"There were," she continued, "some interesting events. Megan Williams produced a shareholder which meant Martin Van Dijl lost the vote."

David leapt out of his chair.

"Right," he shouted, "he was angry with me. Megan's actions in finding the shareholder meant he lost the vote. I WON!" he yelled. "Don't you see he had cause to murder me, not the other way round?? Are you satisfied now?"

"But," continued the detective, "it appeared that Martin Van Dijl had been making threatening phone calls to this shareholder. Jackson Holmes says that you have a misguided morality in business and that you were angry about it."

"Misguided!" exclaimed David. "Have you any idea what people like Jackson Holmes and Martin Van Dijl are really like?

They will do anything for power." He paused, wiped his hand across his face and continued, "it's about money and the power it brings. They'll walk over anybody who gets in their way." He stopped and drank some water.

"Throughout my career I have tried to act correctly. You should ask around the City. I am respected for my values."

DS Rudd moved her chair. "We have asked about you and we get the same response time and again. A decent man with morals – who can get emotional."

"You make me sound like a teenager!" shouted David. "Emotional! No Detective Sergeant Rudd, I do not get emotional. I simply care for my clients and I fight for them. That is why I am successful."

"But," said DS Rudd, "you seem to be getting worked up about a number of issues. You did not even know Alice Kimmins."

"I owed it to Megan," said David.

"Owed what?" asked Sarah.

"She had won the vote by her actions in visiting this Mrs Kimmins. I wanted Megan to see that we had worked together. When she told me the whole story and the phone calls which Van Dijl had made. . ."

"You became very angry," suggested DS Rudd.

Neil Levy stood up. "My client is answering no more questions."

"Of course I was fucking angry. She was an innocent woman! A shareholder through misfortune. That bastard Martin Van Dijl. He thought his money could buy anything. What he did to Justine. . . Can you imagine being forced to put a. . . a thing up her. . . and then the calls to Alice Kimmins. She was scared. He was a fucking animal!"

David sat down and looked at his solicitor. Neil Levy covered his face with his hands.

A few minutes later David Rensburg was charged with the murder of Martin Van Dijl and was told he would appear in front of a magistrate the next morning. He was to be kept in police custody overnight.

He was allowed to make one phone call.

Chapter Eleven

Megan left Abergynolwyn at eleven o'clock on the Saturday evening. She had spent some time on the telephone trying to contact Gillian Edwards but both her home number and mobile were switched off.

Megan decided to take two flasks of coffee and several bottles of water. She would have a break every hour and she calculated she could reach Shrewsbury on the petrol in the tank of her car. She packed a toilet bag and hung a suit on a hanger, which she laid across the back seat of the car. She chose to keep the radio and CD player turned off. She knew that her journey would require her complete concentration.

She was undecided what to wear. The Cardigan Bay area of West Wales had been hot and bright throughout the day and it was still warm. At first she chose jeans and a sweater, but then she changed her mind and put on a tracksuit. She placed a jumper on the passenger seat for the coolness of the early hours.

Her first stop was the car park in Aberdovey. She locked the car, crossed the road and entered Swn-y-Don. She checked the whole house, although she knew there was no real reason to do so. She had to do something. She refused to think about the news she had been given. Her position was unequivocal. David was not capable of murdering anybody. It was a mistake which she would sort out. She just had to get to London. She sent a text message to Matthew.

She by-passed Machynlleth by taking the back road through Llanwrin, saving three miles, though taking the chance of running into stray sheep eating the grass on the verges. She reached the east turning and within an hour was approaching Welshpool.

She wanted to explain the events to herself but there was so much she did not understand. Was Matthew telling her all he knew? He had been distraught on the phone. She had to reach London.

She stopped at the top of the hill near to the entrance to the golf club. She took five minutes of fresh air and rejoined her route, stopping at the services on the Shrewsbury ring road. She filled up with petrol and checked her oil level and the pressure in her tyres. She used the water tap to top up the screen wash. She locked the car and washed her hands in the ladies.

Before long she had reached the M54 and was travelling eastwards towards Wolverhampton and Birmingham. She noticed that there was a steady stream of caravans and other holiday vehicles travelling in the opposite direction, using the night hours to reach their destinations.

She found that her mood varied. At times she felt exhilarated. She was on her way to London to sort out the problem and to get back with David. She would then focus on the truth. She knew little of the detail. What was she getting herself into and did she really understand the risks? Might she unintentionally do harm? Matthew had sounded nervous, in itself unusual for David's son.

As she reached the western parts of Birmingham she slowed to fifty miles per hour for a long stretch of road works. She stopped at the services shortly after the toll road rejoined the M6, drank half a bottle of water, spent ten minutes on stretching exercises, went to the toilet and rejoined the motorway.

She turned on the radio and listened to music. She was now more relaxed and focused. The doubts had dissipated. She would provide the momentum to sort out this issue and be reunited with David.

At 4:30 in the morning she reached Primrose Hill. Matthew and Josh were waiting for her. Matthew had promised to wake Josh when she arrived. He could not sleep and had sat in the kitchen awaiting Megan's text messages. Over coffee and toast they talked. Megan went to bed at 6:30 and rose three hours later to take a shower and to change. She had left some clothes at the house on previous visits and made her selection. She wanted to feel smart for the day ahead.

David lay on the bed in his solitary cell. He could not sleep. The air was thick with the smell of disinfectant. There was noise throughout the night and at one point somebody started shouting. He repeatedly went over the events in his mind. It was his decision to walk around Regent's Park without his mobile phone that perplexed him the most. Why had he decided that he needed to think about things? He had never been more certain in all his adult life. He had found Megan, he had bought their new home in Aberdovey, he was financially secure, the boys were well provided for and Michelle seemed settled again. He would soon be writing his books and fulfilling his dream.

He stopped for a moment. Why had he used the word 'dream' in the singular? That was his turmoil. All his dreams had been coming together centred around Megan. She was the catalyst to his future.

And now it was all slipping away. If only he had taken his mobile phone with him.

On Sunday morning Josh made a pot of tea. He tried to cover up the tears which were inching down his cheeks. Matthew was leaning on the breakfast room table with a writing pad and pen.

Megan came in wearing a white blouse and a dark blue two-piece suit. They discussed yesterday's developments and Megan took extensive notes. She then told Matthew and Josh that she had a number of visits to make and left the house without further debate.

This agitated Matthew. While Josh settled at the table with some holiday homework, Matthew decided to run round the parks.

Megan arrived back early in the afternoon. She asked Josh and Matthew to sit in the kitchen with her. She took off her jacket and accepted the gin and tonic which Matthew placed in front of her.

"Matthew, Josh," she said, "I've seen your father. I've also met Detective Sergeant Rudd who arrested him. I've been to the home of your solicitor, Neil Levy, and I tried to find Justine Hathaway but she has left for Greece. I've had a quick phone call with Jackson Holmes who, as you know, was your father's business partner."

She lifted the glass to her lips and drank quickly.

"In summary, Martin Van Dijl was murdered in his flat in the Docklands two weeks ago last Friday evening, between the hours of 9:30pm and 11:30pm. Your father was walking on

Primrose Hill and then in Regent's Park at the time. We'll come back to that. The other evidence the police are using is the fact that Martin had caused your father problems with a business deal and was an unpleasant man."

She went into lengthy and, at times, graphic detail about the events leading to the injuries sustained by Justine. She had already decided that Matthew and Josh had to hear virtually everything, although she withheld the most lurid facts about how Justine had sustained her injuries.

"The real evidence is that the murder weapon was left at the scene of the crime and has your father's DNA on the trigger. The police are saying the gun was wiped clean by the murderer because it was left in the hand of Martin Van Dijl, in an attempt to make it look like suicide. Neil Levy says the Defence Counsel will try to wreck that theory but the DNA is absolutely certain."

"Sarah Rudd, the detective, says she thinks the gun was left because the murderer knew he or she would never use it again. The police are certain that Martin Van Dijl knew the person who killed him because there were no signs of a struggle."

Megan paused and lifted her glass. She wanted to check on the boys' reactions to the facts. They were sitting entirely focused on her.

"In the two weeks that the police have been working on the case they say they've built a pretty clear picture of the man and, apart from Justine Hathaway, they can find nobody else with a motive to kill Martin. It was definitely not Justine for several reasons, not least because she was recovering from an operation."

"It's as cut and dried as that?" asked Matthew.

"No," said Megan. "This detective, Sarah, seems half decent. She admitted that Martin had a number of enemies, but they simply couldn't find anybody with the opportunity or motivation as strong as your father's." Megan paused. "Matthew, Josh, the police did not have to speak to me. I could push only so far. I have to tell you that your lawyer confided to me that your father's last interview with the police went badly against him. He lost his temper."

"Of course he lost his temper!" shouted Matthew. "He's being accused of a murder he didn't commit!"

"Still. . . he really did lose it, Matthew, I'm afraid."

Josh looked at Megan.

"Do something please," he said.

"We need to tell Mum," said Matthew.

"Yes," agreed Megan. "I have thought of that. I suggest that. . ."

"Mum's here later," said Josh. "Sorry, I forgot to tell you, Matt. She phoned last night. She's at The Westbury. I got upset during the call. She said she had a doctor's appointment this morning."

"On a Sunday?" asked Matt.

"That's what she said. She's got *him* with her. She said they'll be here this afternoon," explained Josh.

"When Josh? When are they coming?"

"Mum said she and Maurice were having lunch in Mayfair and then they would come on to us." Josh wiped his eyes.

"That gives us a little time," continued Megan. "I'm certain that Sarah Rudd doesn't think your father did it. The real problem is the two hours he spent walking around Regent's Park. He did not take his BlackBerry with him, which we know is unusual. Your Dad says he just wanted to think. He says you and he had been talking, Matthew, and he wanted to think about the future."

Matthew nodded but said nothing.

"And he cannot remember where he walked. He thinks he went near to St. John's Wood because he recalls thinking about cricket. In two hours you are likely to walk six or seven miles. A week last Friday evening Detective Sergeant Rudd and six police officers spent those two hours in various parts of Regent's Park. They had taken a photograph from here. They only found four people who had any recollection of seeing your father and not a single one was credible."

Megan stopped and asked the two sons what they thought.

Matthew spoke first.

"We've no hope of finding out who did it if the police aren't able to," he suggested. "What we have to do is prove that Dad didn't do it. And the only way I can think of is to find somebody who saw him in Regent's Park."

Matthew took a swig of lager before continuing.

"If it *was* Regent's Park he walked around," he said. "Dad's been in a world of his own over the last two weeks. You two have got engaged, he's moving to Wales, he's writing a book. I doubt if he knew where he was walking."

Matthew stood up and opened another can of beer. He poured it carefully into his tankard.

"He is certain he walked in Regent's Park," continued Megan, "because he says he cannot remember crossing more than one road. . . and that would be Prince Albert Road to get from Primrose Hill to the park."

She paused and drained the last drops of her gin and tonic.

"Something Detective Sergeant Rudd said might help us," Megan continued, "she said she was frustrated during the Friday night search that, because of budget restraints, she was only allowed six police officers for the evening. She said it needed more like twenty-six."

"Well. . . I have twenty-six university mates," said Matthew.

"Yes, exactly," said Megan. "Next Friday evening, get as many of your pals as possible and we'll blitz the park."

"And find somebody who saw Dad!" cried Josh.

"There has to be someone out there," mused Megan.

At just after four o'clock in the afternoon there was a knock on the door of the house in Primrose Hill, which Matthew answered. Michelle le Grande walked in. She went straight into the kitchen and made coffee for herself and her husband, who had now reached the hallway.

"Right, Matthew," she said. "What the hell is Josh talking about? Your father is in police custody? For what?"

Before either Matthew or Josh could reply, Megan walked into the room. She glanced at Michelle, quickly summing up her immaculate appearance and air of self confidence. She wore pearls around her neck which offset the pink two piece outfit. Her hair had been styled that morning.

"Could you accompany me to the lounge, please?" Megan said.

Michelle looked at her, angry and surprised.

"Yes," responded Michelle, a beat too late. "You and I need to talk. Matthew, Josh, stay here until I call you."

"No, they stay with us," said Megan. "It is your husband who'll be staying in the kitchen. *Comprendez, Monsieur?*"

Michelle stood up, kissed her husband and stalked into the front lounge. Maurice le Grande was engrossed by Megan's more physical aspects as she left the kitchen followed by David's two sons.

Michelle sat down in the single chair.

"I gather you had a hospital appointment this morning," said Megan.

"Yes," said Michelle. "I'm pregnant. Bit late in life, I suppose, but it's what Maurice and I want. My doctors wanted me to have a scan immediately. They had arranged for one at St. Thomas's. I came here to tell Matthew and Josh that they are going to have a step-sister."

There was a silence for several moments.

"Is everything ok?" asked Matthew.

"I want the baby to be born in London," replied Michelle, "which is why we are over here." She paused.

"I've been quite sick, but the hospital say they can stop that. I'm fine, Matthew."

Michelle looked at Megan.

"So you are *la nouvelle femme*?"

"Yes, I'm Megan and I'm now engaged to David. So, Matthew and Josh will become my step-sons."

"You're Welsh," said Michelle, pointlessly.

Megan looked her in the eyes.

"So, what's David done now?" she went on.

Megan pulled up a chair and sat in front of David's ex-wife. She spoke quietly and factually and told her the whole story. Both Matthew and Josh remained silent.

Michelle pondered on what Megan had said.

"Can I see him?" she asked.

"No. Visiting is restricted. I've only been able to see him once and I'm taking Matthew and Josh tomorrow morning."

"What can I do?" she asked.

"Er mwyn ni gyd, cer nol I Ffrainc," muttered Megan. For all their sakes, she hoped Michelle would go back to France.

The visit to see David did not go well. He appeared strained and tense, and Josh in particular became upset. Megan tried to take David through the events leading up to his walk in the park. Matthew worked hard to trace the exact route taken by his father and became exasperated by David's vagueness. Their permitted time expired all too quickly.

On their return to Primrose Hill Megan told Matthew and Josh that she had to go back to Wales briefly. She left on Tuesday morning and reached home in the afternoon. She attended to a number of domestic issues, cancelled a tennis game and retrieved some papers which David wanted from Swn-y-Don.

She returned to London on Thursday evening and spent Friday with Matthew and Josh, planning the campaign in Primrose Hill and Regent's Park. By six o'clock that evening Matthew had assembled thirty university students. Each was given a letter explaining what they were doing, a photograph of David Rensburg, a physical description and a description of the clothing he was wearing, and a pad and paper to record any witness statements. It was decided that they would go in pairs to avoid any complaints from the public. Each couple had a mobile linking them to Matthew and Megan. Josh agreed to stay at the house and work with three other students who were willing to bring around coffee and sandwiches. Megan had asked DS Rudd about her methodology and tried to replicate it.

During the two hours from 9:30pm to 11:30pm the fifteen couples identified seven people who thought they might have seen David. Two were drunks, two asked for money, but there was one elderly couple who seemed more certain than anybody else. They had been walking along Prince Albert Road at 10:30pm.

"My wife suffers from arthritis and does not sleep very well," explained the husband. He looked again at the photograph. "Yes, that's him. I noticed him because he seemed a bit lost in his thoughts. He crossed the road without really looking."

"And you are sure it was this man?" asked Megan, holding out the photograph.

"Yes," replied the old man, "it was him."

"Can I please take your name?" asked Matthew.

"What for?" asked the man.

"I need you to tell the police what you saw," said Matthew.

"That's my Dad and the police have accused him of something he did not do."

"Police? No. No. Leave us alone! You said you were looking for your father. I'll scream if you carry on harassing us."

He pulled his wife away and they hurried down the road.

Megan held onto Matthew's top by his sleeve.

"You can't, Matthew. We have to let them go."

Megan saw DS Rudd the following morning and told her the story of the old couple.

"It sounds to me that a good prosecution counsel would destroy their evidence. You did the right thing, Megan. You had to let them go. The others?"

"Mostly time wasters. It all seems so easy when you watch it on TV!"

Sarah nodded. She noticed that Megan was about to ask her a question.

"Megan, please don't ask me what I think you are going to," she said. "You know I can do no more."

The following morning Megan had breakfast alone in the kitchen of David's Primrose Hill house. At around eleven o'clock Matthew and Josh returned from having breakfast with their mother at The Westbury Hotel, off Regent's Street.

They had not enjoyed the experience. Their mother, occasionally supported by her husband, had launched a tirade against Megan and suggested that all the difficulties their father was facing were due to her. She also tried to extract their sympathy by saying that the strain she was under was down to Megan and David and she, as a pregnant woman, needed more consideration. As they left the hotel she confirmed that she and Maurice were returning to France in the afternoon.

The two boys spent the afternoon glued to the television watching the second test match against India from Trent Bridge. Megan did not like cricket.

At noon the following morning Megan, Matthew and Josh visited Neil Levy's office, near to St. Paul's Cathedral. For over an hour they reviewed the evidence against David.

"We have two problems," stated the solicitor, "the alibi in Regent's Park. You've done so well conducting your own search and finding that couple. I don't think the police are right. They could have put a doubt in the jury's mind. Detective Sergeant Rudd was right though – if any pressure was put on them the judge would almost certainly rule their evidence as inadmissible. I just wish David had taken his BlackBerry with him. The prosecution will be able to find staff at Park Avenue Capital who will have no choice but to confirm that he always had it with him."

Neil took a drink of coffee. "That, on its own," he continued, "we might have been able to manage, but the DNA on the gun. . . We are baffled by that. We cannot challenge it. Of course, we will produce our own expert witness to try to put a doubt on the evidence – but courts are now comfortable with the science of DNA."

"So what do you suggest?" asked Megan.

"Plea bargain," replied Neil Levy. "I had a meeting with Dr Elson this morning. At his recent medical David was registered with high blood pressure and stress and Dr Elson prescribed for the problem. That is fact. Dr Elson feels he can describe the condition in such a way that we may be able to sustain a plea of diminished responsibility. If we can get Justine Hathaway to give evidence it could have a big impact on the jury."

"A plea of guilty, you mean?" asked Megan, horrified.

"If we are able to enter that defence we may get the sentence reduced to little more than eight years."

"And if Dad pleads 'not guilty' and is found guilty?" asked Matthew

"Matthew, it depends on the judge," replied Neil. "My guess is a minimum of twenty years, which would mean at least twelve years in prison."

"But you are forgetting one thing, Mr Levy," said Megan. She stood up and walked over to the solicitor. Suddenly she crashed her fist down on the top of his desk, sending the tray of coffee cups crashing to the floor.

"David is innocent. INNOCENT, Mr Levy! He will never plead anything else but 'not guilty'. That is because he is 'NOT GUILTY', Mr Levy!"

Later that afternoon, Megan left Paddington Green Police Station in tears. She hated being unable to be alone with David.

She hailed a taxi and she and David's sons returned to Primrose Hill. They spent the evening together going over and over the evidence. They considered changing solicitors, but they knew Neil Levy was considered a top professional in his field. Megan had asked Sarah Rudd about the services of a private detective but the idea was dismissed. Megan knew that Sarah did not think David was guilty. She was satisfied that she was doing all she could to discover the truth.

At midnight Megan packed her bag, hugged both the boys and began the return journey back to Wales. By six o'clock on the following morning she had reached Abergynolwyn, parked her car, unpacked, read her post, answered her emails, checked her answerphone and gone to bed. She slept for fifteen hours. She rose late on Monday night, ate some baked beans on toast and went back to bed.

At six o'clock on Tuesday morning Megan drove out of Abergynolwyn, through Tywyn and along the coast road towards Aberdovey. She parked at the cemetery beach and crossed the road to visit the grave of her husband. There, she sat at the tombstone for half an hour, talking to Lance Corporal Rhys Williams.

She kissed her husband's name and crossed back over the road, down the path, across the golf course, along the wooden walkway, across the shingle and onto the beach. She walked a hundred yards towards the gentle waves of Cardigan Bay. She turned south and walked towards the estuary.

She started at the beginning and thought through every single piece of evidence which the police had stated made up their case against David. She could not answer their inability to confirm his time in Regent's Park, but she was completely satisfied about why David had left his BlackBerry at home. The DNA on the trigger of the gun, however, was perplexing. "There has to be an answer," she said to herself.

She returned to the cottage in the late morning and then decided to drive to Aberdovey, where she parked her car in the car park. She crossed Glandovey Terrace and entered Swn-y-Don. She felt closer to David when she was in the house. She made herself a pot of tea and settled in the lounge. She put *The Four Tops*, David's choice, on the CD player. As Levi Stubbs began to sing 'Climb Every Mountain', Megan wrapped her arms protectively around her body.

She took her writing pad and pen and began listing in great detail the whole period, from an analysis of David's state of mind, the problems with Trafford Discount Stores plc, the role of Martin Van Dijl and the final outcome with Margaret Drummond and the General Meeting. She wrote about the consultation with Dr Elson and the high blood pressure. She went further back and reviewed David's decision to hit Maurice le Grande. She recalled David's fearless dive into the sea to save a human life. She wrote at some length about Justine Hathaway and David's concern for her. She recalled every moment of the time they spent together on the beach when David put the engagement ring on her finger. She thought about his decision to leave Park Avenue Capital and begin a new life in Aberdovey. She tried to explain his ideas for writing a book, but she did not really understand his central thesis. She knew it mattered to him. She put the pad down and went for a walk along the seafront, under the bridge and to the station entrance, where she looked up at the house where they wanted to spend their lives together. She returned to Swn-y-Don and went over and over the time David spent in Regent's Park.

She fell asleep on the sofa and woke up at three o'clock. She showered and changed into her bikini, on top of which she wore a loose shirt. She walked over to the beach and went swimming in the estuary. She was in the water for nearly an hour, swimming against the incoming tide out to the sandbanks. These were estuary waters and contained strong currents. Megan was far too powerful a swimmer for these to be a concern.

She came out of the water and walked over the hot sands. She had her answer. She would give evidence at the trial. She knew that a wife cannot give evidence for or against her husband, but she did not have that restriction – yet. She would stand in the witness box and speak of her love for a gentle man. She would tell the jury that she knew that this man simply could not commit murder. She would find a passion and belief that the jury would find compelling. She planned her return to London.

"No, Megan," said David. "It will make no difference and I

can't ask you to submit to the prosecution questioning. I've had a long chat with Neil Levy. I've decided to plead guilty. We're going to play the diminished responsibility line. Neil thinks I'll get no more than eight years."

"But you're innocent," said Megan quietly.

"I can't explain my time in Regent's Park and the DNA evidence is overwhelming." David placed his hand over Megan's.

"Eight years," she mused. "It's not that long for us to wait." Tears welled in her eyes.

"You'll not be waiting, Megan," said David gently.

Megan looked at her fiancé. "I don't understand what you mean."

"It's rather straightforward," said David. "I love you, Megan, in a way I can never believe. I have thought it through. I can't ask you to wait. You have a life of your own. You have your new job for the Welsh Government. You'll be going to Rio de Janeiro regularly. You must return to Wales and forget me."

"But you didn't kill him," said Megan. "Why should two lives be ruined?"

"One life, Megan, and I'll write my book in prison. You must go home and build your future. For you, David Rensburg no longer exists."

DS Rudd sat down and poured a cup of tea for DCS Johnson.

"So, it's all wrapped up, Sarah?" asked her boss.

"Yes, sir," she replied. "We've spoken to the prosecution team and they've decided to accept a plea of diminished responsibility. He'll get eight years."

"Well done, Sarah. A good result in quick time."

"Not really, sir. The job's done, that's all."

"What do you mean?".

"He didn't do it, sir. The courts are going to convict an innocent man."

"So who did kill the man then?"

"We just don't know, sir. The only thing I am certain about is that it was not David Rensburg."

A replacement tray of tea was brought into the DCS's office. Sarah poured two fresh cups.

"This is unusual for you, Sarah. You're normally hanging them from the nearest lamp-post!"

"There are a lot of bad people out there, sir," she replied. "I think I've now succeeded in putting eight murderers in prison. But it wasn't that easy with David Rensburg. I thought from the beginning he was not our man – but, as you said, sir, I had to work with the evidence. The lack of an alibi and the DNA on the gun. I simply could not argue against that."

She paused and drank some tea.

"It was getting to know Megan Williams too. She and his sons have worked tirelessly to try to save him. She's an intelligent woman. Yes, she is in love and I am aware of what that means. But, with a passion, she has never moved one inch from his innocence. You will laugh, sir, but a woman's intuition must never be underestimated."

"You think he's innocent and she thinks he's innocent?" said the DCS.

"Yes, sir," she replied. She closed the folder in front of her. "If I'm right, sir, we're about to watch the destruction of two innocent lives."

She stood up with the file under her arm.

"Please leave the file here," ordered the DCS.

Megan was dressed in a light green shirt and dark green skirt. Her hair was loose, over the top of her shoulders. She was wearing low-heeled shoes.

She placed several books in front of David. She had selected them from the finance section in Waterstone's, on Charing Cross Road.

"David," she said. "I can help you write your book. You'll have a computer and you can email me each chapter. You said you want to write for the general public – well, I can be your consumer panel. It can be as though we are together. The years will fly by. I'll spend the weekend nearby and look after Matthew and Josh."

"Megan, Megan," said David, "you are hurting yourself and you are hurting me."

He moved the books to one side.

"Megan, there is so much time here. The phone does not ring.

I'm having time to think that I've not had for years. I have gone over things time and time again."

David wiped his eyes.

"I did not kill Martin Van Dijl. But I cannot explain my time in Regent's Park, Megan. It's a big area. I could have been anywhere. I can't explain why I did not take my BlackBerry. I can't understand the DNA on the trigger of the gun. In truth, Megan, I cannot explain anything. I'm almost beginning to think I am guilty. . ."

He wiped his eyes again.

"Neil Levy came today. There is no other course of action. I'm pleading guilty and I'm almost certain to serve eight years in prison. Megan, in eight years' time you will be nearing forty. You have some of the best years of your life ahead of you. You overcame the loss of Rhys and, in truth, we've only been together a few months. The easy answer for me is to ask you to wait. But if I do that I'll be using you. This whole business is so completely unfair to you. You have to go, Megan – for the last time."

Megan stared at her fiancé.

"Tell me you don't love me, David."

David looked straight into her eyes.

"Please go, Megan. Please go now."

Megan returned to Primrose Hill and explained to Matthew and Josh what David wanted. Josh clung to her. Matthew shook his head.

Megan left London and returned to Wales.

After DS Rudd had left his office, Tony Johnson picked up his phone and made a call to New Scotland Yard. An hour later he welcomed a former colleague to Paddington Green Police Station.

They talked for half an hour and then turned to the file lying on the desk.

Early the next morning the two men met again in the same office.

"Yes, Tony. Whoever put this file together is a good police officer. Detective Sergeant Rudd – she's careful and thorough. On the basis of the evidence I think you are lucky to get a reduced charge. You're pushing your luck trying for diminished responsibility, but the doctor's statement is compelling. A competent prosecution counsel would almost certainly get murder to stick."

"And did he do it?" Tony asked.

"Almost certainly not," replied the detective.

"How do you reach that conclusion?"

"Very simply," replied his colleague, "because the murderer was cold blooded. It's actually quite difficult to walk up and shoot somebody, wipe the gun and leave it in their hand, walk out of a block of flats, be seen by nobody and go home."

He paused. "Christ, Tony, it's a bit early for one of those," he said, accepting the glass of scotch nevertheless. He drank deeply.

"David Rensburg is emotional. I've not met this Megan woman but he's obviously head over heels. It's interesting that Detective Sergeant Rudd refers to her on several occasions in her notes. Within weeks he is leaving his job, marrying her and moving home. He rescues a man from the sea. He goes to France and hits the man who is belting his ex-wife. That was adrenalin, pure and simple. Not taking his BlackBerry into Regent's Park. Again, a red herring. He wanted to think about Megan. The only evidence you have is the DNA on the gun. On that alone you have to prosecute. There is no doubt it was the murder weapon. It was wiped clean and David Rensburg's DNA was on it. Could it have been on it before? Possibly. But he can't explain it."

"So I have to put an innocent man in prison," Tony summarised.

"Tony, my friend, it is the system. We are part of it. You have no choice."

"And David Rensburg has to go away."

"Yes," repeated the detective. "It is the system."

David received a text message on his mobile.

"Arrived with Mum in Athens. Flying out to the island soon. Thanks again. Justine."

He flexed the fingers of his right hand. He had already written 7000 words of the introduction to his book and he was concerned that he was straining the tendons in his wrist.

David did not know how much pain it was possible to experience. He had recalled time and again the poise with which Megan had left his cell. He wanted to call her back. He wanted to hold her. He wanted to tell her how much affection and love he felt for her. He knew that he would be spending many lonely nights in the future. He also knew he could not, in all conscience, ask her to wait for him. She would quickly become immersed in her new job. She would find a new life. For Megan, David would fade into a memory, a brief interlude.

For David, his chance at the life he had really wanted had sunk into a mire of confusion. All he was certain about was that the dream was over.

Matthew poured some of his lager into the glass in front of Josh.

"I know you steal my beers, Joshy," he said. "You'd better start drinking some proper lager."

"What about the house, Matt?" asked Josh.

"Dad says we can keep it. He's arranged for a housekeeper to stay here. She'll look after us. She's coming round in a few days' time."

"Can we go and see Megan?"

"Dad says not, Josh."

"But I want to see her."

"Let's give it a bit of time, Josh."

Megan arrived back in Abergynolwyn in the dark. She locked the front door behind her, put on a CD, opened a bottle of gin, poured a large glass leaving little room for tonic water and cried herself to sleep.

Chapter Twelve

On Monday 8 August Megan drove to Manchester Airport and left her car in a long-stay car park. She boarded a plane which would take her to Toronto.

She selected a window seat in economy class and made it clear from the beginning to the man sitting next to her that she wasn't interested in any conversation. When the late breakfast was served she resisted his attempts to use the passing of the tray as an excuse to begin talking. As soon as she had finished her meal she turned away from the aisle and shut her eyes, using her jumper as a head rest.

At 12:50pm, local time, she disembarked from the plane and walked through customs and into the arrivals lounge of Toronto Pearson International Airport. As she looked around, a smartly dressed, middle-aged woman approached her. Megan embraced her mother and picked up her case. The two women left the airport and hailed a taxi.

"Jack is sorry he's not here to greet you, darling, but he has an important meeting this afternoon."

The taxi journey from Mississauga into Toronto, a distance of seventeen miles, took over an hour and it was not until late afternoon that Megan was standing on the balcony of a luxury flat, seventeen floors up from ground level, looking south over the huge expanse of Lake Ontario.

Her mother was pouring her daughter a cold glass of white wine, which she served with a plate of tiny cucumber sandwiches.

"Jack and I are taking you for dinner tonight, darling. Jack will be home around 6:00pm and we can drive to the restaurant in a few minutes. Jack will have booked a table."

"There's no need, mother. It's you I came to see."

"Nonsense, darling," replied Sian Zanovisk. "Jack was thrilled when I told him you were coming. Would you like to take a shower?"

"Yes, thank you," said Megan. "Well, mother, you seem to have lost your accent completely."

"Honey, I'm a Canadian now. I managed to get citizenship shortly after marrying Jack. I'll never forget you, and Wales, but my life is here. You'll remember when you were last over here. After Rhys died I couldn't see why you didn't want to move to Canada yourself. Jack has some property. He could still let you have a place of your own. . ." Sian poured herself another drink. Megan retreated to the bathroom and took her shower.

At 5:30pm Jack appeared, dressed in an immaculate pin-striped suit.

"Megan," he said, kissing his step-daughter. "You look good."

They sat down and Megan was regaled with tales from the world of Canadian foreign politics. Her step-father went into great detail about the relationship with the American Democrats and the growing isolation of the North American continent.

"Obama's smart," he said. "The United States is still the richest country in the world by a long way and their military might scares the hell out of Russia and Iran. Obama knows this, which is why he's concentrating on getting the economy back on its feet. I liked his healthcare reforms too. He's got guts, has Barack."

"But I thought he's in real difficulty over the level of Federal borrowing. Trillions of dollars, so they say. . . I can never understand these crazy figures," said Megan.

"Megan. That's smart," said Jack. "It's politics. Obama wants to keep pumping money in to avoid recession."

"Hey, you two," interrupted Sian, "it's getting on. Jack, darling, what time have you reserved the table?"

"Honey, I'm catching up with my lovely daughter. There's plenty of time."

"Step-daughter," said Megan quickly.

"Ok, whatever you prefer, Megan," acknowledged Jack.

At seven o'clock they left to drive the short distance into downtown Toronto. Megan spotted the Air Canada Centre and, as Jack parked the car near to Union Station, she could see the lights of the harbour area bordering onto Lake Ontario.

She was transfixed by a huge and strange looking chandelier in the window of the restaurant. Jack came up to her.

"That was Simon's idea. The owner. It's made, would you believe, of melted wine bottles."

"So why is it called *Lucien*?" asked Megan, still looking at the window design.

"It was the name of his father. This site used to be called *Pravda*. It was a vodka bar. Simon Bower took it over a few years ago and has transformed the place. Your mother and I come here at least every two weeks." He put his arm through Megan's and led her into the entrance where they were met by a waiter.

"Good evening, Mr Zanovisk."

"Simon about?" asked Jack.

"No, sir. He's away for a few days," replied the waiter.

Jack looked decidedly miffed. "You should have told me that when I booked."

"The food will be just as good, sir. The chef has prepared an organic hen dish, especially for you, and there is a bottle of 2001 Chablis on the table, with Simon's compliments. And Simon is phoning in at nine o'clock on the dot, sir, to speak to you."

"Ok, now we're talking," said Jack.

They were shown to their table. Megan noticed the domination of the colour red in the décor, which was offset by the crystal chandelier above them. Jack picked up the bottle of wine. "2001," he said, "Megan, if I could spend the rest of my life drinking Chablis I would be a happy man." He laughed.

Megan absorbed herself in the menu. Her choices were termed 'Beginning', 'Middle' and 'End'. Before she could make any decisions two waitresses arrived at the table, together with the head waiter.

"Mr Bower has selected for you tonight, Mr Zanovisk," the waiter said.

Megan looked down as her plate was served with sliced fish with tomato (which she was to discover was smoked), cured olives, fennel and croutons.

"It's your favourite, Mr Zanovisk. *Octopus Panzanella.*"

"Honey," said Sian, "there's garlic in this."

"Hell," exclaimed her husband, "that's the goodnight kiss out the window!" He started to eat enthusiastically.

The 'Middle' course was preceded by another bottle of Chablis, although Megan was now drinking fizzy water. The 'Fried' Organic Hen was served as a chunky cutlet and was topped with creamed collards and roast onion gravy.

The two Canadians concentrated on their food and it was not until the 'End' was reached that the conversation started to open up. This was interrupted by the arrival of the Chocolate Complex, comprising five cocoa varietals which were intended to be dipped into a bowl of cedar jelly and rose pudding. Megan gave up thinking about calories and decided to have another glass of wine.

As the plates were being cleared away the waiter arrived with a telephone and Jack had a long and loud conversation with the absent owner of *Lucien*.

As coffee was being poured Jack invited Megan to tell him about her new job.

"Your mother is very proud of you," he said. "She was on the phone for a whole day telling all her friends." He tried to kiss his wife but was rebuffed by a turn of her head as a wave of garlic offended her sense of smell.

Megan began to tell the story of her selection for interview at the Welsh Government and the role she was to play in identifying potential Olympic winners.

"Crazy," interrupted Jack. "You'll have about four years. Impossible. You should stay at that school you teach at. Good safe job."

"Actually, Jack, I'll have nearly five years and I've already started. The Olympics are in 2012. It's not crazy, as you say. Wales is a proud country. My report has to be with the minister just after the London Olympics finish. They are really going all out for 2016."

"You should stick to doing a proper job. Sian says you had been promoted at your school before this nonsense. I'd not let my daughter do something like this."

"My *father* is dead, Jack," snapped Megan.

"And *your* daughter has just been given a final warning by her school for failing her exams," said Sian.

Jack laughed. "She's a great girl. She'll pass when she needs to." He called the waiter over and settled the bill.

They returned to the flat in silence. Megan kissed her mother and went to bed. As she fell asleep she vaguely thought she could hear some shouting.

The following morning Jack was nowhere to be seen. Megan looked at her mother in despair.

"Eleven o'clock. Where are you going?" she asked.

"Megan, darling, Jack's been called away for a vital meeting and the plane leaves at midday. I have to go with him. We'll be back on Thursday. I was intending taking you to the Toronto Islands. You enjoyed it last time. There'll be plenty of time to talk then."

"Can we go for a walk?" asked Megan.

"Of course," replied her mother. "I'll get my coat."

They left the apartment and walked towards the shore. They cut across the Gardiner Expressway and into a park.

"Jack's a lovely man, Megan. He's re-building his business because he had to pay his first wife a fortune. But we're on our feet. Life is good. Don't worry about what he said last night. He rushes to judgements. We're both proud of you. You'll make a great success of it. I know you will."

Megan slowed and turned to face her mother. "I need to talk to you."

Sian went over to a park bench and sat down. She patted the seat and asked her daughter to take a seat next to her.

Megan told her mother the full story about David. She stumbled several times as she realised Sian was checking her watch.

"He's awaiting trial for murder and you want to marry him!" her mother exclaimed, when Megan stopped talking.

"No, no. There's much more to it. He's innocent, Mum, I promise you."

"Megan, the police aren't stupid. They don't arrest innocent people and charge them with murder." Sian stood up. "We have to get back. Do not mention this to Jack, whatever you do. We'll talk more on Thursday."

When they arrived home Jack was waiting for his wife.

"Megan," he said, as he watched Sian rush into the bedroom. "This new job. I've been thinking about it. Have you signed your contract yet?"

"I have an interview with the minister next week, Jack," said Megan.

"Email it over to me. I'll get my lawyers to have a look at it."

"I take care of my own affairs, thank you, Jack," snapped Megan. "I suggest you focus on your own daughter. I wouldn't laugh off failing exams if I were you."

Jack looked at Megan. He seemed about to speak.

"Jack," shouted Sian, "the car's here. Come on."

Megan moved towards the front door.

"We'll be back on Thursday, Megan. Have a rest and enjoy Toronto. I've left you my gym membership card on the table. They're expecting you."

Her mother kissed her and rushed to the lift.

Jack tried to hug Megan. She took a step back. He was gone. Her mother was gone.

She sat down and put her hands over her face. Her mother had a new life and she had tried to bring her own problems into it. Megan knew that it was all over with David and there was nobody else to turn to. Rhys was gone and Mam was old and infirm. Time and again at the High School she had tried to persuade her pupils not to reject their mothers. It was something that seemed to happen too often. Megan wanted her relationship to be right. But her mother needed to be with Jack.

An hour later a cab arrived to collect Megan and take her to the airport. She spent half an hour working out her journey home. She settled for a four hour wait and then a flight to London Heathrow. She would be landing at 11:44am on Wednesday morning.

She looked at the statement given to her by the booking clerk. She handed over her credit card and thought of David.

"Have you enjoyed your time in Canada?" asked the clerk. She didn't reply.

Megan arrived back at Abergynolwyn just before two o'clock on Thursday morning. She poured herself a cup of coffee and read through her post. She checked the answerphone and made a list of calls she would make in the morning. She returned to her front door and checked again for a letter she might have missed. She picked up her mobile phone and listened to the six messages on it. She scrolled through 'missed calls', looking for one particular number. Finally, she sent an email to Sian and went to bed.

"You're rather quiet, darling. What is it?"

Sarah and Nick Rudd were walking down the centre of Broadway on the northern edge of the Cotswold Hills. They were booked in at the Lygon Arms for the night. Nick had decided his wife needed a break. The children were with their grandparents in Ruislip.

"Just a bit of a difficult case, Nick," she replied.

They had stopped to look in the window of a bookshop and now carried on walking down the hill.

"But I've always admired the way you're able to leave work at the office," her husband replied. "Why is this case different?"

"Because the man accused. . . well, I think he's innocent. . . and I've allowed myself to become involved."

Sarah stopped and turned.

"Nick, I'm too professional to make mistakes. But I'm human too."

"What does your boss say?"

"Tony Johnson. He knows what I think, but he's right. He says all I can do is follow the evidence."

"So what is the evidence?"

"Nick," replied Sarah, "if I was the prosecuting counsel I would be shouting with joy. He had the motive, he cannot explain where he was and the gun has his DNA on it." She paused. "And, what is worse, there is nobody else in the frame."

"Sarah?" asked Nick. "If he is innocent then somebody else did the murder. Right?"

"Right."

"So who?"

"Who what?"

"You're the detective. Who fired the gun?"

The couple paused and sat down on a bench seat. Nick stood up again.

"What do I know, Sarah? I'm a teacher. I can't even work out who's stealing from the school stores. But I will tell you one thing. It seems to me you're wrapped up in proving that this bloke is innocent. You are convinced on this. But I'm not sure you're spending enough time trying to find the guilty man."

"He has plea bargained. He's going to accept a reduced charge and plead guilty."

"Then he is guilty, Sarah. He would never give in otherwise."

"But that is what Megan argues against - his fiancée. She wanted him to fight on. I think he's just exhausted, Nick. I think that, as a human being, he's had enough."

"Sarah, enjoy today and tonight. Then tomorrow go back and find the murderer. Somewhere you must have missed the vital clue."

Sarah glanced at her husband, held his hand, and walked on.

Megan travelled to Cardiff on the Tuesday morning of the following week. By mid-afternoon she had been waiting for Ieuan Jones for over an hour.

Eventually the door opened and he came in, apologising before he had even put his papers on the desk.

"You'll have a coffee, Megan?" he asked. "I think we'll get a fresh supply."

"So, I hope you were satisfied with my plan, minister?" said Megan, as the coffee tray was brought in.

"Did you see it?" he asked.

"Excuse me?" said Megan.

"During the winter, when we won the cricket in Australia." He paused and smiled. "Don't you remember, Megan, two years ago?" He stopped again because he had noticed what she was wearing.

"The Test Match at the SWALEC Stadium, Megan. The bloody English coming to Wales to play their cricket against the Australians. What is more, Megan, there was every chance England would lose. The Australians were stronger than was expected after their defeats in the winter. England were bloody fortunate to scrape a draw."

"Clearly, you don't like the English," said Megan.

"I like their money. The rest you can keep. There is nothing we can do about them in truth. I know we talk about an independent Wales – and just look at what Alex Salmond is achieving in Scotland. But no, Megan, the way I want to go is to get more powers for the Assembly, which means tax raising so we have a bigger budget."

Megan smiled. "You speak like a future leader, minister," she said.

"Leadership, Megan. That's what it's all about. Just think when the British Lions beat the All Blacks in 1971. Brilliant it was. I cried with joy, Megan. They all talked about the mercurial Barry John and the brilliant Gareth Edwards and the greatest full back the world has ever seen, JPR Williams, but, what they forget, Megan, was the captain. Who was the captain, Megan? You don't know, do you? John Dawes. One of the best captains there has ever been. Leadership, Megan. It was a great side but the important ingredient was captaincy. We beat the All Blacks, Megan, in New Zealand. In New Zealand."

"Isn't the Lions' side chosen from all the four Home Countries, minister?"

"And do you know, Megan, I can name the side that played the final test match. At Auckland it was JPR, the great Gerald Davies, John Dawes in the centre, he was captain of the side, Megan, Gibson, he was a good player, Duckham, crappy Englishman, Barry John and Gareth Edwards; Megan, I tell you that was the best pair of half backs the world has ever seen, front row. . . er. . . Mighty Mouse McLauchlan, great Scottish prop, he was respected by the Welsh boys, Megan, Willy John in the second row, he sorted out Colin Meads, the All Blacks hard man, and at Number Eight, who, Megan? Merve the Swerve. The Great Mervyn Davies. What a side, Megan!"

"1971, minister. You must have been very young?"

"I'm sixty-one, Megan, so I was. . . take away thirty-eight, I was twenty-three. I should have played for the Welsh under-21s but I injured my shoulder against Bath Colts. The bastards. Late tackle, Megan. I had made a break, passed the ball and this English bastard shoulder-charged me. You see, Megan, when you pass the ball you drop your defences because you're not expecting to be tackled. He should've been sent off. English ref. I was out for a year."

"So you see yourself as leader of the government?" continued Megan, pointedly.

"Megan, I tell you, I'm coming into my prime. I'm fit and well. I'm determined to improve Wales. I'd be a dedicated leader."

"Can we get more use out of the powers we now have, minister?" asked Megan.

But she didn't really listen to his answer.

"It really is interesting to feel part of it, minister. But on to my plan. Tell me what you thought of my ideas – and please be honest," asked Megan.

"Yes, of course," Ieuan Jones shuffled his papers and looked in the drawers either side of his desk. "Tell you what, Megan, just summarise what you intend doing."

"Ok, thank you, minister," said Megan. "We want Welsh winners at the 2016 Olympics. I've been concentrating initially on trying to define the special qualities that identify winners. In my report, which is underneath your left hand, minister, you will see that I've studied Gareth Edwards and Ian Woosnam by reading their autobiographies. What I have done, minister, is to identify ten qualities which must be present for any individual to get on my list to start with and. . ." She didn't get any further.

"Woosy. Greatest Welsh golfer. Won the Ryder Cup in 2006. We won again at Celtic Manor last year, Megan. I've got it all planned. After the Ryder Cup, the eyes of the world will be on Wales. I'm going to announce my personal manifesto for the Wales of the future. We'll attract capital from all over the world. I want a new Silicon Valley – but in the Welsh Valleys! I want tax raising powers for the Assembly. I will create the biggest budget we've ever had. I want a new Bank of Wales so that we can offer subsidised mortgages for the young people. I want Welsh people living in Welsh homes."

"And I'll back you up, minister, by discovering Welsh Olympic winners," enthused Megan.

Ieuan Jones stood up and walked over to the door of his office. He checked it was closed and, with his back to his visitor, he turned the lock. He walked over to his desk but pulled up a chair and sat next to Megan instead. He stumbled as he tried to sit down.

"Megan," he said. "I'm so looking forward to our working relationship. I don't want to be personal. . . but obviously I know you lost your husband in the war. I am so very sorry. But now you are free, of course."

"'Free', minister?"

"Yes. You're not tied down. What I mean, Megan, is, er, well, I have a cottage down in the Gower and I thought we could spend some time there this weekend and go through your plan together. It's so well written and it inspired me. Your ideas are excellent. . ."

"Did you like my analysis of the potential of the Welsh schools, minister?"

"One of the best sections, Megan. I read it twice."

At this point the Minister for Children, Education, Lifelong Learning and Skills put his hand on Megan's knee. She was not wearing stockings.

"Please don't do that, minister."

"Ah. Hard to get," he laughed. "Megan, the cottage is isolated. We'll have a wonderful time. Just me and you. What a team."

"Please remove your hand."

The minister lurched forward, slid his hand up Megan's skirt and squeezed the inside of her inner thigh.

Megan pulled back, stood up and slapped the minister across the face, sending him flying into the corner of the desk, where his head glanced across the edge. He collapsed to the floor.

"*Yr hen ddiawl*!" she yelled. What a bastard.

She went over to her case and took out the supplement on Welsh Schools she had forgotten to include in her plan. She stood over the mumbling figure, unzipped his fly, and stuffed the document down the front of his trousers.

She then returned to his desk, picked up the envelope containing her plan, extracted the signed contract, and tore it up.

She left the National Assembly building in Cardiff and began the three hours' drive home to Abergynolwyn.

Sarah poured the two cups of tea and handed one across the desk to DCS Johnson.

Tony Johnson seemed to spend a little more time than normal stirring his drink. He reached across to the tray and picked up a bourbon biscuit.

"Just one. I promise," he said.

He looked at his detective colleague.

"How many days off is it?" he asked.

"Three, sir. We're staying at home. My husband and the children have planned a full schedule. It's the London Eye tomorrow morning."

"I'm told the views are stunning."

"Yes. Though I'm not sure that seeing Primrose Hill is quite what I want."

"We've moved on, Sarah. That's all over."

"I was discussing it with my husband."

Tony Johnson looked at her rather sternly.

"Nick is as confidential as you can get, sir, and anyway, I didn't go into detail."

"So what was his view?"

"I think, sir, he was a bit worried about me. In truth I have perhaps allowed the case to get to me. But he did say. . . he thought I'd committed myself to trying to defend David Rensburg rather than finding the real murderer." Sarah picked up her cup and drank quickly.

"And is he right?"

"I followed the evidence, sir, as you instructed. But Nick has a point. I don't think David Rensburg murdered Martin Van Dijl. So, who did?"

"The person who fired the gun. Not even Rensburg's lawyer has questioned that and he challenged just about everything else." He paused. "DNA is so safe these days. Again, the lawyer didn't want to try and undermine us on that. In fact, that was the point I could see him give in. Sure enough, he began plea bargaining shortly afterwards."

"Sarah," he continued, "please use your three days off to relax. Move on. That's an instruction."

"I envy you, sir. You seem much more certain than I am and yet we're both looking at the same evidence."

"No, Sarah. It's just that I'm dealing with the doubts better."

Sarah looked at her boss.

"So you are uncertain, sir?"

"I. . . well. . . "

"Sir, is there anything you're not telling me?"

"I had the case reviewed. A pal in Scotland Yard. They do not come any better than this guy."

"And?"

"He thought you had maintained an excellent file. He was very complimentary."

"Thank you, sir. But what did he say?"

"He could not be sure, of course – but he thought that David probably did not commit the murder."

Sarah sat back in her chair. She breathed out heavily.

"Did he say. . . ?"

"All the points we knew," replied Tony. "His main focus was that the murder took place in cold blood. He felt that David is emotional. When he hit the Frenchman – my friend thought that was an example of how David behaves. He said that he could not see him walking through an open door, calmly walking up to the victim and shooting him."

"The other point, which we have missed to some extent." continued Tony, "is that, if David had committed the murder, he would have had a better alibi. He would have done better than this story about walking around Regent's Park."

"So where do we go from here?" asked Sarah.

"You go home, Sarah," he instructed. "The case is closed until the court hearing. Please enjoy your break. And please turn your phone off."

She looked him straight in the eye.

"My mobile will be on at all times." She stood up. "Good-night, sir."

Charlie Bartlett completed the mooring of *Mikatcha* to the retaining chain that ran down the near side of the Dovey estuary, and which allowed over forty boats to harbour during the summer. In late October most would be lifted out by crane and secured on the quayside, or taken to one of the repair yards.

The twelve fishermen he had taken up to the Barmouth Bar were now on their way back to Wolverhampton. They had re-booked for the following year.

The town was busy, as the summer weather encouraged people to enjoy the beach. This was the peak period for the coastal area as home owners and families filled the available accommodation. The tide was out. The Outward Bound staff were directing their charges in the securing of their two boats to the harbour walls. The last jet-ski was being loaded on to the trailer before being taken back to the Midlands. The children were still crabbing in the shallow waters beneath the pier. The pubs were full.

Charlie reached land and walked round to his car. As he left the village and went under the railway bridge he looked up to his right and to the white house on the hillside. He knew it was where Megan would be living.

Charlie was surprised that he had not seen either Megan or David recently. Unusually for Charlie, he stopped the car. Most evenings he was so tired he drove back to Tywyn and settled down for his evening pint. But he sensed something. When he was out in Cardigan Bay he had learnt to read nature. The birds were creatures of habit. The sudden disappearance of the seagulls immediately put him on storm warning. The fish also could tell their stories. The shoals followed the warmer water. There were the sounds. Some were quite eerie, particularly at sunset.

Charlie could sense malfunction. He walked around the recreational area and studied the hill again. The white house stood all alone. Empty. Silent.

It was time to go home. Charlie shook his head. Something was wrong.

Matthew put the phone down after a difficult conversation with his mother in France.

"Come on, Josh. Pub," he said.

"But Matt, what about. . .?"

"Josh, I'll read it later. Dad said I could leave it, with my comments, with the security people. Actually, he is writing quite well. He'll be a bestseller when it comes out."

"What did Mum say?"

"It's all *that woman's fault,* is all she can say. She's struggling with the sickness."

"Will Dad be ok, Matt?"

"Dad is a fighter, Josh. Never forget that."

David was thinking back to his conversations with Megan about his book. She was a good and intelligent listener and considered each phrase he spoke. He remembered telling her about the three card trick.

So what was the real message of the book he was proposing to write? He believed in financial and economic cycles and had never forgotten the lessons he had understood after reading Bob Beckman's *'The Downwave'*.

Many of the City books written were really semi-autobiographical. After years in the financial markets many financiers thought theirs were stories worth telling. Others were historians and wrote books to supplement their earnings. Some were journalists, others politicians.

David tried to isolate the special features of his work which might be of interest to the general reader. Unless a person had experienced the months and years of corporate finance work it would be impossible to convey the lessons that were learned: the relationship between the professional advisers, the lawyers and accountants, living for their chargeable hours, the brokers calculating their commissions, the corporate financiers relying on a 'success-fee' deal which could (and did) collapse at the last minute. He thought about the sponsors. The 'leeches', as he called them. Many had been affected by the 2008 financial collapse, but they would be back and they mostly made so much money in the good times they were quite happy to retreat for a year or even two before resuming their activities.

The time spent in his cell was an unusual experience for David. His life was normally planned at a frenzied pace and he was almost beginning to enjoy the sense of relaxation.

He wondered if he should tell his story about money, in a novel. His mind began to roam. *The Deal* by David Rensburg. A corporate financier becomes infatuated with the Public Relations executive acting for his client. In meeting after meeting he cannot take his eyes off her body. Her skin is tanned and radiates good health. Her dark hair highlights her face. She has hypnotic breasts and athletic legs. She never wears stockings. The Deal is not going well and the financier has to apply all his skills. One evening, after a late night session, he and the girl find themselves drinking wine together. She tells him she knows he wants to go to bed with her. She reminds him that the chief executive of the client company is her brother, whom she loves dearly. She agrees a compromise. If the financier pulls off the deal she will go to bed with him. Much happens over the next few weeks. Nothing, however, can stop his growing infatuation with the PR girl.

David took a sip of water. He realised it would need a surprising ending. He thought for some time. When the deal is successfully completed the corporate financier prepares to meet the PR executive. He stops off at the cocktail bar and finds himself with one of the analysts from his company. She had played an important part in ensuring the deal was successful by writing an incisive research note which was accepted by several of the funds as a basis for their decision to invest. They find they are enjoying talking to each other and he orders a second bottle of champagne. They decide to book in for the evening at The Tower Hotel overlooking the Thames. He sends a text to a luxury flat in North London.

David sneezed and wiped his nose with some paper tissues.

"It's the air conditioning," he said to himself. He thought he probably had a cold coming on.

He thought about the central character in *The Deal.*

He tried to imagine a beautiful woman who would fit the role.

Tears began to inch down his face.

Chapter Thirteen

Ieuan Jones bowed his head.

His friend over many years, the former first minister in the Welsh National Assembly, took a deep breath. He looked down at the copy letter in front of him and read it again. He asked himself whether he had employed the right tone. He was skilled in political prose. But corresponding with a woman who had been. . . he paused. . . a woman who had been assaulted.

"I've written to Mrs Williams, as we agreed, Ieuan," said Richard Morgan.

"Thank you," Ieuan replied.

"But whether she will respond is an open question."

"And if she doesn't?"

The diplomat knew the answer to this question. If Megan proceeded with a formal complaint, Ieuan's career would be over, and a possible police charge would follow.

"We will have to make a statement. The real problem is, we do not know if Mrs Williams intends furthering the matter. She is entitled to do this, you know that, Ieuan. What you did. . .well, it is a police matter."

"She hit me."

His friend exploded. "And where was your damn hand when she did, you stupid, stupid man? Yes, I know you are lonely, Ieuan. But this was sexual assault. You are guilty."

The two men lapsed into a few moments of silence.

"I'll not harm you, Richard. You're one of the truly great Welsh politicians of modern times. I'll make a statement and resign."

Ieuan put his head in his hands.

"Well, first we'll wait and see if Mrs Williams responds to my letter," said the first minister.

"She was very angry," said Ieuan. "Although I was dazed, I knew how angry she was."

Richard Morgan looked at his friend in utter bewilderment.

"Of course she was angry – do you have any idea what you really did, Ieuan?" he asked.

Megan listened as Dolgellau High's school secretary continued in great detail about the problems being experienced by the principal.

"I tell you, Megan," she continued, "Mrs Edwards thought it would be a simple process. She had been so careful. Asked all the right questions she did. She read all the documents. I myself downloaded stuff from Google for her. She was so excited because she wanted to be free of glasses and contact lenses. She was never happy with those things. And now what, Megan? Told to rest for a week. She's lying down at home, she is. Cannot be disturbed. This of all weeks, Megan. I've got so much to do. Strict instructions. That is what I've been told. No calls. No visitors."

The phone rang on her desk and Megan took the opportunity to exit the office. She spent the remainder of the morning helping one of the senior teaching staff complete the closing down of the sports facilities for the summer. He made comments on her new role at the National Assembly which perhaps, in different circumstances, she would have appreciated.

She left the school in the early afternoon and drove south through Happy Valley and into Aberdovey, along the seafront, under the Penhelig Bridge and up the drive to the Outward Bound School. It took her over half an hour to ascertain that, earlier that day, Zoë Wallis had been one of three leaders who had taken a party of newly arrived teenagers from Liverpool on their first night out on a mountain side.

She left the school and drove back into Aberdovey. She parked her car opposite Swn-y-Don and walked down to the harbour. The early evening sun was lighting up the busy scene, as families lingered on the beach before returning to their holiday accommodation. Several people were swimming in the estuary waters, having to avoid the wind surfers and the various craft mooring up after their day in Cardigan Bay.

Megan called in at the Harbour Master's office and discovered that Charlie had taken *Mikatcha* over to southern Ireland. She walked over to the Britannia and, as she reached the doorway, she heard a roar from the bar as India at long last managed to lose a wicket. For England, the first day of the third test match at Headingley was proving hard work.

She turned around and walked slowly towards Glandovey Terrace, past the Londis where she and David used to buy their newspapers, past Nandora's where David had bought her a bikini, past Medina's where they had indulged in cups of coffee and local cakes, and into David 's holiday home.

She collected the post from the door mat and went into the kitchen. The cold water tap was dripping and so she tightened it. She looked through the envelopes and put two official looking letters into her back pocket. She climbed the stairs to the first floor landing. She opened the back door, walked over the wooden bridge which Richard, the helmsman from the lifeboat, had built two years earlier, up the slate steps to the second tier, where she noticed that Jonathan the gardener had been rebuilding the bank, on to the third level, where Jonathan had repositioned the table and chairs on the cut grass, and to the top of the garden.

Megan turned around and looked at the Dovey Estuary. The view stretched for miles westwards over Cardigan Bay. The tide was out and the evening sunshine was reflecting off the surfaces of the sandbanks. There were myriad colours from the red of the horizon, the dark blues of the waters, the green and sand of the coastal areas, and the pure quality of the skies which provided a canopy of light blue and a hint of occasional white cloud.

She spent twenty minutes lost in thought and then she returned, back down the steps, over the bridge, into the house, and to the living room where she switched on the CD player. She slumped into her chair, leaving the window seat for David. Then she realised there would be no David.

The baritone voice of Levi Stubbs filled the room and she remembered the evenings of Miles Davis and Mahler. She listened to the music and, when it finished, she switched on the television and watched a news bulletin. David Cameron was locked into another row with the European Commission.

Megan switched the television off and climbed to the top floor, where she went into the small back bedroom, lay down on the bed, wrapped the quilt around her and fell asleep.

At 5:30am the next morning she went through the drawers in the front bedroom and put on a top and a pair of shorts. She left the house, crossed the road, climbed down the steps to the beach, crossed the sands and felt the chill of the gentle waves as the water washed around her feet. She began the walk to Tywyn, round the headland and across the firm sands provided by the low tide. She splashed through the pools left by the outgoing sea. Somehow the dangers of weever fish seemed suddenly unimportant.

As she reached the far part of the route she looked across and spotted the white sand bags which had been placed in a futile effort to prevent further erosion of the beach side of the 12th hole of the golf course.

She recalled her first meeting with David. She wondered how significant that moment had been when she had heard him commenting on her appearance through the wall of the changing room. She remembered how Gillian Edwards had suggested she was letting herself down. She remembered the evening with Gavin Davis when she had hated herself afterwards.

She remembered that first beach walk with David, how he had talked about his split from his wife. She shook slightly as she relived David's rescue of the sailor from *Aunty Betty* and that night when they had first made love. She stopped and looked up at the cemetery on the hill where her first husband was buried.

She walked on and remembered singing some words from 'The Bells of Aberdovey' for David. She listened carefully but she could only hear the sound of the waves.

Megan had now reached the two drainage pipes which marked the end of their walk. It was here that David would turn around and begin the return walk to Aberdovey. She sat down on the rocks and saw in her mind David take out his banana and throw the peel into the outgoing waters. She never ceased to be amazed how quickly it would be swallowed by the Bay.

She stood up and slowly began to walk. There was so much about David she did not really understand. She tried so hard to offer intelligent comment but the world of Nomads and brokers remained beyond her. She remembered the Friday evening when David told her of the three card trick and how City people made money.

She pondered over their differences. She was a Welsh girl who asked for nothing. It had taken her a long time to recover from losing Rhys, but she never questioned the Iraq war. Rhys had chosen to be a soldier. He had been so proud when he wore his Welsh uniform. And so he was a soldier, and soldiers die in war. Rhys had died. Megan had worked hard to move on. She paid all her own bills. She knew she was lucky to have her cottage in Abergynolwyn, paid for by the early death of her father. She just shrugged her shoulders when she thought about her mother. She was welcome to Jack Zanovisk.

Megan found herself recalling her job interview at the National Assembly and the dash David had made from London. She relived the evening of rehearsals in the hotel bedroom. She laughed to herself as she remembered the sex and then David's refusal to allow her to drink wine. She groaned as she was made to repeat her presentation for – what was it? – the seventh or eighth time before David allowed her to go to sleep.

She passed the end of the golf course and looked out to sea. It was still cool, as the early morning sun was only just appearing over the eastern hills. She walked slowly on and remembered David's despair over Martin Van Dijl and his difficulties in raising the money for Trafford Discount Stores. Megan had struggled to keep up with the individuals involved. She never met Jackson Holmes or Jemma Shah. She could not understand the role played by Justine Hathaway.

She thought of Matthew and Josh. She had wondered about visiting them again but Matthew was a man now. She had seen him, in a matter of weeks, take charge of the situation. She knew he would stand by his father and take Josh with him. When she had left Primrose Hill for the last time he had been unable to look at her.

That early morning walk down the estuary had stayed in her memory. The man jumping up and down on the sand bank. She could taste the paella which David had cooked for her that evening.

Was there any point in thinking yet again about the murder of Martin Van Dijl?

She remembered Ieuan Jones's hand on her leg, and the feel of his fingers on the inside of her thigh. He had left four messages on her mobile phone and sent text after text. She shuddered.

So who had killed Martin Van Dijl? Megan had tried so hard to prove that David had been walking in Regent's Park. On one evening she had gone out at eight o'clock and managed to walk for three hours around the paths and walkways, along the Grand Union Canal, towards St. John's Wood and back along Prince Albert Road. She had returned and written down all the people she could recall meeting. Her list was no more than six and even those were vague. There had been two runners, a couple who took her attention and even then she could not remember the colour of the girl's top, yet alone her face.

Yet DS Rudd was certain that Martin Van Dijl had been murdered by somebody he knew. Sarah Rudd had sat down with Megan and explained the murder scene, the open door and the lack of a struggle. She explained that he had sat in the chair and allowed a person to shoot him. She was absolutely certain that Martin Van Dijl knew the murderer.

Megan also knew that DS Rudd did not believe that David was the killer. They had discussed the DNA evidence at great length. That, more than anything else, puzzled the police. Sarah had wondered whether the killer had tried to wipe the gun clean but leave the DNA on the trigger. The laboratory staff had convinced her that this was an impossibility.

Megan had reached the turning back to the harbour. She crossed over the sands and went into a dune, where she lay down. For some reason she thought about snakes. A dog had been bitten by an adder the previous week, according to the local newspaper.

She lay back and her thoughts returned to David. She had re-read *The Downwave* and thought more and more about David's idea of writing a book to explain money. She had searched the business book section of Waterstone's on their website and had been engulfed by the hundreds of experts who were keen to write about their subject.

But she wondered whether it really mattered. David was exhausted after the General Meeting. She laughed as she remembered his suggestion that he expected to be charged with causing the heart attack suffered by Cyril Trafford. He had told Megan he was on his way to becoming a mass murderer.

So who was the man who had come into her life in April? The person who, a few weeks later, she had agreed to marry. The man to whom she was willing to give her whole life. The man to whose sons she was willing to become a step-mother.

Megan really had no more thoughts to offer. They had been through so much together, from the winning of the Bells of Aberdovey Tennis Cup, to the rescue of the skipper of *Aunty Betty* from the turbulent waters of Cardigan Bay, to David's trials raising the money for Trafford Discount Stores plc, to the stress which his doctor was treating, to his personal wealth and the deal with Jackson Holmes which gave him the financial freedom to leave the City of London and move to Aberdovey and write his book, to his developing relationship with his sons following his visit to Monsieur le Grande in France – and to his need to find his life partner.

At one point this last issue had caused Megan great worry. Was David simply escaping and was Aberdovey no more than a convenient bolthole? Was Megan 'the woman' he needed? But those thoughts had been swept aside by the sheer power of his personality. Yet again, she went back to the hotel room and the preparation for her interview with the National Assembly. David had given everything that night. With a passion, he had wanted that job for Megan. He knew exactly what it meant to her. He had been so proud of her.

She thought about his final words to her. Why would he not allow her to wait for him? Was eight years, perhaps 200 visits, too much to endure? But she thought she knew, in her heart of hearts, what the real problem was. David had realised that in a community such as Aberdovey there was no way that his background would remain a secret. They would never be free as a couple. David's life was in tatters.

He had been forced to make the ultimate sacrifice. He had had to let go of the woman he truly loved.

DCS Johnson was not in a good frame of mind. England were losing wickets rather quickly and facing a three days' innings defeat.. He would be downcast at any time in the face of a poor England performance.

He groaned, as another English batsman lost his wicket. He switched his radio off and looked at the budgets in front of him on his cluttered desk. He was struggling to finish the figures for the next financial year. Why should he, a senior police officer, be spending a Saturday afternoon on administrative matters when he joined the police force thirty years earlier to solve crimes?

There was a knock at his door and before he could give an answer a young police officer entered. She was dark-haired and of medium height.

"Sir, I'm sorry, but this man is insistent. We're quite short staffed downstairs. He just will not fill in a form. He says he'll not move from the front until he has seen you, sir."

"What's your name?" asked the DCS.

"PC Amanda Page, sir. I'm on the graduate programme."

Tony Johnson smiled at the young recruit.

"Just relax, PC Page," he said. "You've done exactly the right thing. Never ignore any member of the public, PC Page. Do you have the man's name?"

"He won't give it to me, sir. He just says he must see you." She ran her hand through her hair, pushing it back from her face.

"Right. I'll come downstairs and we'll talk to him then."

He closed his budget file and stashed it away in a drawer. He went through the open door, thanking PC Page for her manners. He climbed down the two flights of stairs and went into the reception area of Paddington Green Police Station. He walked up to a man sitting in the waiting area.

"You want to see me?" he asked.

The man was around six foot when he stood up. He was wearing a white, creased shirt and dark blue slacks. On his feet he wore sandals. He was holding a rolled newspaper.

"It's in the paper, DCS Johnson. You've charged the man for murder," he said.

Tony Johnson asked PC Page to find an interview room.

When she returned he invited the man to enter and sit down. He instructed PC Page to stand at the back.

"Shall we start with your name, please?"

"How long will he get?" asked the man.

"Who?" replied Tony. He could smell the alcohol on the man's breath.

The man opened the newspaper and turned to an inside page. He put it on the table and tried to straighten it out.

"This bloke who shot the stockbroker," he stuttered.

DCS Johnson turned the newspaper round and read the article. It covered his role in arresting and charging the suspected murderer of a London stockbroker, Martin Van Dijl.

"I need your name," repeated the detective.

"It's not right. It says sixteen years. Just for shooting somebody. Why should he be locked away for all that time? Anyway, it says here the victim was a nasty guy. . ."

"Sir, do you have any knowledge of this case?" Tony asked.

"No. I just wanted to say – you shouldn't put him away for so long."

The DCS stood up and walked out from behind the table. He stretched to his full six feet three inches. He wandered over to PC Amanda Page and then turned abruptly and faced the man sitting at the desk.

"So," he said, "you've just walked in off the street after a visit to the pub to tell me that somebody, who has not even been tried by a court of law, should not get sixteen years in jail for a crime you know nothing about."

"Well, what evidence have you got?" asked the man.

Tony Johnson began to show some anger. He put his fist on the table with a certain amount of force.

"Sir, please give me your name. If not, I will arrest you for wasting police time."

"How can anyone face a prison sentence that long?" the man went on.

The DCS walked around the table and put his hand on the man's shoulder and his mouth near to his left ear.

"Please tell me. Why are you here? You want to tell me something, don't you?"

"He didn't do it. This David Rensburg in the article. He didn't do it. Sixteen years. It can't happen." The man put his hands up to his face.

"How do you know he did not do it?"

"Because I shot Martin Van Dijl," said the man. He slumped forward and put his hands over his head.

Tony Johnson picked up the phone on the table.

"Duty sergeant in here now!" he instructed.

The door of the interview room opened almost immediately and two police officers entered.

"Search him and take great care. He may have a gun," he cautioned.

The search was completed and one of the police officers confirmed that the man was unarmed.

"Stay here with him. He touches nothing. You watch him like a hawk. Keep his hands on the table. Any movement, cuff him. Stay here, PC Page."

DCS Johnson returned to the front office and ordered the officer on the desk to contact Sarah Rudd at home. The phone was passed to him.

"Detective Sergeant Rudd," he said, "I'm sending a car. You're coming in."

David had decided not to follow the Test Match, despite his love of almost all English sports. Instead he re-read the paragraphs he had written that day. Never before had he had the chance to concentrate for such long periods of time. The structure of his book was taking shape. He had decided that it should fall into four sections. The first the history of money; the second the evolvement of credit; the third the growth of the banks. This would be a major part of the tome. Finally, in the last part, he would tell the story of the banking crisis over the last four years. He wanted to use language that the general reader could follow.

He was aware that finance, like all professions, used esoteric words, phrases and mnemonics that made their understanding more difficult. Stockbrokers still refer to 'call' and 'put' when they mean 'buy' and 'sell'. He wanted to select words that would allow the reader to understand the argument he would be putting forward.

He was still unsure about the final conclusions of the book.

He realised that there could be no ending because economic periods are cycles. He knew that as the UK came out of recession, there was, further ahead, another burst of irrationality. In the late 1990s, and the early part of the 21st century, it had been the dot-com bubble which burst, in spectacular fashion. Over the last five years it was sub-prime and banking mayhem. The next fashion? Possibly climate change financing, especially with the vast amount of government money available in this sector. Perhaps with low interest rates forecast to continue it might be an explosion of interest by the private investor in the stock market.

For David, nothing was certain apart from his coming trial, a plea of 'guilty' and a sentence of sixteen years, of which he was likely to serve half.

He would come out in his late forties. He had decided to pull out of the house purchase and complete the sale of Swn-y-Don. He would never return to Aberdovey.

Matthew was sitting on a bench seat at the top of Primrose Hill. He was studying a photograph which he had taken from his back pocket. It was crumpled. He took out his mobile phone from the breast pocket in his white shirt. The sun was streaming down. He was alone. He had decided he needed to feel smart. He would be visiting his father later that afternoon.

He looked at the latest text message.

He had made his decision. He would not return to Wales.

He looked down again at his mobile and the message he'd just received. He pressed the 'delete' button. He would never see Emily Bowden again.

Stephan Andrew beamed. Margaret Drummond smiled. Tea at the Ritz in Piccadilly was not a usual event for her. The glass of cold white wine helped maintain the conviviality of the meeting. Alice Kimmins accepted another sandwich.

"I am a lucky man to be allowed to entertain two beautiful ladies," announced their host. He sipped some iced water.

"It was kind of you to invite us, Stephan," said Margaret.

"I am staggered," continued the Swiss financier. "The business plan you have produced is outstanding. You've employed a local Yorkshire firm of accountants and we cannot fault their analysis. We disagree on the return on capital calculation because we believe we can structure the trading so that the tax bill is reduced to under 10 percent. But that is a small matter we will let the boffins argue over. Not a bad word for a Swiss man: 'boffin'," Stephan laughed.

Alice smiled at Stephan, who blushed.

"I don't really understand what you're talking about, I'm afraid, Mr Andrew. I'm just pleased to be here to support my sister."

They had now had several meetings and caught up, to some extent, on each other's history.

"Now, Margaret, I had suggested that my friends and I would make €10 million available to Trafford Discount Stores."

"That's what you said, Stephan," replied Margaret.

"That is what I said," repeated the Swiss financier. "But now I see you are asking for €20 million!"

"Stephan, my father was a great man. In truth, over the last two years he was deteriorating. This held us back. I would not do anything to hurt him. But now we can fulfil our true potential." Margaret took a sip of her wine. She held Stephan's eye.

"What if we call it €10 million and a further €10 million against certain financial targets?" suggested Stephan.

"Then I will find the funding elsewhere. My phone has not stopped ringing."

"I'm sure that is the case, Margaret," said Stephan. He turned to Alice.

"And what do you think I should do?" he asked.

Alice smiled, said nothing and took her sister's hand.

Stephan laughed. "Lucky for you, there are only two things in this world that I cannot say no to – the chess board and beautiful women. You have your euros, Margaret."

Alice squeezed her sister's hand.

Stephan took a piece of paper out of his briefcase.

"Here are our conditions," he said.

Margaret read the details quickly and nodded.

"I will have to check with the other Board members and the AIM corporate advisers but consider them all agreed except. . ." and she seemed to swallow rather suddenly.

"Yes," said Stephan, "the proposed chairman. It is sad. We can't believe it. My solicitors have spoken to Neil Levy, who's acting for David. He's pleading guilty. He is not guilty, of course, but it is a plea bargain agreement. Madness."

"So we need to find another chairman?" said Margaret.

"It is regrettable," said Stephan.

Megan was shaking. She was sitting on a hill above Aberdovey, overlooking the harbour. Her car was parked in the lane below.

She had lost her job. She had slapped her new boss across the face. She had torn up her contract. She knew she would get no sympathy. She trembled at the thought of her next meeting with Gillian Edwards.

There was simply no way back for her.

"Rwy'n teimio'n oer" ddywedodd hi wrth i hun." She was feeling cold and very lonely.

DCS Johnson and DS Rudd sat opposite the interviewee. PC Amanda Page and a police constable stood silently against the far wall. On the desk were three glasses and a bottle of still water. The two detectives each had a writing pad in front of them.

Sarah explained that she was turning on the tape recorder. She announced the names of the four law officers in the room.

The man sitting opposite them had accepted the caution and refused the offer of a solicitor.

"Let's start with your name, please," said Sarah Rudd.

"Thomas Payne," replied the man.

"And you admit to murdering Martin Van Dijl?" she continued.

"Yes," he stated.

"How did you murder Martin Van Dijl, Mr Payne?"

"I shot him once in the head."

Sarah looked intensely at the man sitting opposite her.

"And what did you do then, Mr Payne?"

She was already certain that this was the man who had murdered Martin Van Dijl. She was later unable to explain to herself why at that moment she also thought of Megan.

"I wiped the gun clean of prints and put it in his right hand to make it look like suicide. Stupid, of course. You saw right through that."

Suddenly his tone changed. He looked at the tape recorder to his side.

"My name is Thomas William Payne. I live in Rutland Road, London, NW4. I am a printer. I killed Martin Van Dijl in cold blood and I accept I'll go to prison for a long time. I print financial documents and Martin Van Dijl persuaded me to put all my savings into a share offer, Trafford Discount Stores. But I could not get at my money."

Thomas sat still and stared ahead of him at the window in the wall.

"And you killed him for that?" exclaimed DCS Johnson. "How much did you invest?"

Thomas looked at Sarah.

"I killed him because of what he did to my father."

"You will have to explain that to us," said Sarah.

Thomas wiped his arm across his face.

"My father, Albert Payne, developed prostate problems. He became very ill. He was taken into hospital. The conditions were poor. There were no nurses. He pleaded with me: 'Get me out of here, son', he kept saying. I found a private hospital but the fees were beyond belief. My business is struggling. I heard about this share offer. Trafford Discount Stores. We printed the document. I read it at home."

Thomas paused and poured himself a glass of water.

"I asked David about it, but he was pretty cautious. But one day Martin Van Dijl came in to collect a box of share promotion documents. We often do this. We print the whole order and then the finance people collect them as they want them."

He paused again.

"I asked Martin about the shares. He met me that night in a hotel. He was professional and answered all my questions. I had £30,000 left from my pension money. I put it all into Trafford Discount Stores. I also signed a piece of paper saying I wouldn't sell the shares for a year. When my father became ill I went to see Martin again. The first time he was polite but said he could not sell the shares. I went to see him again. He completely changed. His eyes were bloodshot. He shouted at me. He called me 'pathetic'. I saw him a third time. He was again different. He just said 'no', he would not sell the shares for me."

Thomas looked again at Sarah.

"By now my father's condition was terrible. I so wanted to get him out, but I couldn't find the money. When he died he was in agony."

At this point, Thomas broke down in tears. A tray of tea was ordered and the two detectives waited for him to regain his composure.

"Two questions, Mr Payne," continued Sarah Rudd. "You have mentioned the name 'David.' I presume by that you mean David Rensburg?"

"Yes. I know him quite well. He works for the finance company I do the printing for and he came into my offices regularly."

"And," continued DS Rudd, "the gun you used to shoot Martin Van Dijl – had it ever been handled by David Rensburg?"

"That is what I could not work out," replied Thomas. "I knew you must have something on him. It was only last night I remembered that earlier this year David was in my office and we were talking about civil disorder. You know what I mean. The recession and all the social problems we're seeing. I told him I wouldn't let anyone attack my property and I showed him a gun I had bought. I got it off one of my printers. David told me to throw it in the Thames. I knocked it on the floor and David picked it up. I suppose I missed something when I tried to wipe it clean."

Sarah Rudd composed herself and entered the cell. She looked at her watch. It was early evening. Earlier she had visited Primrose Hill and to her relief had found both Matthew and Josh together in the front room. It had taken her thirty minutes to tell them of the afternoon's developments and for the two boys to collect themselves. Matthew had wanted to phone Megan but Sarah had said not to do so yet.

They were now waiting in the family car outside for their father.

David looked up at the detective. He stood up and indicated she should sit down.

"Detective Sergeant Rudd, thank you for coming." David smiled.

"I've just finished planning chapter two. I'm writing a book," he said. "It's just the final section I cannot get right in my mind. I'm trying to convey the financial news in a way that a non-financial person can understand. Let me ask you this, Detective Sergeant Rudd. If I say to you, 'The national debt is 40 percent of GDP', what does that mean to you?"

"Sit down, David," ordered the detective. David sat down.

"You are a free man, David," Sarah said, feeling emotional but revealing nothing. David just stared at her.

"You have him?"

"Yes."

"Who?"

"Thomas Payne," she replied, and she told David about his confession that afternoon.

"But the DNA. . ." said David, ". . . of course, I picked the gun up in his office. Why didn't I remember that?"

"Because you were not looking in that direction, David. You were searching for a witness in Regent's Park."

Sarah Rudd stood up and walked around the table. As David got slowly to his feet, she hugged him and kissed him on his cheek.

"And don't you dare tell Chief Superintendent Johnson I did that!" she laughed. "Come on, David, your sons are waiting outside to take you home."

A few minutes later Josh flew into his father's arms and Matthew clasped his hand with emotion. They drove away together towards Primrose Hill.

DS Rudd composed herself. She took out her mobile phone and made a call to a number in the coastal area of West Wales.

Chapter Fourteen

About an hour before DS Rudd made her phone call Megan had turned off her mobile. She had disconnected the landline from its socket and switched off her computer. She had then walked round to a terraced property in Abergynolwyn and spent forty minutes with Rhys' aging mother.

They sat on the sofa together. Megan wrapped her right arm around Mam's shoulders and, with her left hand, gently stroked her frail mother-in-law's face. They talked about the weather and the level of the river that ran through the village. Megan went into the kitchen and brought out the three prescriptions which Mrs Williams took daily. She checked the level of each plastic bottle and reminded the old lady that she needed to ask the surgery for a repeat of her angina pills. She asked her mother-in-law if she would like to walk, but Mrs Williams declined. They gave each other a hug and Megan straightened the shawl around her shoulders. She quietly closed the front door behind her.

She took a detour around the village, crossed over the bridge and looked at the church where she and Rhys had been married. There was another broken window and the notice board to the one side of the entrance reminded the local population that Christ offered hope to the afflicted, and that there was a jumble sale in aid of the church roof appeal next Tuesday.

Megan returned to the street leading to her cottage. She looked at the Alpha Romeo parked in front of her home. She then went into the cottage and locked the front door behind her, before going upstairs and getting changed. She returned to the kitchen, opened a bottle of wine and washed out a glass which she dried carefully. She carried both out to her patio. She put them down by the side of the sunbed and decided to enjoy what she calculated would be the last two hours of evening sunshine.

She was unaware of a series of increasingly urgent phone calls and emails. DS Rudd phoned the police station in Tywyn, only to be told that all available officers were dealing with the arrival of some gypsies who had set up camp in a field leading to the seafront. The cottage hospital, which was located on the Aberdovey side of the town, was already dealing with three injured local people who had tried to tell the gypsies to move on. But they were decent people and the local reaction was out of proportion.

Megan listened to the birdsong and let the calm of the evening wash over her. She thought about the afternoon she had spent in the village. She had deleted an email from her mother and a text from Ieuan Jones. She had read a letter she had received from Richard Morgan. She had spoken briefly to Emily Bowden and confirmed that she had Matthew's home number in London.

She began to slumber and went back to the beaches of Aberdovey. She wondered how many times she had walked along the sands. Hundreds, probably. The beach at Tywyn was full of pebbles and she could only recall playing there as a child. Over the last few weeks she had experienced so many new adventures with David.

She mentally revisited the start of their walk, exiting Swn-y-Don, crossing the road and the car park, climbing down the steps onto the sands and reaching the edge of the water. The first part would often be on the slopes of the estuary banks, depending on the tide, and it was not until they had reached the circles of stones that the beach opened out into the flat sands leading to the turn towards the north. They would usually remain quiet in the early stages as each of them recovered from their week's work.

Even on the best of the summer days there could be cloud over the hills, more often in the north over Barmouth and to the east over the southern hills of Snowdonia. The sand dunes on the right hand side hid from view the golf course and the coast road, but the start of Happy Valley would be visible. For some reason, Megan wondered whether Elwyn Jones had succeeded in collecting his stray sheep.

She poured herself another glass of wine. Why had she thought of that? It was many weeks ago. Her mind drifted. She was concerned she had not given Emily Bowden the right number. Was it 0207 455 4?. . . and then she could not remember the final three digits.

Megan could not think where they were on the walk. Perhaps they had now reached the pipes at the Tywyn end. This would be the point where David would start talking, usually about Trafford Discount Stores. Why did he want to write a book? He seemed convinced that people would want to read about money.

She no longer needed to find Welsh winners. Would she have succeeded? They were out there in the towns and athletic clubs of Wales. Lately she had been focusing on those stars that seemed to come from nowhere. She had studied Andy Murray. Yes, he was a Scotsman, but he would probably win Wimbledon one day. He had been unknown two years earlier. Wayne Rooney. He came from nowhere. She had read that the Manchester United scouting system would often identify potential players at the age of nine or ten. Who was that English diver who had gone to the Beijing Olympics at the age of fourteen?

She thought about Jack in Canada. She had never really known her own father, although she kept a photograph of him in her lounge. Why was her mother not in the photograph? She decided that she had no opinion about Jack. Jack was Jack. That was her mother's problem.

After she had drunk the bottle of wine she stood up and put the lounger away in the shed at the bottom of the garden. She went indoors and cleaned her cottage from top to bottom. She tidied her paperwork and wrote out two cheques for bills, neither of which were yet due for payment and left the two envelopes on the kitchen table. Megan then opened a bottle of gin, poured herself a large measure and added a small amount of tonic water. She went into the lounge, closed the curtains and lay down on her sofa. She slowly sipped her drink and enjoyed the silence.

She went to bed at 11:08pm.

Tony Johnson put the glasses of Chardonnay down on the hotel bar table and smiled at his companion.

Sarah Rudd was reading a response to her text message.

Having sent: *"Nick. Am taking you out for dinner. Love you lots. Sarah"* she was wondering how to reply to her husband's *"It is 9:30 and the supper is burnt. Fondly, Nick"*.

She had to tell her husband: *"David R is free. You were right. We were looking in the wrong place. Home shortly. Oodles of love. S."*

"So what happened, Sarah?" asked Tony.

"Well, Matthew Rensburg is quite a mature young man, sir," she replied. "He took charge of everything. They both wanted their father back as quickly as I could get him. I heard him phone his mother in France. I thought that was terrific."

"And David?"

"Quiet. Controlled. He and the boys were as close as ever, straight away. They never doubted their father."

"Have you reflected on our conduct at all?"

"We always questioned his decision to plead guilty. It was a perplexing situation."

"But you knew he was innocent, Sarah?"

"No, sir. I followed the evidence. We both know, in our work, tomorrow will always be different."

"And David Rensburg. Was he angry with us?"

"No, sir." Sarah paused and drank some wine. "Once he realised that Josh and Matthew were in good shape he moved on almost straight away. It was as if his mind was elsewhere."

And the detective knew where David's thoughts were taking him.

She checked her text messages. The screen was blank.

On Sunday morning, just around dawn, Megan rose from her bed. She swilled her face in cold water, put on a top and shorts, left her cottage and drove down the valley, following the Talyllyn railway, through Tywyn, along the coast road and into Aberdovey. She turned right into the car park and stopped her car so that she could look at Swn-y-Don. After a few minutes she left the car park, turned left under the railway bridge and turned left again into the road leading to Aberdyfi station. Again, she stayed in the car but looked up at the hillside and at one house in particular. She started the engine and drove out of town, past the start of the golf course and along to the cemetery beach lay-by. She got out of the car, locked it and threw the keys into the bushes.

She crossed the road and entered the cemetery through the iron gate. She climbed the slope to the row of headstones and found Rhys' grave. Before sitting down on the grass, she wiped the sand off the individual letters of his name and with her fingers she tidied the soil. She rearranged the small bunch of flowers she had left the week before.

She spoke in a quiet voice to her husband.

"I seem to have mucked things up, Rhys," she said. She bowed her head and paused.

"I've tried hard, Rhys – I so wanted you to be proud of me."

She sat with crossed legs for a few more minutes. Her lips were moving but there was no sound.

She kissed his name, stood up and then knelt down again. She traced his name with her fingers.

She rose again and walked down the slope. She walked out of the cemetery, across the road, past her car, down the hill, across the golf course and stood at the start of the wooden pathway, which led over the dunes and the pebbles onto the sands.

She hesitated. She then started to walk over the wooden floor, through the dunes and onto the beach. The morning tide was a long way out. There was nobody in sight.

David had given up trying to contact Megan. Both her phones were engaged and there were no replies to his emails.

At Matthew's insistence he lay down on his bed for two hours and at one o'clock on the Sunday morning he left London and Primrose Hill, joined the M1, and exited at the junction for the M6. He decided it would be quicker to stay on the motorway through Birmingham and so didn't take the Toll Road. He stayed on the M6, through Birmingham, until he took the turning for the M54. He stopped at Shrewsbury for petrol and an opportunity to stretch his muscles. He had maintained a daily exercise routine in the police cell and felt comfortable. He checked his mobile phone and sent a text message.

David resumed his journey through Welshpool and on to Machynlleth. He took the faster route through Llanwrin and reached Aberdovey in the morning sunshine. There were some early walkers wandering around the village centre.

He stopped at the car park opposite Swn-y-Don. He went inside and checked it was unoccupied. He raced up to the fourth floor and the bedroom where Megan had, on occasions, stayed.

He returned to his car and continued out of the town, under the railway bridge and past the golf club.

He sped past the cemetery beach lay-by and glanced in his mirror. Was there a vehicle parked at the top of the steps?

He reached Tywyn Hospital where he stopped and looked again in his mirror. He then checked his mobile. There was a text from Matthew: "Sorry, Dad. Nothing."

He thought again. Had he seen a car stopped by the cemetery? Why would it be Megan? It was seventeen minutes to Abergynolwyn. Was it his instinct telling him something?

Megan had finished the walk to the water's edge. It was now low tide at the start of another glorious Aberdovey summer's day. The water was tranquil and even the seventh wave failed to make much of a stir. Her feet quickly warmed to the chilly water as she paddled around. She looked to her left and towards the Dovey estuary. She thought for one moment she had spotted somebody coming through the early morning mist, but quickly realised the beach was empty.

She looked out into Cardigan Bay. She could see the marker buoys which showed the entrance to the harbour. On the far western horizon there was a sailing boat just visible to the naked eye. To the north low clouds obscured the hills. She watched the birds fishing for breakfast in the shallow waves.

She let the sea water reach above her knees and rubbed moisture over her face. She felt calm. There were no more decisions to be made. She felt happy on the beach of her birthplace. She was standing on the coastline of the Welsh country she so adored. She felt at home. She allowed the water to reach her thighs.

David continued to sit in his car. He watched an ambulance arrive from the Tywyn village. It drove quickly up to the cottage hospital with its flashing blue lights colouring the entrance.

He remained unsure. Had he seen a car in the cemetery lay-by? Could it have been Megan's car? Surely she would be in her cottage at Abergynolwyn. Why would she be on the beach at this time of the morning? He calculated it was no more than fifteen minutes to her home. He made his decision.

Megan was alone. She had nowhere else to go. She looked for the dolphins out in Cardigan Bay. She felt the sea water reach her shorts.

Within five minutes of turning his car around outside the cottage hospital, David had returned to the cemetery beach. He immediately recognised Megan's car and screeched to a stop beside it, before jumping out of his vehicle and checking the doors of Megan's car. They were closed. He looked around and up at the rows of gravestones. He turned and ran down the hill towards the golf course. He searched the area in both directions. He cried out Megan's name.

David ran across the grass fairways and – just as he reached the wooden bridge which took him across the dunes and onto the beach – tripped and fell.

Megan was thinking about the time at the hotel in Cardiff when David had coached her in preparation for her interview at the National Assembly. The water around her waist was feeling quite warm. She wondered whether to start swimming when she heard a shout.

She was not sure, as she peered through the mist down the beach to the Dyfi estuary and then northwards towards Tywyn, that she had heard anything. She must have been mistaken. She put her arms out in front of her. She heard another shout and hesitated – she was sure she had heard the word 'Megan'.

She turned around and waded out of the water. There was a figure running towards her. It was a man. He was slim and dark-haired. . . it was David.

They stopped about five feet away from each other.

"David!" Megan cried.

"It was the printer, Megan! I had handled his gun when I was in his office!"

"Printer. . . who. . . what. . . why did he murder Martin. . .?" She laughed suddenly. 'Martin whatever-his-name was?!"

"It's a bit of a long story, Megs, but Martin had lost Thomas Payne a lot of money – he killed him as an act of revenge." David held his arms out.

"But the DNA, David, on the gun?"

"I'd handled the gun when I was in Tom's office a few weeks ago. He'd not meant me to be involved. He thought he'd wiped the gun clean."

"So what happened?"

"He walked into Paddington Green Police Station yesterday afternoon and confessed. Sarah Rudd came last night to secure my release. I phoned and phoned you, Megan."

"So what does all this mean?"

"What it means, Megan, is that I will be writing my book in a house on a hillside in Aberdovey." David took a step forward.

"But you stopped me coming to see you, David. I wanted to share everything with you. I could have made the time pass more quickly. You didn't want me!"

David looked at Megan.

"Is that what you really think?" he asked.

"No. No. You did it for me. I know that." She paused. "David. I have to tell you something. I've lost the Assembly job. He put his hand up my skirt and I slapped his face. I tore up my contract."

David stared at the beautiful, fair-haired woman standing in front of him.

"You've had a dreadful time, Megan. We can talk about everything later."

"Later?" said Megan. It was slowly dawning on her that her life was coming together again.

Out in Cardigan Bay a flock of seagulls had detected a shoal of mackerel and was diving deep into the sea water.

Megan took two steps forward and put her hands on either side of David's face. Their tensions exploded and their lips found each other's, Megan holding onto David with an iron tight grip. He picked her up and took her into the sea, dragging her down into the shallow waters. They rolled over and over, clawing at each other. Megan's tears were being washed away by the sea water but she would not let him go. They edged back onto the sands and Megan lay on top of David. The waves lapped over them. She simply could not get closer to him.

Finally they stood up and started to walk toward the Dovey estuary. They spoke and spoke – each telling the other of their thoughts, their pain, their anguish and their despair. As the sun rose in the east the bright daylight flooded the beach. The tide had turned and was coming in.

As they walked David took his arm from Megan and slowed to a snail's pace. He stopped and started to rub his left leg.

"Megs," he said. "You know, I think I pulled a muscle running over the bridge."

Megan smiled. "Normal service has been resumed," she said to herself.

They reached Aberdovey, crossed the car park and entered Swn-y-Don. David phoned Matthew at the same time a police officer phoned DS Rudd from outside a cottage in Abergynolwyn.

They climbed the stairs and showered together. Later, in bed, Megan entwined herself around David.

"Byth, byth eto fyddai'n gadael ti mynd," she murmured as she searched for his lips. "Never, ever again, do I let you go."

Richard Morgan invited Megan to take a seat in his office. He seemed nervous and took an exaggerated amount of time to pour cups of tea for the two of them.

"Thank you for your letter, minister," said Megan.

"Thank you for coming to see me, Ms Williams."

There was a silence. Megan remembered her instructions and sat still. She wanted to run her fingers through her hair. David had advised her not to wear a headscarf.

"This is no easy matter, Ms Williams. I cannot apologise enough for. . ."

"Apologise for what, minister?" interrupted Megan.

She was wearing a dark grey suit and her fair hair flowed loosely over her head. She wore no make-up and a single crucifix around her neck.

"What happened, Ms Williams, with Ieuan Jones. He's one of my best friends, and last year his wife died of a brain tumour. He'll be such a loss to the Assembly. Do you want to press charges? He knows what he did was wrong. He will not fight you."

"And what did happen, minister?" Megan asked.

"In Ieuan's. . . er. . . Mr Jones's office, Megan. . . er Ms Williams. . . when he. . . er. . ."

The politician looked across his desk. He studied the face of the young Welsh woman. Megan remained silent.

"It goes without saying that Ieuan is deeply, deeply sorry for what happened," said the minister. "He wondered. . . he wondered if you would reconsider your decision. He very much wants you to work with him. He has promised me there will never again be – shall we say – this sort of. . . problem. . . again. I have a contract here, Megan."

Megan looked across the desk. She and David had discussed how she should respond in this situation.

"With respect to Mr Jones, minister, what I think is important is what *you* feel at this moment."

Richard Morgan sat back in his chair and ran a hand through his hair. He had come to the end of a distinguished political career. He hesitated before he spoke.

"I am thinking two things, Ms Williams." He paused.

"Firstly, I think I'm sitting in front of a very special person."

Megan waited.

"And secondly, I'm thinking that I would like you to open the package I have here."

He handed her a large brown envelope with the Government crest on the front. It was privately addressed to Megan Williams.

Megan radiated a smile and opened the envelope. She took out the papers and carefully read them before asking the minister if she could borrow his pen.

She carefully signed her contract and handed the documents back.

A few moments later the former first minister of Wales stood on the steps of the National Assembly with his new colleague. The crowds were dense as the city of Cardiff continued its growth into an international capital of the world.

"They are out there, Megan. Our Welsh winners," he said, and then he paused. "It has just struck me – Megan Williams – what a beautiful Welsh name."

"Well, not for much longer!"

Richard Morgan turned and looked at her.

"Soon I'll be Mrs David Rensburg."

The minister smiled.

"I'm pleased for you, Megan. I'm sure you'll be very happy together."

Megan had started down the steps and was walking towards a slim, dark-haired man who was waiting to take her home.

"I'm sure we will," she said to herself.

For Megan the game was finally over but, this time, there were no winners and no losers. There were just two people who had been through so much together and who were now happy at last.

They walked along the beach. The tide was out and Cardigan Bay was a deep shade of evening red. The seagulls were hungry.

Megan took hold of David's hand.

"*Mae'r clychau'n dan y mor yn canu,*" she said.

And she was right.

The bells under the sea were ringing out.

About the author

Tony Drury is a corporate financier based in the City of London. He is a Fellow of the Institute of Bankers and a Member of the Securities Institute.

A keen squash player, coach and referee, Tony is also passionate about rugby and picked up his smattering of Welsh from watching the game in Aberdovey, where he and his wife Judy had a holiday home for 12 years.

Tony has written extensively over the years and is particularly well known for his financial and political books. He blogs weekly for www.enterprisebritain.com - both in his name and that of his alter ego Mr Angry.

He lives in Bedfordshire with his wife, and they have a son and daughter, both now married.

Megan's Game is his first work of fiction.

Find out more about Tony Drury at www.tonydruryauthor.com

Coming next...

The Deal

The pressure is on for corporate financier Oliver Chatham. If he can raise two million for a publishing house, City Fiction, then the woman of his dreams, Amanda, will go to bed with him. If not, no deal. Yet the course of true love never did run smooth. Things are complicated along the way by a kidnapping, an alluring young corporate researcher and some Russian coal mines – to name but a few.

Will Oliver get what he bargained for – or will he learn the hard way that you should never mix sex and the City?